Esha Patel is a contemporary romance writer with a love for diverse romances and empowering stories. She is a full-time college student in the Midwest, and has a knack for overbaking so greatly that the resulting yield can probably feed multiple eleven-man soccer teams. When she's not writing, you can find her drowning in papers, spending time with family and friends, dancing, or watching Real Madrid matches. You can follow Esha on social media @eshapatelauthor or visit her website at eshapatelauthor.com to learn more.

T0318057

Offtrack

ESHA
PATEL

Overdrive

avon.

Publised by AVON
A Division of HarperCollins*Publishers* Ltd
1 London Bridge Street
London SE1 9GF

www.harpercollins.co.uk

HarperCollins*Publishers*
Macken House,
39/40 Mayor Street Upper,
Dublin 1
D01 C9W8
Ireland

A Paperback Original 2024

1

ISBN: 978-0-00-869396-1

Set in Birka by HarperCollins*Publishers* India

Printed and bound in the UK using 100% Renewable
Electricity at CPI Group (UK) Ltd

*For the daughters who forgot to look for happiness
because they were too busy giving it to others.
I hope you find the love you have doled out
for years in these pages.
And I hope that, one day, that same love finds its
way to you when you need it most.*

Content Warning

Overdrive, although fictional, tackles some events and issues that some may find distressing. If you'd like to find out more, please read the 'Content Warning' note at the back of the book, but be warned that it does contain spoilers.

Formula One Grands Prix Schedule

1. Bahrain Grand Prix
2. Saudi Arabian Grand Prix
3. Australian Grand Prix
4. Miami Grand Prix
5. Singapore Grand Prix
6. Japanese Grand Prix
7. Emilia-Romagna Grand Prix (Imola)
8. Monaco Grand Prix
9. Canadian Grand Prix
10. Spanish Grand Prix
11. Hungarian Grand Prix
12. British Grand Prix (Silverstone)
13. Belgian Grand Prix (Spa)
14. United States Grand Prix (Austin)
15. Azerbaijan Grand Prix
16. Italian Grand Prix (Monza)
17. Dutch Grand Prix
18. Jaipur Grand Prix
19. Las Vegas Grand Prix
20. Brazilian Grand Prix (São Paulo)
21. Mexican Grand Prix
22. Abu Dhabi Grand Prix

SEVENTEEN YEARS AGO

Prologue

Darien

'He doesn't even speak English!'

The boys in the expensive custom karts ahead laughed as they buckled in for the qualifying round. Their parents watched from the sidelines, comfortable beneath parasols and cooled awnings that shielded them from the brutal California sun.

I looked down at my small hands encased in their karting gloves, gripping the steering wheel tight. I knew the words. 'My name is Darien.'

But all that came out was '*Eu sou Darien.*'

I was six, and English was hard. Whatever I knew was learned from Hollywood movies with Portuguese subtitles.

'*Quero voltar,*' I whispered. *I want to go back to Brazil.* Mãe would never have it.

'Good luck, *amigo.*' The boy next to me was smiling, but there was a nasty glint in his eyes. Even so, I shifted in my seat to face him, curious. He had just spoken Portuguese. Could I talk to him?

'Magalinho!'

My head snapped to the right, towards where the parents were. Mãe crouched in the sand just behind the wire fence that separated the track from the stands. She shook her head, saying to me without a word, *Not worth it*. The heat beat directly down on her unprotected black curls. Sweat was seeping through her orange tank top and dirt dotted the knees of her flared jeans. Her gold hoop earrings glittered, the names in each circular piece of jewellery catching the light: Nico, my father's name; and Darien, mine.

She pointed to the starting line in front of us, making the gilded cross around her neck swish. '*Apenas dirija, menino!*' she shouted. *Just drive!*

I nodded and gave her a thumbs-up.

Maybe the rest of the world saw it as a silly sport that well-to-do families entertained their rambunctious kids with, but to me, even then, racing was my way out. Karting was my *only* way out.

Karting was also cutthroat. You built up your kart, practised till you had blisters on your palms that burned so hard you couldn't even pick up a pencil when you went to school, and when you lost, it was crushing. But it was just entertainment for a lot of these boys.

For me, karting was life. Karting was how I got my Mãe and myself free from the loans and into her very own car garage.

The boy who had spoken Portuguese snorted and snapped his visor down. One of the dads beneath the awnings waved to him and yelled, 'Send him right back across that border, Ryan!'

Mãe's eyes narrowed. She didn't look happy, and this wasn't the kind of upset she got when I talked about home. This was a different kind of upset – the kind of upset she got when people looked down their nose at us, called us names. I might not have known exactly what Ryan's father had said, but I got enough of the message to know that I had to win this race.

The man standing off to the side of the starting line waved us forward to make a formation lap. I began to drive at a steady pace, wiggling the steering to warm my tyres up. We rounded the track before coming back to the main straight and stopping in fifth position, where I would start this race.

Our karts' motors revved loudly, the sound of thirty little tractors vying for a standout performance, trying to catch the eye of sponsors and prestigious karting teams. The same man waited by the line with a green flag.

'*Mostre a eles quem somos!*' yelled Mãe. '*Pa' papai!*'

Show them who we are. For Papai.

The man raised the flag.

He waved it.

I pressed my little foot to the gas pedal. Racing here on this track was not the same as racing back home, but I could imagine. I imagined I was still in Santa Teresa, practising with Tio Julio and Pai in the streets, the sun hanging low in clear skies crisscrossed by thick cable lines.

The karts puttered around me, and grass flew as one or two clipped the corners of the track. I picked my way up the grid, grinning wildly. I had so much power here; the kind of power other kids my age could only dream of.

On the next lap, one of the boys, the one running in second, came around from the inside. I thought he would overtake me, but instead, he stuck right across from me, gluing himself so close to my kart that his wheels threatened to push me off the track. I was losing control with each second.

'People drive dirty,' I remembered Pai telling me. 'They will want to run you off. They'll do it regardless of the consequences. And when that happens . . .'

I felt my father guiding the steering wheel as I sped up and turned wide on the next curve to cut the other boy off. A neat arc, just the way Pai used to drive.

'*Vamos*, Magalinho!' I heard Mãe cheer.

When I finished that race in first place, my debut race in America, I thought my heart would explode out of my chest. I parked my kart and struggled a bit to get my stubby legs out of the seat but, eventually, I succeeded. I ran across the dry grass, straight through the gap in the fence, till my mother's strong arms caught me and lifted me.

'*Mãe, eu venci!*' I squealed. 'I win!'

'Oh, *parabens, meu amor.*' She unbuckled the chin strap and removed my helmet, ruffled my curls before pressing a kiss to my forehead. '*Seu papai também sabe.*'

'Papai?' I echoed incredulously.

Mãe nodded. She smiled then, but there was a hint of something sadder there. Her eyes shone with unshed tears.

The other parents had also come down to join Mãe in the sand. As they reunited with their children, there were sharp words and brusque helmet taps from the fathers and excessive mollycoddling from the mothers. They glanced over at us with disbelief in their eyes, gaping at my mother as she hefted me upon her shoulders, held my hands, and danced in total and utter bliss.

Ryan's dad looked on, appalled, before turning to his son. 'I thought I told you to send that Mexican home!'

At first, I didn't think my mother had heard anything.

But nothing ever escaped Célia Cardoso-Magalhães's ears. She stopped singing just like that, and turned around with me still on her shoulders. Ryan's dad regarded her with what was almost a look of disgust. He was an idiot. Everyone in our neighbourhood in Oakland loved Mãe. They said she had the face of an angel and the work ethic of our greats: Pelé, Ronaldinho, Senna. Even the grandmas and grandpas spoiled her rotten.

'Brazilian,' Mãe said to Ryan's dad.

Everyone within twenty feet turned to peer at us, as if no one had ever stood up to this man before.

'I'm sorry, what?' he spat.

'We are Brazilian, *monte de merda*,' she repeated. I giggled. The last part I could translate easily. 'And for the record, my son has the trophy. It's you who's going home. What's more . . .' She made a flicking motion with her wrists. 'Empty-handed.'

'*Caraca!*' I blurted.

Mãe tugged on my leg with a chuckle. 'Let's go, Magalinho.'

Ryan and his father and everyone else just stood there speechless as Mãe carried me to the car, laughing and joking all the way.

Maybe my mom didn't have a lot to her name back then. Maybe we weren't well-off enough for her to teach me how to fit the newest kart model with the best engine on the market. But she did teach me that compared to money, time is a mountain of wealth, and when you race, when you *live*, time is everything. We have none to waste on hatred.

So we spend each second doing what we love, with the ones we love.

January 2024

Chapter One

Darien

The tram screeches along its cables with a shriek that rivals upset children. I chuckle as I check my phone to find at least ten messages from Mãe. I might only be in California for another handful of days, but that hasn't stopped my mother from putting me to work in her garage.

Mind you, I suck at anything cars most of the time – regular cars. I possess only the bare-bones skills with karts and single-seaters. I can't do much else. But I am good at drawing and painting, which translated to bodywork, making people's rides look pretty. Painting, tints, wraps: that was what I grew up helping Mãe to do in the auto shop she founded, deep in San Francisco proper and about twenty minutes from our Oakland home. The garage was where I picked up one of life's most important lessons: you want something done right, you'd better be willing to get your hands dirty.

I hear the garage before I see it. The boom-boom bass thump of Brazilian funk tells me the day's already begun.

I heft my backpack further up onto my shoulder and blow a hair from my forehead. It's not quite as hot here as everyone makes it seem, now that we're closing in on the fall and getting ready for the winter. I've put on a hoodie and sweats to combat what is basically a light chill for us here in San Francisco, but I never wear anything too nice to the shop. Oil stains tend to get you in that line of work.

'Mãe!' I call, rounding the corner to where both of the big garage doors are open so you can see all the work going on inside. You wouldn't think that anyone in there is cold with all the heat the cars and tools generate. This is nasty, greasy, smelly work, contrasting starkly with the pretty blue neon *Magalinho's* sign over the two white doors, plastered against the brick façade.

I see her sneakered feet peeking out from beneath a Civic that's in less-than-ideal shape, so even though she doesn't answer, I let myself in. I drop my bag near the big black rolling tool chest. 'Mãe!' I repeat over the music.

'*Oi*, Magalinho!' My mom rolls herself into view on her mechanic's creeper, a broad grin on her face as she sits up. I keep telling her she should take Manuel up on his offer to do the undercarriage repairs, but she's just way too stubborn. Maybe I'm also extra, because Miss Célia Cardoso-Magalhães is coming up on her mid-forties and still in the best shape of her life. She's been working on cars since she dropped out of school at thirteen and took up a job at the local garage, if you could even call it that, in Rocinha, to help her parents pay class fees for her younger siblings.

'Hey.' I raise an eyebrow. 'What'd I tell you about the undercarriage?'

She clicks her tongue and waves a dismissive hand my way. 'No, this is my life. It's been my life since I was younger than you. I can't stop now.'

'You love the bottoms of cars that much?'

'Look, Darien.' Something in Mãe's voice changes, something sterner and more fragile. 'It was your father who taught me how to work on the undercarriage. We were just kids then. It's . . . it's a silly thing that keeps me close to him.'

Oh? I hadn't actually known that. I sigh. 'Okay. If permanent back damage brings you closer to Pai.'

'Maga-*lin*-ho!'

'Mãe!' I throw my hands up in surrender. 'I'm done. Promise. So what do you need me to do here?'

My mother glares at me, but she gestures to the Civic. 'This Honda, customer wanted a new paint job, maybe to race or something. We will take care of the internal, but you can start on the body. Matte black and white, he said.'

I can't help but laugh at that one. 'He's gonna look like the cops.'

'Hmm.' Mãe steps back, regarding the Honda as if trying to imagine it with the new paint. 'Reminds me of when you almost got arrested. Remember, that one summer? When was that, you tried to take the Chevy out on the street and—'

I groan like only a kid being perpetually embarrassed by his mother can groan. 'That was *so long* ago!'

'So, it being long ago means I cannot remember it?' She gives me the *I'm still your mother* look, complete with a twinkle of mischief in her eye – where I get it from, I've been told. 'I am not that old yet, Darien.'

'Oh, god. Let's just start on the car.'

The garage begins to come alive as the rest of my mom's crew trickles in. I recognize all of them. Mãe was reluctant to look for new sets of hands once she'd found mechanics she could trust, and her mechanics didn't want to go anywhere else, so they stuck. The team that made up our Magalinho's family were the best around.

'Hey, look who decided to pay a visit!' a stocky, bronze-tanned guy just years older than me calls out as he strolls into the garage.

'What can I say? Mom wants help, I have to respond,' I joke. Manuel Soares da Costa brings me straight in for an enormous hug. It's been almost a year, as it tends to be with Formula seasons. Off on the winters, that's about all the holiday we get other than the brief summer break, now that they're cramming our schedules full of races at every possible turn.

'Good to see you. *E parabéns!*' He wolf-whistles, gripping me by the shoulders. 'I saw that contract you signed. Dude! The numbers on that thing!'

'Ah, best part is still having that car,' I point out with a smirk. 'She's the queen of my heart.'

Manuel presses a hand to his forehead and swoons, which goes wrong when he has to hop over a fallen wrench. 'Can you imagine popping the chassis of an *F1 car* and stripping that engine?'

'Just you, bro,' I tease him. 'You and your engine fetish.'

'Hey, there's a reason your mama trusts me with her cars! And there's definitely a reason you trusted me with yours,' he teases me back. He's quite right, though. Something about engines and their many parts just lines up in Manuel's brain. We used to work together to get my kart going absolutely nuts in local races. Manuel was, I like to say, my first engineer, and – without a doubt – my best.

'When do you go back?' he asks, dropping his bag beside mine.

'Like, three weeks.' I smile at the thought of home. 'Can't wait. Bro, I hear that trolley going outside, and it's . . .'

'Santa Teresa.' Manuel reads my mind with a snort. 'Damn, you talk like my *vô*. All you need's a cane and dentures.'

'Shut up.' I elbow him in the ribs. 'You need to go. I'll take your ass there myself.'

He rolls his eyes. 'Of course, I *want* to go. And I would, but I've got Vanessa here, a kid on the way . . . not quite the time to jet off.'

It takes a minute for that one to sink in.

'Yo . . . you got *what?*'

Manuel's my age. We literally grew up together. I guess with the way I live, I forget that everyone else's lives keep on going. Even this guy, the dude who won a bet and made me pierce my ears before deciding that he wanted his pierced too, the guy who got so drunk he went skinny-dipping in someone's pool the rich neighbourhood over. And now he's having a *child*.

'Pick your jaw up off the floor.' He laughs, partly shy, partly proud.

'Dude! A *kid*,' I yelp, pulling him into another hug. '*Parabéns*, brother. *Wow*.'

'Thank you, Dar.' I can hear the happiness in his voice.

'Well, then, all three of you better come over sometime,' I prod him, trying my best to sound more upbeat than I feel. Maybe it makes me a terrible friend to say it, but man . . . this news has me all up in my own head.

'You said it.' Manuel winks and rolls over to his tool stand. 'Are you guys going to see Teresópolis when you go back? *Please* take good photos if you're there. Ness loves that Paquetá guy.'

'Yeah.' The nostalgia fills me like a can of my favourite cold, fizzy Guaraná. 'It's been a pretty long time.'

For the most part, my early memories of Brazil were nonexistent leading up to Pai's death, save for bits and pieces. But I remember my whole family piling into a minivan and driving the nearly two hours to Teresópolis. The place was pretty, lots to see and do, nature and hiking if you were into it. However, it was also home to Granja Comary, the training facility of Brazil's national football team, the stomping ground of the CBF, the Brazilian Football Confederation. I remember looking up at Granja Comary, with its big lawn bearing the shield of the national team, gated and unreachable. It looked like some kind of top-secret police headquarters, or a military fort. Four-year-old me, dreaming the dreams of every Brazilian kid, thought to myself, *Dang, I'll make it up there some day*.

That was my first and only time in Teresópolis, but I think about it often. Now, it's no longer about visions of going pro in football, it's about what it means to be at the very pinnacle of your sport. And after years and years of work, it's crazy to think I've finally reached the motorsport equivalent: Formula 1.

'You think they'd let you into Granja Comary?' Manuel echoes my thoughts.

I grab my spray gun. 'I could call in a favour from the guys.'

'The guys . . .' Now it's my friend's jaw that goes slack. 'Bro. That's crazy. *A seleção?' The team?*

'Just maybe.'

'Get *out*,' hisses Manuel. 'I should be asking you to get Ness a signed jersey or a voice message or something!'

'I will!' I say with a laugh. 'You know I will!'

'God.' Manuel is still reeling as he begins to take a look at the engine. 'Getting into Granja Comary . . . imagine training there . . . and the *food* . . .'

His musings make me chuckle. I load up the black paint for my spray gun and don my safety goggles and mask.

'Or how about a Granja Comary of your own. For driving and karting, big track all around the whole thing.' Manuel is really getting into it now. He looks like he's just had an earth-shaking vision, a dreamy look all over his face. He is so much sometimes.

'Now that,' I snort, 'is crazy.'

Chapter Two

Shantal

I stare down at my suitcase blankly. It's as if I've got an undeserved pile of riches before me. Stolen, perhaps, a luxury I didn't earn.

This isn't right.

The last time I had taken a plane was with my mother and father, to Georgetown, Guyana. It had not been a happy trip, but it was what was right for Sonia, at least according to the *pandit*. Going home to spread the ashes was the only way to grant her soul peace. I tried my best to assure myself the trip was necessary, but even that felt wrong without her there next to me.

'Soni,' I whisper, 'I can't do this.'

I sit down on the side of my bed and rake my hands through the remains of my hair. It's been over six months since I chopped most of it off in our upstairs bathroom, right after we got back from Georgetown, but I'm still not used to it. I had hair down past my waist before, grew it out because Sonia did, and I wanted to be *just like her*. Now, the waves just skim my shoulders.

Ma hated it. She let out a strangled scream when I came out of the bathroom. 'Shanni, what in the—'

'I had to,' I replied shortly. We didn't talk about it after that. Babu saw and looked at me sadly. He had never been one to yell.

I pick up my phone and scroll till I find my mother in my contacts. The photo of Sonia on my desk stares at me as I hit call and the dial tone drones.

'Hi, Shantal?'

'Ma, I just . . . I can't go.'

'What? No.' There is scolding in her voice. Maybe Babu never yells, but my ma, as wonderful as she is, makes up for this threefold. 'This is so big. Don't joke with me.'

'Not without her, Ma,' I manage.

On the other end of the phone, Ma stays silent.

'What?'

'Shanni,' my mother says, voice as fragile as my resolve. 'It's been six months.'

'Six months won't bring Sonia back.'

'Listen to me, Shantal.'

'Are you back to normal, Ma?' I snap at her. 'Tell me you don't think about Sonia. Tell me you don't try to text her or go to look for her in the house and realize she's left.'

More silence.

'Yes,' she finally admits. 'Yes. Of course, I do that. But this, Shantal, this is the chance of a lifetime. And maybe getting out of this place is what you *need*.'

I swallow hard. 'I love Clapham.'

'I know,' sighs Ma. 'I know you love Clapham. I know you two did everything together.'

'Every decision I made, Ma, I made it with her.'

Sonia and I had dreamed of this for years, an opportunity for me to take my career to a level of leadership. Losing her before I made it to that point was as painful as a knife in my heart, a pain that six months had done nothing to dull.

'Don't make yourself suffer. You've been . . .' I could swear my mother's words threaten to crack with tears. 'You've been living like this long enough. Go and enjoy your life.'

Ma doesn't wait for a response. A beep signals to me that she's hung up.

I throw my phone aside and take the photo of Sonia in its gold frame off my desk. Long black hair, big brown eyes that constantly held a smile, grinning lips outlined in a russet shade she always had on, even if it was only for a supermarket trip. The photographer had caught her mid-laugh. She had the best laugh, and when she smiled, she lit up the room. She was Miss Guyana Great Britain for a year. She was a Bharatanatyam graduate. She was a schoolteacher. You can see it in the picture: she is beautiful, inside and out. Vibrant, gentle, loving. She was full of *life*, and yet Ma thinks I can go on with mine as if nothing happened to my brilliant sister's.

'I've wanted this for years,' I whisper to her. 'But it doesn't mean anything without you.'

I don't think I can do this without her. My heart will scream at me to turn around the second I reach the airport terminal. But I do what I always do, anyway: I force my mind to believe that maybe Ma is right, and maybe I will be able to pick up the pieces of myself and move forward in this new stage of my life.

Chapter Three

Darien

I squint at the missive that my PR manager has sent to me. Judging from the all-caps *READ ASAP* and the many red exclamation emojis following that subject line, it looks to be worth checking out.

Diana puts down her coffee across from me, quirking an eyebrow at my laptop. 'What are you looking at?'

'Revello has that big thing in Calabria or wherever, right? With the track and the development stuff.'

She nods. 'Only because the team is ancient, though. Like, older than Ferrari. Why?'

'God, you guys are so old money.'

She shoots me a blank look. 'What is old money?'

'Unimportant.' I scroll further down the email on my laptop with a badly concealed laugh. 'Apparently Heidelberg finally wants to do the same thing. They've got a centre in progress, this says. Absolutely insane. A development track designed especially for their cars . . .'

'And?' demands Diana.

'This is supposed to open in *Rio* in a *week*,' I say with a disbelieving laugh. 'No way.'

'Heidelberg? In Brazil?' Diana takes a huge swig of coffee from her mug, eyes wide and attention piqued. 'What? When? Why did they contact you?'

'I think you've had enough of that for today.' I grab the mug emblazoned with CERTIFIED CAR GUY (a gift from my mother) from her and set it on the counter near the sink. 'Dude. You've been here for no more than a week and *already* you've cleaned out all our coffee twice.'

'Hey, it was your mom who said to make myself at home,' she points out smartly. 'Is it a crime that I wanted to see California for the first time?'

Diana is now a frequent flyer over at Heidelberg Hybridge Formula 1 Team, ever since she got engaged to my teammate, Miguel de la Fuente. She's not only the sole woman on the grid, but also the driver who has lived under a rock the longest. To date, she still hasn't seen snow fall. She didn't know what 'gaslighting' was until a month ago. She's like a really poorly adjusted older sister. You can see why my mother took pity on her and let her stay over till she leaves to canoodle with her trophy fiancé in a few weeks.

Also, Mãe is just *way* too nice.

I roll my eyes. 'Fine. But we need to adjust your caffeine intake.'

'Shut up, Darien.' She slaps the table in front of me, making the wooden toucan napkin holder jump a foot in the air. 'Now. What is with this Heidelberg drama?'

I keep going on the email, and there's a postscript there, typed out by my PR manager. *They're gonna need you there for this one. Call me as soon as you can.*

Before I've even finished reading, my phone starts to vibrate in my pocket, and I fish it out with a grip so unstable that my hands could be coated in butter. The caller ID, as if by fate, reads my manager's name: KATRINA (HERE COMES THE HURRICANE).

'Answer it!' Diana hisses, peering over my shoulder at my phone.

I nod frantically and hit the accept button on the screen, trying my hardest not to drop the thing. 'Uh. Hey, Katrina?'

'Darien?' There's the tinge of an Australian accent in her voice. Katrina, who's been putting up with my crap for years (as in, since I joined with Vittore in Formula 3), and helped me build up my public persona, is essentially the determiner of my fate. She's kept media disasters far away from me and taught me to suppress my temper during the awful time I had with Vittore's Formula 1 team before I moved to Heidelberg. She's kind of a blessing. 'I hope you've seen the email.'

Diana watches me with eyes the size of dinner plates.

'Yeah, read the whole thing just now.'

'So, Darien. *You* compete under Brazil's flag in Formula 1, the only one on the grid to represent the country. You have an excellent story. Pocketed your first win at home, grabbed multiple last year, all the works.' Katrina clears her throat. 'You're young, and you're drawing fans. And as you can now see, Heidelberg has chosen to put down roots in Brazil. Do you start to see how you come in here at all?'

'Um . . . not quite, to be honest. Like . . .' I trail off. 'What am I coming into? And why Brazil?'

'Well. Let's start at Redenção, shall we?' says Katrina in what I know to be her 'down to business' tone. 'Darien. The Regional team you founded is literally *based in Rio*. Heidelberg already loves you as their driver. I don't see why they wouldn't do this in Brazil. Heidelberg is willing to take a chance on you and let Redenção *share* that centre next year.'

I feel the hairs on my arms stand on end. I can't believe that this is happening. Rio Redenção is the team that I started and then have worked on expanding for the past two years through my place in Formula 1. It's a Formula Regional fixture, focused on giving homegrown Brazilian drivers from all backgrounds a chance in motorsport. Bringing Redenção into the Heidelberg family definitely explains why Heidelberg would want to start a centre in Brazil. Our team principal, at the end of the day, isn't much different from me – his team is a progressive new addition to a rich old man's sport. Both of us need connections to carve out a place in motorsport: Redenção needs Heidelberg to vault our young athletes into the sport; Heidelberg needs Redenção to establish a feeder team for itself, a steady stream of new talent. But I hadn't thought for a second that Heidelberg cared enough to *partner* on a place for our athletes to train.

'Redenção will *what*?' I match Diana's expression of confusion, and she shakes her hands at me, as if to say *what is going on?*

'Yes, Darien. You're a PR dream, like I said. Heidelberg is young and fresh, what with you and Miguel. It's a perfect opportunity for them to make moves to show their commitment to finding talent all over the globe, and put themselves in the limelight. You know what their image is: growth, improvement, but only the best,' Katrina goes on matter-of-factly. 'So this is a *huge* deal. They've spared no expense on this project. You'll have top-of-the-line technology, living quarters, everything in one place.'

My jaw drops in the direction of the polished tile floor.

'They want you to join them quickly,' continues Katrina. 'This is short notice, I am well aware, but they'd like you to be there when the centre opens. That's in just about a week. The plan is for the entire Heidelberg team, our new reserve driver included, to be out in Rio till that first winter testing, which, for the first time in Formula 1 history, will take place in Brazil, at the new track attached to Heidelberg's facility. The press is going to be all over this going into the new season. It's a huge change for Heidelberg, and you're at the core of it, Darien. Do you understand?'

'I understand,' I echo, dumbfounded.

This is amazing.

This is *everything* to me. This is everything I've been hoping for since I was a kid growing up here, dreaming I'd get the chance to do my home country justice. There isn't a day that passes by when I don't long to feel closer to Brazil. Now, that day is here.

My F1 team is coming to my home, and my entire country will be watching.

'Good. We'll be talking in person soon,' says Katrina. 'In the meanwhile, all your itinerary information will be sent to you via email. I'm aware you're already flying over, but we'll be moving your flight date up to get you here in time. You'll be in Rio the day before the grand opening. We're delighted to have you – trust me, Darien. This project will be an exciting one for the team. But you should know: there's a lot riding on this launch going well.'

'Yeah,' I murmur. I feel like I'm trying to drink water from a fire hose with all this information, but I'm attempting to grab onto the most important parts. Like this one. 'A lot?'

'Well, we didn't want to stress you during the off-season, which is why we've decided to greenlight this all now, but Heidelberg will need evidence, you know, that this state-of-the-art facility is working. The funding is no light matter. The sponsors will want to see results.' Katrina clears her throat.

'And that will be in the form of bettering last year's Drivers' and Constructors' Championship standings. Without which . . . it's possible your contract could be on the line, as well.'

At that, my heart sinks.

Last year, we were third in the Constructors' Championship. That means we'll need first or second this year. And last year, I was fourth in the Drivers'. Now, I have to podium.

'Just . . . just me?'

'Darien, Heidelberg is investing in *you*. Your home country, partnership with your racing team. You're going to have to deliver if we want this new facility to keep its funding for next season, not to mention if we want Heidelberg to keep you for next season too. And ideally . . . you know you're young, doing well for yourself. They'd love to see a title back in the trophy case.'

I've picked up my jaw now, but it's just so my mouth can form an *O* of shock.

'I'll be sending you that itinerary. Speak to you soon,' Katrina finishes far too peppily.

I don't let the phone move away from my ear till I hear the dull tone that tells me she's hung up.

Frantically, I open my laptop again. There's a gentle chime as my inbox tab lights up. I've never clicked on something so fast. I lean back and let out a low whistle. There it is.

Re: Heidelberg Hybridge Ring

'What? What is it?' Diana scrambles to get out of her chair and stand at my side so she can see it for herself.

'Look at this thing.' I exchange a slack-jawed look with Diana as we glance over the floorplan of the new building. 'It's huge. This is gonna be the bridge between Heidelberg and Redenção, man. This is unreal.'

My head spins like I've just downed a whole bottle of tequila.

I suddenly remember what Manuel had been going on about: a Granja Comary for drivers. Apparently, as if by magic, here it is now: a chance to attract more drivers from home, to show everyone that Brazil can hold its own against all-comers. New equipment, analytics, it would level our game up massively. Redenção drivers would have a fast track, a direct affiliation to F1 through Heidelberg, a shared facility.

But at what cost? I need to get third in the World Drivers' Championship.

That's insanity.

'Well, look at you go!' hoots Diana, stealing back the CAR GUY mug for one more sip. She studies me for a second, calming down to ask, 'They'll want results from you, won't they?'

I let out a laugh, awkwardly hiding how nervous I'm feeling at the prospect of even more weight on this next season. 'It's not just gonna be the average expectations this year. They're doing all this extra stuff, bringing new people onboard . . .'

'The WDC,' finishes Diana. 'Bit of pressure there.'

'Yeah,' I stare at the email, at the open reply text box yet to be filled in. There was always going to be pressure; it's the price I pay to drive in F1. It's the price I paid when I took it upon myself to get Mãe and me out of Oakland. But I had never felt it so intensely before.

Looks good, I type. *I'll be there in a week.*

Chapter Four

Shantal

Marcus shoves his phone in front of my face. 'Shantal!'

'What!' I yelp, nearly slapping the phone right out of his hand. 'Oh, god, you scared me.'

He waits barely a second for me to compose myself before coming back with a vengeance fuelled by multiple cups of cold brew. 'Do you realize what you're going to do? Look at this!'

The staccato music absolutely pouring from his phone speaker, dripping with bass, repels me instantly. 'My days. Marcus, turn that down. What is that?'

'It's Brazilian funk, *Miss Rio*.' Raya pokes her head out from behind the wall of her cubicle.

'Yes, it is. Look!' Marcus attempts to bring the screen out one more time, but I wave a hand and turn back to my monitors.

'I would, but if I want to go to Brazil, I have to finish all the prep work first,' I counter slyly. It's true. I've been given a laundry list of things to sort through prior to my flight out. This new sports centre they're setting up is no small operation, and their expectations of my simulator program are equally enormous.

'No, Shan, seriously.' Now Joel has rolled out of his workspace in his beloved gaming chair, which takes a lot, because Joel is the sort of man who minds his own business as a principle. 'Darien Cardoso-Magalhães is Brazil's *future* of motorsport. That song—'

'Is Brazilian funk. I know.'

'It's about *him*,' Joel corrects me. 'They made this guy a song.'

'As a citizen of the United Kingdom, you're really gonna say you've never had exposure to Formula 1?' prods Marcus. He's the biggest fan of this racing stuff I know, but I can't say I share his enthusiasm.

I squint, trying to remember the last time I watched a race. 'I mean, I've seen Silverstone on TV, I think, but I don't follow it religiously enough to know names.'

'You're about to.' I detect a chord of envy in Raya's voice. 'All the guys on that Formula 1 grid are . . . lord, I'd at least learn to pick out Darien in a crowd, if I were you.'

Okay, this may be true. I am going into the chance of a lifetime poorly armed. My heart clenches as I think of all the deep googling my sister would have had us doing.

'Sorry, all, but like I said, I've got a bunch to get done.' I gesture to the sticky notes all over my monitors. 'Heidelberg Hybridge Ring isn't going to get its own sims up and running.'

Maybe doing this entire thing halfway across the world while my family's in a state of emotional fragility isn't a part of my dream – I'd have loved to stay in London – but it's an opportunity to bring my brainchild to the very top of motorsport certainly is. I've worked for Conquest since midway through university, picking up an internship that became a career. Since that point, our company's been primarily linked to one of the many South

London football clubs we share home base with, Crystal Palace. I'd always dreamed of working in sport, maybe coaching or something, so running training using virtual reality and simulation for world-renowned footballers, bridging my physiotherapy education with new-era machinery . . . it's pretty close. And now, with a little help from our friends in the programming and tech departments, our task team has finally finished the motorsport simulator I hope can completely change how drivers practise – starting, unbelievably, with Formula 1. We worked for ages on this, and everything is ours from the ground up: the parts for the sim, the program we wrote.

It's still hard to believe that Conquest has given me the chance to manage an entire operation across the ocean on my own, not to mention in a whole new sport. *Team simulator specialist*. A title they've created just for me. It's amazing, but it's a terrifying burden, and without Sonia, this giant step just feels like one I can't take.

'All right,' Marcus gives up, voice shrouded in an air of annoyance. 'But don't work yourself into the ground, Shantal. Have some fun. This trip is a chance for you to test your limits, yes, but it's also an opportunity for you to *finally* let loose. You've been . . . kind of tense lately.'

Oh? I know for a fact I'd become aggressively highly strung in the past couple of months, but I take that one straight to the chest with a look of irritation at Marcus.

'Exactly,' adds Joel enthusiastically, which doesn't help at all. 'An opportunity to . . . get funky.'

Raya shakes her head, looking away with a roll of her eyes. 'Please never say that again.'

As the two of them get straight to bickering as usual, I turn to my monitors. The wallpapers, our Conquest team posing with Crystal Palace FC's, remind me of everything we've built here. I can't back down out of fear now.

Like any project this far from the normal for us, the stakes are high. I'll be with Heidelberg for at least the first half of the season, up until summer break, with the second half optional if I do my job well enough.

Everything pertaining to the simulator technology in that building, all Conquest's doing, has to pay off. If this doesn't benefit Heidelberg – if they don't see significant improvement from their standings last year, and move up from third in the Championship – then they won't find any value in spending millions on us any longer. They'll sever ties with Conquest, the tie in question being me.

I open the tab holding the immersive floorplan for the Heidelberg Hybridge Ring Complex, just landed in my inbox from *the* principal of Heidelberg's F1 team. It's a humongous facility, nestled within its own track, two expansive storeys high, even equipped with drivers' living quarters. All of this is wonderful, but I immediately click and zoom in to the gym, stacked with what will be a state-of-the-art simulator room. As always, it's not the building but the powerful technology inside I'm interested in, waiting to take Heidelberg Hybridge to Championship victory.

I adjust the photo of my sister on my desk, beside my tiny portrait of Shri Ram and Sita. I think of nearly breaking down over the phone to my mother. *Go and enjoy your life*.

'Those birds went extinct years ago!' Raya's voice soars over the open tops of the cubicles.

'I refuse to believe that. Macaws are *resilient*,' insists Joel.

They could have chosen Joel or Raya or Marcus, anyone who worked on this sim, but it's me going to Brazil.

You earned this, I think to myself as I click into the technology menu. *Now come through.*

Maybe I'm not going to Brazil to let loose, but I've never been one to half-ass a project. This could be my big break, and I'm not letting it go, no matter how wrong all of it feels.

Chapter Five

Darien

On account of getting thrown onto a new flight two weeks before my mother to reach Rio in time for training, there's no one to keep me awake on the plane. I sleep through most of my trip in the cushy cabin, but my eyes flutter open to breakfast. This is perfect because, as I eat, I get to watch us begin the stunning descent into Rio de Janeiro.

We soar over the expansive city, so close, yet so high up. I make out the beaches of Copacabana, dotted with umbrellas, the psychedelic mosaic sidewalks of Ipanema and Leblon, where all the hotels stretch up to the sky and the rich tourists do their shopping and bar-hopping. Just past it, I can see Rocinha, the biggest favela in Rio, a mishmash of brightly coloured buildings perched precariously all over a massive hill – my mother's home. And the backdrop to it all, our national park, Tijuca, with its seemingly never-ending greenery, climbing upwards till it reaches a peak, where Christ the Redeemer stands, arms wide.

It's the best welcome I could ask for.

We touch down at Rio de Janeiro International Airport in Galeão. I don't actually enter the airport; stairs are folded out from the plane, and I'm shepherded down them by several security guards.

'It's good, man,' I try to tell one on my way out, but he just shakes his head, stern-faced. Funny, the security is never this tight in the Euro countries. I don't think all the people putting it in travellers' heads that Rio is one of the most dangerous cities in the world are doing Brazil any favours. Either way, I know how to get around here much better than anyone on my detail, so escaping their clutches won't be hard.

We get out of the airport unscathed using a deserted back gate. My car will be in the garage of my Santa Teresa house, not far from the neighbourhood where I grew up. I offered to let Mãe use my house when she's here, but she stays in our old one, telling me I'm grown and need my own space. Truthfully, I know that's partly bullshit. Other than me and the Chevy, the house is all that's really left of my dad. Mãe keeps her distance from the memories all year, but the break is her chance to feel close to Pai again, even if it's only for a moment.

Before I know it, the driver has pulled our black Porsche right up to my front gates and scanned in, the journey quick due to the clever route he took to get here. The fact that there are no fans around is really refreshing. Of course, I love them, but sometimes it's worth lying to the media about your date of arrival to get a day's peace. I'll let myself drown in a sea of hats, posters and driver cards tomorrow, when training at the new facility will begin, and my team will place a new weight on my shoulders. For now, I'm afforded some semblance of calm in this place.

Santa Teresa is on a hilltop. All the roads here are very curvy and very narrow. We are beautifully untouched; our town never quite left the nineteenth century. We have the only tram in the city that still operates, canary yellow paint peeling just slightly, but charm still fully intact. My childhood here plays out in my mind like a dream. Santa Teresa is so stunning it's surreal, like someone has drawn this caricature of a small town nestled in a crazy city and thrown me into it. I could have chosen a place anywhere in Rio, but nothing will ever top Santa Teresa for me. Even San Francisco can't match it. This will always be home.

I feel that the moment I enter my house. It's not much flashier than anywhere else in town. One floor, white plaster walls, arched windows, a roof of curved terracotta tiles. It bakes during the day and simmers at night. I kick off my Sambas once I'm inside, and slip on the well-worn pair of flip-flops lying on the tiled floor. It's just the way I left it from summer break; even the houseplants look the same. Granted, they're fake because I'm away half the time, but it matters to me. This house is my order among the chaos, my safe haven, my breathing space.

I collapse into my armchair with such force that I'm surprised the shawl draped across the back of it doesn't fall right off. I close my eyes, and I listen. I relish how distant the chatter, the beeping of the horns, and the rattling tram are. Here, it's just the faint rustle of the leaves, the chirping of birds rarer than a blue moon.

And, apparently, the loud default ringing of my phone.

I groan and roll over to grab my phone from the coffee table. Tranquillity never lasts long. The call is, of course, from my trainer. I love Celina Valdez to death, but in this moment, I want to throw her phone in one of Rio's many lakes and make sure it never sees the light of day again.

'*Tudo bem!*' Celina chirps the second I hit the green *accept* button. 'I've been practising. Tell me that was good.'

'It was good.'

'Perfect. Then hit me with a reply.'

'Well, *foi beleza*, until you disturbed my peace . . .' I drawl sarcastically.

'I don't know what that means, but thank you. I love to hear that I'm excelling at my job,' Celina shoots right back. 'Just calling to make sure you're aware that tomorrow's centre orientation begins at eight a.m. sharp. It's a brand-new facility. Let's be on time, yes?'

'Sure.'

'So no partying.'

I should have seen that one coming. As much as I loved the calm of my corner of Santa Teresa, there was something about the party scene, most likely the sense of anonymity that went with a roomful of inebriated clubbers, strobe lights, and smog. I could have a good time without scrutiny or recognition (which, unfortunately, wouldn't be happening again anytime soon).

'Where's this complex, again?' I cleverly gloss over Celina's unpopular directive.

She makes a disapproving sound. 'Not far from some area called Urca. It's a wonderful location.'

Celina is right about that. The views from the track will be crazy. Spaces near Ipanema get to be ridiculously crammed with tourists, but Urca is typically much less congested and can be much more low-key. Heidelberg seems to have made a wise decision.

'Great. I'll be there at eight.'

'You will.' My trainer's proclamation sounds almost like a threat. Like I said, I can't help loving her. 'Because if not, you'll have worse people to deal with than just me.'

Chapter Six

Shantal

'I think this map's upside down.'
I attempt to give the map on my phone a look from a couple of different angles, but none of it makes sense. This place, as beautiful as it is, has turned out to be a maze as complex as London.

Raya groans from the video call. We've never been too fond of each other, co-workers who kept one another at a distance, but I wasn't sure who else to call. In hindsight, Raya Almeida probably should have been Conquest's number-one choice for this job: well-travelled, social butterfly, half-Brazilian and fluent in Portuguese. She has a framed photo on her desk, where she stands at a party in a sparkly gold dress, Neymar Jr's arm around her waist from the left, Richarlison de Andrade's from the right. She also knows both Rio de Janeiro and São Paulo, the site of the F1 race that will take place later in the year, inside out. She probably grew up next door to this Darien. I have the feeling that if it weren't for the high quality of my work on the sim and all the sleepless nights I'd contributed to this project until we finally got to a 'eureka' moment, it could very well have been Raya here instead of me.

'Your map is not upside down,' Raya is doing a bad job at hiding her smile. 'That's how Rio *looks*. Where are you exactly, again?'

I look around for some indicator, but it's all just people everywhere. I swear the taxi dropped me off right where I'd be staying, unless my poor pronunciation landed me somewhere else entirely. Wherever I am, it's extremely loud, samba blaring as people congregate around small tents stocked with drinks, and yet more start to dance in the middle of the street.

'There's some arches here,' I attempt. It's the best I can do; there are, in fact, rows of arches that form what looks like an aqueduct behind the crowds and tents. 'Old looking. People are partying here.'

'Arcos da Lapa,' determines Raya off-handedly. 'Great, so you are near Santa Teresa. There's a tram that goes over the arches, have you seen that?'

'I think so.'

'Good. Then what you're going to do is—'

I wait for a directive, but none comes. Raya's face has frozen. A little exclamation point pops up, above the words *No Connection*.

'Shit!' I give my phone a desperate smack – nothing. My lifeline is gone.

With shaky hands, I turn the screen and give the photo of the map one more try, but I've already lost my composure. I'm working on my own here, completely and utterly. I have to keep my wits about me, or at least pretend to. I take a deep breath. Rio is huge. Where am I, even? Santa Teresa, what is that?

I knew coming here was a stupid idea. It's what my gut has been telling me the whole time. I feel the gaping hole beside me where Sonia would be, solving our map problem in the jab of a finger, more now than I have in months. But it's not our problem. It's mine, and I can't, for the life of me, figure it out.

'*Oi, tudo bem?*'

I jump a little at the sound of a distinct voice. Portuguese, of which I know about two words. I ignore it at first, until I hear it behind me again.

'Um, are you good?'

This time, it's English, a distinct American accent permeating each word. I turn to its source: some guy who looks rather amused by my map.

'Do you speak—'

'English,' I finish. 'And I'm fine.'

'Hmm.' He shoves his hands in the pockets of his black football shorts. 'Your fake map says otherwise.'

'My what?' I glance down at my map. 'This is perfectly real.'

'No, look, *your* Ipanema is, like, on a big-ass hill. Ipanema's that way.' He points in the general direction of the beach. 'It's *flat.*'

His cocoa eyes crinkle as I take in this information. This man is holding back laughter right now.

'Are you sure?' I reply, sceptically.

He looks slightly surprised at this. He tilts his head, making just a few strands of the blond-tinged curls from the top of his undercut of dark hair fall out of place. 'You really . . .'

'I really . . . what?'

'Nothing.' It's like he's trying not to burst out laughing as he peers at my map. 'But actually. Find a new map.'

My eyebrows slowly climb up my forehead. 'I'm sorry, why should I trust that advice?'

'Dude. I'm a Rio native,' he says, miffed. 'Pretty sure I know what I'm talking about.'

You sound American, I'd love to mention, but I keep my mouth shut and instead focus my energy on finding another map. Unfortunately, the search engine stalls and gives me that same error. *No Connection*.

'Listen,' I sigh. The guy has got on my last nerve, but I admit it, I need help. 'Could you just point me to, um Vila Atlântica?'

'Oh . . . for real?' He grins, this time with no sarcasm or snark. 'You're a ten-minute walk from here.'

My mouth nearly falls open. Seriously? A ten-minute walk? That's *it*?

'Every "ten-minute walk" I've tried so far hasn't turned out that way,' I say in a fairly horrible attempt to justify my lack of direction.

'Okay. I'm being a dick. Rio is a hard city to navigate, I don't blame you,' he admits rather sheepishly, scratching the side of his neck. I catch a glimpse of angel wings tattooed there. It looks like that's not the only one; I catch sight of more ink on his forearms, lines forming detailed drawings across his dark tan skin. 'Do you want me to walk you?'

I'm not sure what my expression betrays, but he adds, 'It's not far. I could just show you how to get there, if you want.'

So I either get hopelessly lost in the streets of Rio de Janeiro (again), trying to follow this guy's instructions, or I go on a walk with said guy and hope I make it to my lodgings alive.

This is why I was never the travel-savvy sister.

I sigh. Here we go. 'Could you possibly walk me, Mister . . .'

From the crowd of dancers and drinkers behind us, someone suddenly yelps. My eyes travel back to where a quickly growing clump of people have begun to gesture towards my new guide, murmuring in rapid Portuguese. One or two bring out their phones.

'Uh. André,' he manages after a beat, gaze flickering to the makeshift paparazzi for just a moment. The lights around us cast shadows on his face, highlighting his strong nose, well-defined jaw and muscular neck. His eyebrows knit together and create a small furrow in his forehead.

'Are you on the national football team or something?' I joke. At least, it's intended to be a joke. André, who's already starting to walk off, doesn't seem amused. He waves an arm with urgency.

'Let's go,' he calls.

We pick our way through the sidewalks, me trying very hard to keep up with André's clipped pace. Fortunately, he slows down a couple of minutes in, enough for me to catch my breath.

'So,' I huff as I match his steps, hiking my backpack straps up on my shoulders, 'you never answered my question.'

'No, I'm not on the team . . . What's your connection?' He points to my shirt, Heidelberg Hybridge's kit from last year. It has the ice blue and white, and the printed logos of the sponsors. 'The city's got Formula fever with that new track out here, and that livery's one they know well. They can probably smell the affiliation on you.'

'I'm no driver,' I start.

'What are you? Paddock team?'

'Here to set up the training program,' I explain. 'I'm integrating it with their practice plans.'

'That's pretty cool,' remarks André. 'Are you a fan of the sport?'

There's humour in his voice, as if he sees right through me, but I just shrug. 'I watch on and off. Maybe Silverstone each year, nothing much.'

'Okay.' He nods. 'Is there something you have against it, or . . .?'

'I don't know. It's a little long.' I struggle to find the right words. 'Two hours of just racing? The same path, over and over?'

41

'Two hours isn't the worst.'

'That's true, but I'm impatient.'

He chuckles. 'Yeah. Speaking of which, this should be you.'

I follow his line of sight, and indeed, there it is: Vila Atlântica, as promised. It's not a traditional hotel, with just a few floors and a terrace rooftop. The exterior is a fresh cream colour, illuminated by both sconces and pole lights.

'Is that the only bag you've got?' André remarks of my backpack.

'They said the rest will be sent over.'

'Ah. Sure you aren't a driver?'

I roll my eyes. 'Fairly positive.'

He smirks, still apparently amused. It's a great first hour in Brazil if my stupidity has already been exposed by a local who's also had to serve as my tour guide. That would be enough on its own, but the laughter dancing in his dark eyes sends me spiralling into a pit of questions. If this André finds me so funny and inept, what will that say about my work here?

'Don't worry.' He seems to know just what's on my mind. 'Rio gets easier as you spend time here. She's not as bad as she seems.'

The diamond studs in André's ears glint under the streetlights as he waves with a charmingly dimpled smile, stepping back the way we came. Lights cast perfect shadows on his strong nose and slightly stubbled jaw. 'Good luck.'

He's around the corner and out of sight within the minute. I look up at the cosy villa and, with one last tug of my backpack strap, I make my way up the stairs to the door.

Chapter Seven

Darien

The streets become more and more crowded with cars and foot traffic as I drive closer to the Urca neighbourhood. I've never seen this many people in the area, but it's evident that the arrival of Heidelberg Hybridge to our new state-of-the-art facility has snagged their interest. I take in the sights of sidewalks awash in pedestrians beneath endless blue skies as my silver AMG putters along happily.

Watching all the locals interspersed with tourists, I think of the girl from yesterday. I'd say the map situation was hysterical but, as well as I know Rio, I can't say I'm much better on race weekends, when I'm on unfamiliar turf. I don't know quite how to explain it. Just the fact that she didn't have a shred of an idea about the crazy half of my life . . . it was like having my goggles on in the garage. It felt good to fly under the radar for ten minutes, so I rolled with it.

The drive into the complex tugs me back to reality. It's a

nightmare. I can hear the screams of anticipation, the heavy thump of funk music.

But beyond it all, there's the Heidelberg Hybridge Ring Complex. It's not tall so much as wide, the exterior glittering white beneath the Brazilian sun. I have to do a full left-to-right scan to make out the individual sections: the squarer block towards the back likely houses the drivers' rooms; the circular offshoot in front is possibly a gym. What stands out most, though, is the track. It weaves around the building, with its own mini pit and garages embedded behind the complex. The reality of the project almost makes all the pressure worth it. Maybe I could have imagined something this groundbreaking in America or in one of Europe's many wealthy, racing-crazy nations, but in Brazil? I'm still processing it.

I'm led to a kerb by a few officers on scooters, where I park my car and turn it over to a valet. He informs me that there's a car park gated off just past the complex.

Although now, I notice, a lot is gated off. It's more like Granja Comary than I had imagined, with crash-fencing cutting the track off from the greenery, and the open black gates I'd come in through. I'm not yet sure if I like that.

'Darien!' someone yells. My time to think is limited as the officers, now on foot, clear a path towards the complex.

I've decided to go effective for today's outfit: the new kit hasn't yet ended up in my hands, so I went with a white Balenciaga tee and beige sweat shorts, paired with a Heidelberg cap, as per usual. Naturally, shoes had to carry the outfit, so I pulled out one of my favourite pairs of white Dunks to match.

I move pretty slowly, though, wary of the excited fans here. Without them, I doubt I'd even have reason to race. They wave flags and posters and caps my way. I grin and sign all I can with a flourish. Every so often, an avid group of fans hand me a phone for a selfie.

I'm almost to the doors when a young journalist off to my right shouts, 'Do you know who else is joining you on this project?'

I just chuckle and shrug the journalist's way. I have my guesses, people in the motorsport world I could name who might help with all this tech, but I can't say anything for sure.

As I continue into the complex, the same crowd of officials is holding open the doors as if parting an ocean of metal and glass. But just past them, interacting with the press inside by the staircase to the next floor, I see a familiar face.

The first thing I notice is the glint of her nose ring, winking at me as if to grab my attention. It works. I stop directly in my tracks as I take in the slightly upturned chocolate eyes, the perfect lips shining with a brown gloss, the proud tilt of her chin. She holds herself with poise. Her hair is down now, instead of in the scrunchie ponytail of yesterday, just sweeping her shoulders in waves. She looks freer, effortless yet confident, determined. It's a good look on her. A really good look.

Her gaze shifts just slightly my way. 'Oh, shit.' I cough as we make the briefest eye contact, and slip behind an officer. Ah, yes. *André*.

These days, like I said, I don't get a moment's peace. F1 has vaulted me further into the public eye than I ever would have chosen. And now, it's pushed an enormous responsibility onto me for the coming season. So sure, maybe our interaction was funny, but maybe it was also nice to have some anonymity. For someone to look at me and see nothing but another dude who knows all the nooks and crannies of his home, who floats around the Arches looking for good beer and a party and maybe a pickup football game. In her eyes, there was indifference, and I don't want to lose that.

But now we're here. She'd mentioned helping with the set-up around here; I thought it might be in passing. Yet she stands here surrounded by media. I suppose I'm not the only one who understated their role in this operation.

'Darien, you there?'

Crap. That's Celina, nothing if not right on time. I'll do anything to keep this situation from going sour, but I can't in good conscience hide from my trainer (and life coach, for the record).

Slowly, I creep out from behind the officer still standing on guard. Celina is at the door, arms akimbo, eyebrows raised.

My dear Celina is not the kind of person who likes to blend in. She is both my confidante and my tormentor. Her blonde-rose-dyed hair is thrown into a high ponytail. There is no mercy in her grey eyes today. She is inches shorter than me and still manages to make it feel like I am cowering beneath her.

'What in god's name are you doing?' she demands. 'Are you *hiding*? Darien, this is your chance to make a *good* impression!'

'I know,' I grumble in reply. But my eyes still unconsciously float to the circle of reporters, double-checking that this woman hasn't found me out.

Too late, though. She's been replaced by some old white man. Which means she could now be anywhere.

Celina and I walk through the doors, beneath built-in metal detectors and into the lobby of the facility. The glossed floors glimmer and, over our heads, the ceiling is a great big window that lends a complete view of the clear sky.

Immediately, the press envelop us without mercy. A million questions are shouted as we go elbow to elbow with packs of reporters. I just raise a hand and forge towards the elevators, which is what (I think) Celina had instructed in her 'arrival plan' email. I'm not one for minute details, as I'm sure you can tell.

'Someone should meet us here,' she says. 'Help us find our way up to the conference room.'

I almost gag. A conference? I won't survive it.

'Excuse me?'

We turn around. Our guide is here . . .

. . . and it's her.

Her eyebrows furrow as the math starts to click. She exhales slowly and deliberately, sweeping a curl from her round face.

She forces a smile that doesn't reach her eyes. It makes me shift slightly in my spot. I've screwed up . . . clearly. 'Darien Cardoso-Magalhães and Celina Valdez?'

Celina nods happily. I can't bring myself to do the same. An invisible vice grips my chest as I watch the acute discomfort cross our guide's face.

'Pleasure to meet you. I'm Shantal Mangal.' Shantal swallows hard, straightens a minuscule crease in her white team top. 'Let me take you up.'

Chapter Eight

Shantal

The elevator takes longer than I would like to reach the second floor. I try my best to avert my eyes from so-called André during this time, but he's a better liar than I am – clearly – and is bold enough to attempt eye contact. I'm confused and insulted all at once. I'm not sure what kind of a sick joke it was for Darien Cardoso-Magalhães to capitalize on the fact that I didn't know who Darien Cardoso-Magalhães is. It only stings further as I put two and two together, realizing that his stupid smirks and laughs were probably because this was all pretty entertaining as far as he was concerned. Not to mention the fact I've now got to *work* with this guy, who made a joke of my ignorance. Is it too late to go back to Clapham?

'Right this way.' I lead the two of them, Darien and his trainer, down the hall dedicated to office and board meeting spaces, and into the main conference room.

André – *Darien* – stops his trainer. 'I'm just gonna be out here a moment. I have a couple questions for Miss, um, Mangal regarding this facility.'

Celina looks pleased at what she may be misinterpreting as his proactivity. 'Sounds good.'

She heads inside, and I stare directly at him, my irritation refusing to take a back seat.

'Oh, so you have a few questions?' I cross my arms in an almost protective gesture. 'I think I'll start with one of my own. Who is André . . . Darien?'

He flinches a little on the last word – his real name. It's been quite a while since my tongue was this sharp.

'Um . . . me?' he tries, pairing the sentiment with an extremely uncomfortable megawatt smile.

I just stand there in disbelief. 'Are you really *smiling* at me right now?'

He gulps like a scolded child. 'Okay. So. André is not completely my name. Hear me out—'

'How could I hear you out?' It's a miracle I keep my voice even, what with the wave of temper rising in my chest. 'You are a *Formula 1 driver* who is not, in fact, named André. Maybe I don't know you, but the fact that you thought I was gullible enough that you could lie to my face about your *identity* hurts. Why, tell me, should I hear you out?'

'Because I *liked* your ignorance. It wasn't stupid.'

Now I'm even more confused. I squint. 'What?'

'I didn't want you to care about who I was,' he says quietly. 'You didn't even know. I liked that. I wasn't about to change it.'

I hate to admit it, but that soft tone of his files away at the sharp edges of my internal rage. I feel my hands slowly uncurl from the fists they've made at my sides. The tension seeps away.

I imagine being in his situation. Poor guy, millions of dollars and fans, multiple cars and houses. Right. But no privacy. No ability to truly know if your circle is real or fake.

'Hmm.' I put my guard back up the second I realize it's coming down. He won't win me over that easily. 'At least one of us benefited from your charade,' I observe.

He does that dumb head-tilt again, peering up at me from beneath the shadow of his cap. He smiles for real, the sort of smile that reaches his eyes, making them narrow happily, and reveals just the right number of pearly whites. 'If I'm remembering correctly, we both benefited. You got to your hotel safely.'

I feel my cheeks go warm. Ugh. 'You're infuriating for someone who's apparently so loved, do you know that?'

Darien laughs. Initially, his little confession seemed like it could be fabricated, but his casual manner erases any doubt I had of his honesty. Every movement he makes is so easy, from the way he messes with the hem of his T-shirt to the way he twists the back of one of his earrings in thought.

'So my teammate likes to tell me,' he replies, rich voice surrounded by a chuckle.

He breezes easily through the door to the conference room. I grit my teeth and file in after him.

We're about the last ones in. I take my seat beside the Heidelberg team manager, a man named Afshin Demir. He's not nearly as old as I thought he'd be – the guy is as young as his Formula 1 team. I'd been briefed on him the second I took the project, given that his vision had essentially shaped Heidelberg. Despite the team's namesake being some exceptionally ancient German man, Demir has built it into a constantly evolving force keen on new talent. I suppose it was this philosophy that made the team decide they would build a training centre in Rio de Janeiro, of all places.

Like the rest of us, Demir is wearing the team shirt and jeans, off-putting given his role on the team. His salt-and-pepper hair is combed neatly off his forehead, smile lines wrinkling his olive skin as he grins in greeting.

All the other spots at the table are filled by six people: Celina, and another five members of staff, all of whom are predictably unfamiliar. It's possible I've seen some of the others in passing, but there's nothing that sparks recognition. Darien, on the other hand, takes his precious time after I sit down to greet the others with grins, laughs, and a ton of back-slapping. He takes his seat beside a dark-haired man with big brown eyes and a shadow of stubble across his strong jaw. The two of them can't stop giggling like little schoolkids, elbowing each other and cackling before exchanging an aggressive '*shh*' and nodding towards an amused Demir.

The team principal stands at the head of the table. 'Welcome. Or should I say, *bem-vindo*, Heidelberg. Everyone is thrilled to have you all with us here today in beautiful Rio de Janeiro, as I am sure you will have gathered from the greeting you were given outside.'

I may not have been mobbed by the drivers' adoring fans, but I did have to suffer through some terrible traffic, during which I got a good look at the mania. Demir is right. The fans are absolutely elated. Brazil clearly loves its sport.

'Either way, our agenda for today is fairly brief. We will tour, get you all connected to the software, get you IDs, and finish our social media welcome photos. But let's start with introductions for the newest member of the team,' Demir begins with a nod in my direction. 'I'm Afshin Demir, as you know, team principal for Heidelberg Hybridge F1 Team. I've headed up the Formula 1 division since the team was formed about ten years back. We are the newest constructor on the grid, which necessitates some extra effort from us in proving ourselves. You may have seen us in the headlines in 2021, with Peter Albrecht claiming our first Drivers' Championship.'

This sentence earns a couple of proud whoops from around the table. Out of the corner of my eye, I see Darien bob his head appreciatively.

'Let's make it two, why don't we?' the man beside him quips, which only increases the volume of the cheers. This team hasn't even begun their season, and they're already giddy with excitement.

'Why don't we?' echoes Demir with a laugh. 'Yes, going into the 2024 season, that's our goal – we want two, and we want a Constructors' trophy out of it as well. So we've put in a little extra this year, a little extra in the form of the facility we stand in right now. Not only have we built this centre with Heidelberg's advancement in mind, but we have also cemented our commitment to our own Darien's Regional Formula team, Rio Redenção, for whom the Ring will hopefully serve as training facility next season.' He beams and nods my way. 'Which brings us to a short introduction from the woman of the hour, perhaps?'

Woman of the hour? Oh, no.

I manage an awkward half-smile. 'I'm here on behalf of Conquest Athletic. We were instrumental in the development of the technology involved in this centre, and will be driving the accompanying equipment changes that will follow across Heidelberg. My name is Shantal Sanjeevani Mangal, and I'll be here for at least the first half of the season as your team simulator specialist. I'll be working very closely with drivers to make best use of some of the new fixtures this centre comes with, particularly the groundbreaking simulation system,' I explain. 'Pending that and external matters after the summer break, I'll either remain with the team physically, or continue to work remotely from London as your round-the-clock specialist.'

'Excellent. Let's do a quick round-the-table. We'll start with our drivers,' suggests Demir, though it's less a suggestion and more an obligation.

Darien grins his dumbass grin. 'I'm Darien Cardoso-Magalhães.'

He sneaks in a mocking wink my way, just subtly enough that no one else gives any indication of having caught it. I fight the urge to roll my eyes.

'Raced for Heidelberg Hybridge for the past two years, this being my third. It's super exciting; I can barely believe that we've got our team rooted in Rio now. So let's make this off-season a good one, and let's head into testing ready to bring that P1 home,' he finishes, with a tip of his head to the guy next to him.

As much as I hate to say it, he's well-spoken. You can see it in how easily he conducts himself, that same casual demeanour I'd seen before.

'Miguel de la Fuente, with the misfortune of being Darien's teammate,' the next in line jokes, earning a cuff of his ear from Darien. 'I've been with Heidelberg a year, this is my second; as for F1, I'm now six seasons deep. Pleasure to meet you, Miss Mangal. Really excited to see where things can go, especially with last season being pretty great for us.'

Miguel cues in another man, who's easily the youngest person in the room. I hadn't even realized he was a driver. 'My name's Henrique Oliveira Miranda, but you can call me Henri,' he says with a smile, albeit a slightly nervous one. He looks like he could be just over eighteen – the Formula 1 age threshold – and appears as anxious as I feel. I decide I like him right away. 'I'm in development this season, my first with the team. You guys are all actually new to me,' he says with a wry laugh, 'so it's good to meet you all.'

The next three members of the team are trainers to each of the drivers. I already know Celina, who works with Darien. There is also Louie, Miguel's trainer, and Jack, who works with Henri. The other remaining staff member is named Katrina, press officer to Darien and overseer of the Ring's PR. She's got pin-straight blonde hair, stands inches above everyone else in the room on towering stilettos, and looks as if she will suffer no fools.

After introductions, Demir leads the bunch of us through a quick tour of the place, after which it's time for formalities. I make my way through the rest of my obligations over the course of the morning: scanning in IDs, pointing out personalized sims and trackers in the gym that are issued to each driver. Darien is thoroughly enjoying himself now that he's no longer got to hide behind that André act, humour dancing in his eyes as he cracks little jokes. Poor Henri looks as if he's been positively overloaded with information. Miguel breezes through it all. The trainers, naturally, listen in like there's prizes at the end.

Which, evidently, there are.

Before taking photos, the session that is supposed to be my cue to leave, Demir rounds us all up merrily as the trainers gawk at the sim sensors. 'So I have heard that we have here *someone* who is brand-new to Rio de Janeiro.'

Oh . . . no.

The three drivers glance about at each other, for the most part at Henri, in an attempt to single out the weak link, but he just shrugs and shakes his head like, 'Wrong guy.'

'Miss Mangal has never been to Brazil before,' says Demir with a show-and-tell air to his voice. 'She will also work as closely with you as your own trainers. Why don't you all get to know each other? Show her around. See the beach.'

Demir bustles off with the trainers, gesturing as he announces something about an in-depth brief on the 'state-of-the-art gymnasium'. This leaves me with three race-car drivers, and the prospect of the most uncomfortable afternoon of my life.

Chapter Nine

Darien

'Do they need to follow us around?'

Henri isn't loving the security detail flanking us as we leave the complex and walk towards the parking lot. Thankfully, they back off once we're well among the cars.

'Not any more.' I click my tongue. 'Four of us. I can fit us all in, but it'll be tight. Anyone else?'

'Two-seater,' declares Miguel.

'Same,' Henri says. Is that guy even old enough to drive?

'All right, squeeze it is.' I lead the walk to the AMG, just a short way across the lot.

'Shotgun!' yelps Henri. He's still got a baby face which, paired with big green eyes, makes for the happy visage of a pre-schooler. He can't be a day over eighteen.

Miguel laughs and gestures Shantal's way. 'Hold on, mate. You can't call shotgun when you're driving with a woman.'

'I don't really mind,' Shantal tries. 'It's all the same to me—'

'No!' Henri protests. 'What would it say about us if we made

56

you squish into the back seat? Sorry, Miss, um, Shantal, you go ahead.'

'It's just Shantal.' She shoots Henri a quick smile. The kid looks as though he's going to pass out. Miguel and I exchange a look of amusement.

Over our last year on Heidelberg together (and because he put a ring on the finger of the woman who's basically family to me), I've got a lot closer to Miguel de la Fuente. He has loads more experience than I do – he's twenty-six-ish years old with a World Championship under his belt. However, I'd hardly consider the guy to be a mentor. He causes more chaos than almost anybody, drives like he's still a teenager, and sets up pranks in the paddock. Once, he even snuck a bottle of Jack Daniel's into his suite when we were in Austin and had the thing shipped all the way back to Barcelona. It's a miracle his trainer never found out. I can't lie – before I knew him well, it was hard to separate him from his family name. But the more you learn about Miguel, the more he tends to prove you wrong.

I unlock the car and we pile in like we're on our way to family dinner – Shantal to my right, Miguel and Henri in the back.

'Ready to see Rio?' I ask Shantal.

'It depends.' She pointedly raises an eyebrow. The effect is startlingly attractive, whether she realizes this or not. 'Is Darien showing me around, or is André?'

I choke on sheer air, managing a violent cough of surprise. 'Who is André?' Miguel prods.

'Oh, no one,' I start. I don't need him having that particular bit of ammo on me, but Shantal, evidently, would love nothing more.

'Well, see, Darien here lied to me about his identity when we met yesterday because it made him feel like one of the common

57

folk,' Shantal takes over dryly. 'Our own little Princess Jasmine from *Aladdin*.'

Henri and Miguel explode into a chorus of 'What the hell?', Henri's exhortations punctuated by an exasperated 'mate'. I groan and press my face to the steering wheel. 'Can we drop André, please, Shantal?'

'Maybe' is her one-word reply.

'*Maybe?* But—'

'Drive!' everyone in the car demands in unison.

I roll my eyes. It's 'hate on Darien' day, I guess. 'Fine. First stop, Sugarloaf.'

The track is located conveniently near Sugarloaf Mountain, best described as a slab of giant grey rock sticking up from Urca. The view of it from the Ring is spectacular on its own. Seeing it up close is somewhat horrifying.

As much as I'd love to go further up, we don't have that kind of time on our hands and we still have plenty of spots in the main city to hit. I start by taking us to Copacabana, from where, I warn the others, we'd best walk.

Shantal is undeterred. Henri stares at her in disbelief as she swaps her sandals out for a pair of sneakers she brought in her bright pink tote bag.

'Someone came prepared.' Miguel nods in approval, and Shantal returns him a small smile. Great, Miguel has gotten on her good side. To my knowledge (and judging from the way she looks at me with murderous intent), I've made no progress in that direction.

Shantal throws her hair into a quick Founding Father-esque ponytail. She looks like a genuine tourist. We've all changed to blend in, but Shantal understood the assignment too well to be intentional. The white strapless crop top and blue skirt combo is selling it hard. She's even got the sunglasses and crossbody belt bag.

'Do you own any flip-flops?' I ask her with a raised eyebrow.

She shoots me a look. 'I didn't bring those. I'll be on my feet all the time.'

'No flip-flops?' I gape. 'In Brazil?'

'What, should I have some?'

'Maybe,' I remark sarcastically, although I am being truthful. Flip-flops are every local's shoe of choice, whether you're walking a foot or a mile. We'll certainly solve this problem for Shantal along the line.

Copacabana, naturally, is *packed*. There's barely room to breathe. Seeing it full is one thing, but today, the umbrellas are nearly overlapping. Some great big sand football thing is going on; people are gathered all around. The boardwalk isn't any better, with throngs of *cariocas* – locals – and tourists alike flooding the area.

'It's . . . crowded,' remarks Miguel. Out of us all, it's he and Henri who are most shell-shocked by real Rio. I can't quite get a read on Shantal, even when she removes her sunglasses. She doesn't look quite as turned around out here as she did near the arches.

'Is this familiar to you?' I go out on a limb and ask her.

She startles when she turns my way, but she nods. 'Somewhat. I grew up near a . . . slightly less chaotic beach.'

'In the UK?'

Shantal glares at me. Her irises flash a paler brown than I'd initially thought they were in the light of the sun.

'You've got an accent,' I say nervously.

'I know.' She turns back to the beach, and a smile lights up her face as she watches the crazy football game. 'We lived along 63 Beach in Guyana until I was maybe ten.'

'Not far from here.'

'A little far.' She tucks a wave of hair behind her ear. It gets caught in the back of her gold heart earring, and even the breeze doesn't make it budge.

I think about that for a moment. Obviously, Brazil is big, and Guyana *is* far, but we share a border. Maybe we'd have crossed paths somehow. Maybe if Shantal had stayed in Guyana, she'd be up in Teresópolis with the CBF, running their football training programme instead of ours. I wonder how the world can be so big and yet so small all at once.

'Let's go!' calls Miguel. Looks like he's enjoying this unusually jam-packed version of the beach much less than he's letting on.

'Wow, he's loving all the buzz,' Henri jokes. Shantal purses her lips as if holding in a laugh. I notice that about her: she keeps her feelings to herself, unless you lie to her about your identity, in which case you'll have your ass handed to you on a platter.

We stick to following the boardwalk for a while, though I'd argue the experience is inauthentic without visiting the favelas just past the beach. I'm biased, with my aunt and uncle living near one of the two in the *bairro*, Cantagalo. Sandwiched between Copacabana and Ipanema, Cantagalo-Pavão-Pavãozinho is what I'd call a safer favela. It used to be pretty nasty back when I was younger, but it's gotten a lot better. The food can't be beaten.

'What's up there?' Shantal gestures to the houses and buildings built against Cantagalo Hill like a landslide of life, as if she's read my mind. 'That's a neighbourhood?'

'Yep, neighbourhoods,' I tell her. 'Favelas.'

'Favelas,' she repeats. 'Is it true what the guides say about staying clear?'

I shake my head. 'Not quite. Some are worse than others.

60

But it's like in any big city: crimes, gangs. Mostly, it's just people trying to make a living. They have shops, crafts, food, all of that.'

'Can we go there?' asks Shantal, shielding her eyes from the sun as she looks up at the hill.

'Maybe when we have more time. It's a bit of a hike.'

'What about that tram up there on the arches, back towards Santa Teresa?' Shantal continues to enquire. It's almost funny how methodically she's extracting information from us.

'Well, that's a way off,' Henri helps out. 'I remember this. My mom's from here, Dad's from Perth. We came here once when I was younger. That tram's on the other side of Christ.'

'Right,' I say, searching for the appropriate analogy here. 'Rio is like a . . . Pac-Man. If *Cristo* is the eye, Santa Teresa is the top of the mouth. We're on the chin.'

Miguel stops and blinks at me. 'Pac-Man?'

'We have Pac-Man here,' I say by way of explanation. Miguel just rolls his eyes.

We just make it to Ipanema on foot before giving in and buying ice pops for the walk back. We weave through some of the streets, glimpse storefronts, residentials, and the beginnings of the favelas. It's always brought a smile to my face, so I feel pleased to see it does the same for Shantal. Except beneath her smile is a layer of melancholy. This reminds her of something else, something sad, and I don't think it's just Guyana.

And as much as I'm sure it's intrusive of me, I wonder what this girl is hiding. I barely know her, just met her, but it's the way she looks at our beach. Something in me wants to find out more.

Chapter Ten

Shantal

I arrive at Heidelberg Hybridge Ring the next morning at seven a.m. for the first track walk of the new facility. In tow, I've got my things for the rest of the week. The hotel is not, according to Afshin Demir, as convenient as having the team in one place, hence living quarters. So naturally, he's indicated we try to stay at said living quarters during the week. I'm not complaining – each room is huge and beyond comfortable.

I find this when I scan into my room first thing after getting inside. The living quarters building is ultra-secure: fingerprint to get in, ID to unlock your room. It's just two floors with ten rooms total. We've got the five on the upper floor, because of the views.

The promise delivers. My suite's sitting-area window opens straight out towards Sugarloaf Mountain, the big rock-like slab surrounded by greenery that we drove past. Yes, *sitting area*. I have well-cushioned leather couches, a TV, and a kitchen space with appliances and an island in an adjoining wing. My bathroom and bedroom are connected, just down a short hall. You can tell it's designed for athletes: the shower has these acupunctural pressure jets, and you can adjust the mattress all kinds of ways for customized support. The physio side of me says it's smart, but the business side only sees the expense.

I just have time to drop off my bags and change before heading down. At Crystal Palace, as a training specialist on the coaching staff, we had red and blue team windbreakers designating our roles, intended to be worn with as many layers as possible. I remember wearing leggings under my sweats to combat the chill. But Brazil is baking. Rather than layers, I've got running shorts and a bright white team livery T-shirt matching the rest of our drivers and staff.

'Morning,' I greet the trainers with a yawn when I arrive in the garage for the track tour. They murmur echoed good mornings all around with bleary eyes. We nurse iced coffees that are already beginning to melt in the scorching heat. Someone mentions that the cars are still somewhere in Germany being worked on for the great reveal come February, which is slightly disappointing, at least to me. Testing will be the first time I've seen F1 level cars live and, unfamiliar as I am with the sport, I've got plenty of questions.

'Do they just adapt to the new car, then, when winter testing comes round?' I ask Henri's trainer, Jack. Jack Lyons is world renowned, I've learned (from googling, something I clearly should have done long ago). Before he became Henri's physio, Henri weighed maybe sixty kilos, struggling to hold his head up against Gs. He's nearly seventy kilos now, with the F2 G record under his belt.

Jack nods firmly. 'New car's always a bit of a challenge, but they'll be great.'

'Is there a reason they don't, I don't know, turn down the

power and crank it up as they get used to the car or something?' I carry on around a sip of coffee. 'So that when they max out, the team can obtain a pretty true baseline safely?'

'Clever,' says Louie Alvarez, Miguel's trainer. 'But would the guys see it that way? I mean, deprivation of speed can be offensive to these sensitive egos.'

I smile tightly. 'This is one of the most dangerous sports in the world. Wouldn't they accept the fact that we prize survival over speed?'

'Welcome to Formula 1, my friend.' Louie just shakes his head. 'It's speed over survival here. You either go fast, or you lose your seat.'

'These are for you.'

The last thing I expect when the drivers arrive is for Darien to approach me with a ridiculous gift bag.

He just stares at me expectantly, tugging at the arm of his white hoodie, a bold choice in this kind of stifling climate. Rather than world-class race-car driver vibes, he's giving off small-child energy. What on earth has he brought me?

I take the bag and look inside.

It is a pair of the ugliest slippers I've ever seen. They are a criminally radioactive green, made of some sort of silicone material, with a slightly misshapen bedazzled thong to them. Alphabet beads glued to the strap spell out SHNTAL.

'You don't have to give me . . . these.'

'You said you don't have flip-flops.' Darien gives me a weird look, like I've entered London during rainy season without a coat. 'Everyone here has flip-flops, remember? You can't be walking around the compound in those sneakers.'

'Hokas,' I reply slightly snippily. 'I am fond of my Hokas, Darien. You might know. All the Americans wear them.'

'But here, we flip-flop.'

'You brought me flip-flops,' I proclaim in disbelief.

'Okay, Queen of England.' Darien gives the slippers a little nudge. 'Take them.'

'You've misspelled my name.'

'The first "A" fell off. Sorry.'

I raise an eyebrow, but I gingerly pick up the slippers as if they are as poisonous as their colour. Dare I wear these in public? The odds of them falling apart beneath my feet seem dangerously high.

'How did you . . .' I trail off, allowing him to infer the rest of my question.

'Five-Minute Crafts,' he says as if this should explain everything. 'Henri helped. Miguel said he was too old for this bullshit. Then he glued on the letters anyway.'

'Indeed.' I try to picture Miguel squinting to attach small beads to my brand-new flip-flops. 'What'd you glue these together with?'

'Wear them and find out.'

I nod drily. Interesting. If these were created with a five-minute tutorial, the odds of them lasting the walk across the training facility itself are quite slim, but I can't be so rude about it. Maybe Darien is an inveterate liar, but he has also made me a pair of shoes. There is something strangely endearing about the effort.

'It's a peace offering, Shantal.' He crosses his arms. 'It's peaceful. I'm not trying to sabotage your feet.'

'I mean . . .' I pick them up and glance at the soles. They don't look like they'll hold up too well given all the walking I do in a typical day. 'Maybe not intentionally,' I acknowledge.

With a dismissive eye roll, Darien turns to the space in the currently empty garage marked with bright yellow paint, signifying the parking spot for the as-yet-incomplete Heidelberg car. 'So. What's the plan? Will we give the car aero rakes in February? Flow-vis paint?'

Maybe I'm beginning to lose some of my edge towards Darien/André after he read my mind clean yesterday at the beach, but the judgement in his voice brings out the snark in mine. It doesn't help that I have a bare-minimum understanding of all the technical jargon he's just spewed. 'Sure, we'll do all of that. But for the time being, we won't just be testing the car,' I tell him. 'That's the simplest part. We'll be testing the three of you as well. Pulling old numbers to try and adapt to the new stuff. And the sims have little sensors that will give us precise data—'

'Sorry. Testing *us?*' Darien's eyebrows fly up his forehead far too extravagantly. 'You don't trust us?'

'Well, it's going to be a new car. The sim is the closest we have in the meantime. We have to get data to tailor your season practice plans to what we have available in the system. After all, there will only be a month between testing and the first race.'

'I'm a Formula 1 driver.'

'And I'm now partially responsible if we have incidents during the season. Keep in mind. Bringing me here isn't just Demir playing games. Maybe I'm only running the simulators, but everything in that building is Conquest tech. Hell, parts of your car are going to be Conquest's now, too. Not to mention the duress you're under to produce results. I've got information from the company. I know what's on the line for you, and for us. I know about Redenção. I'm going to do this right. We're your new sponsor, Darien. We go down with you. If we have an incident—'

'I won't have an incident.'

With each retort, we get in each other's faces just a bit more, and as I shoot back, 'Anyone can have an incident,' I find myself having to look up to Darien, mere inches from me now.

He stays there, an almost amused look on his face as his dark eyes glint with an unspoken response I can't identify. I refuse to lose this one. I'm not about to have the whole team see me as a pushover.

'Okay.' Darien sighs with a doctored smile that looks more infuriated than anything else, running a hand through his curls. 'We'll do things your way.'

I nod. 'Thank you.'

'You're a menace to society, you know that?' he quips, one last attempt to get a hit in.

'That's what I'm being paid to be.' I throw him a smirk. 'I'm glad it's working.'

We get the entire bunch of us on the track, beginning at the starting line. I give my team tee a little shake to dispel the sweat that seems to be following me around in this place, either because of heat, nerves or both. This is my first time watching any kind of motorsport track session so closely. I've already exceeded my quota of dumb questions for the day, so I'm praying I'll be able to understand whatever foreign motorsport language they throw around as we walk the Ring.

Being our primary drivers, it's Darien and Miguel who are up at the front of the pack when we start the tour. They start to exchange talk about things like corners and torque and drag with their trainers and engineers, Henri and his team echoing the sentiments I'm hearing. Team principal Demir is not here today, but Jack loops me in plenty since Henri, like me, requires a bit of extra explanation, having just entered Formula 1.

'Straights are, obviously, portions of the track that go straight like that,' says Jack, gesturing to the main grid area that we've just walked down. 'Turns can come in a few varieties. Single corners, there's only one apex, or point of the turn, to hit. F1 cars don't aim to go around the turn, they go through. Like someone's drawn a line tangent to the curve. Chicanes, you get a series of those turns, so you've almost got to try your best to draw a line that touches the apex of every turn, with a modicum of yanking around. So Turn One, that's just your first corner, right-handed corner. Goes into a curve, and then up ahead,' he points towards a section of track just beyond us that wiggles like a child's unsteady attempt at a line, 'that's the chicane. Then past that, there's a sharp corner, I'm guessing Turn Four. And further down, maybe a couple of easier curves. Those are still considered turns.'

'So what happens to the driver on those turns? To the car?' I down the last of my long-held coffee.

'The harder the turn, the worse the Gs,' a new voice joins us. I realize it's Darien, grinning cheekily as he falls back to give us his unsolicited input. 'Entry and exit of any corner, it's basically this heavy decel that presses your whole body, pulls at your head so hard you think it's gonna leave your neck. Every corner is different. Just depends on how the car responds.'

'And, of course, on human error,' Celina pipes up, shooting me a wink when Darien harrumphs at the mere notion. I grin, because anyone who can get Darien to squirm is automatically at the top of my list of allies here.

'Not if you practise well enough!' he insists, although we all know it's in vain since everyone in our group is chuckling at this point, including Darien himself. I find it astonishing how easily he drops the grudge to let out a laugh. There's something so straightforward about it. I wonder if the man has a *single* enemy in the world.

For a moment, his eyes catch mine watching him, and my stomach instantly drops. I look away as fast as I can, sucking in a sharp breath, training my eyes on Miguel's back in front of me instead.

Chapter Eleven

Darien

'Take a look at this data.'

I've seen my data a million and one times before, but I let Celina, Afonso – my engineer for the past three years – and Shantal walk me through it all again. She looks slightly less unhappy with me than she did yesterday, at track walk. I spin idly in my chair at the counter of the Ring's pit wall. Shantal had requested our most recent testing stats to make a start on calibrating all the training tech and regimens, which, for me and Miguel, meant our Pirelli tyre tests from December in Barcelona, and for Henri, the free practice he'd done for Heidelberg last season at Abu Dhabi.

Afonso pulls up a graph of speeds on turns, peaks and troughs, indicating measured speeds for each turn number at Barcelona. He zooms in on the Turn Fourteen section, the toughest one on the Spanish track, a ridiculously fast right-hand that sends the best of drivers for a toss. There's a yellow and green zigzag on the graph, and though the yellow arcs over the green, both represent the same value: turn speed over the course of the corner, averaged from the total practice laps.

'Green is the averages we calculated for Miguel's Turn Fourteen,' Afonso explains, turning to Celina. 'And yellow—'

'That's you,' finishes Celina, tracing the line on the screen with an index finger. 'Your turn speeds are outrageous, as I've heard. But seeing the numbers . . . you're tens of kilometres – miles, sorry, American boy – ahead of your teammate.'

'There's more than turns,' adds Shantal. She locks eyes with me, an eyebrow raised. 'You have a pretty odd driving style. You speed right through corners. You weave faster than the clips I watched of the others. We looked at your race tapes, too. You overtake mostly by forcing opponents wide and utilizing that gap quite aggressively. Your defence is immaculate.'

'Watched my race tapes. High praise,' I remark, and shoot her a mischievous smile that sends her gaze far from mine, turning her cheeks pink.

She clears her throat. 'Well. Where did you learn to drive like that?'

'Here.'

Shantal blinks. 'Sorry?'

'I learned here. In the street.'

She appears to be processing this information very slowly and deliberately. Then, 'Sure, okay. But I would, respectfully, like to see how. Because, Darien, if we can implement that into the programming in the simulator, if I can figure out exactly *what* you learned and use those exercises on a simulated track . . .' She shakes her head. 'All three of you would be absolutely deadly for this season. And I can tell you the Ring has the resources to make that possible, if I can just crack exactly how.'

'That'll be a challenge,' Celina chuckles, echoing my

thoughts exactly. 'You don't know how he got his start, Shantal? It's an urban motorsport legend.'

'I'd like to see it for myself,' she insists. 'This really could help in developing a program, as I've said.'

I tilt my head. 'You did say you wanted to go up to Cantagalo, didn't you?'

'Darien . . .' Celina's tone is warning. She obviously knows exactly what I'm about to do, and she's not buying it.

Shantal is quick to notice. Her big brown eyes narrow, making the dark liner around them stand out. 'What's going on here?'

'Let's leave the matter where it is, Shantal,' Afonso puts in with an awkward cough.

'I'm kidding, anyway,' I say with a laugh that earns me a sharp nudge of Celina's elbow.

'Yes.' Shantal doesn't look amused. 'Darien, how about we have a bit of a chat, may we?'

I exchange a glance with Celina. She widens her eyes at me as if to yell, *WHY?* I just shrug and follow Shantal. We leave behind the monitors and headsets of the pits for the open garage, where Shantal stops. I mimic her.

She crosses her arms. 'I'm *not* joking.'

I don't know whether to laugh or yell at her. I settle for a fairly even tone, the most serious one I've got. 'Listen, uh . . .' I gulp. 'I don't know if this is the kind of thing I would want to have someone do, Shantal. I get that you want what's best for the team, but I can't offer you this. It's dangerous, no matter which way you look at it.'

I know I'm not the most straitlaced of people, but I mean every word I say. This is beyond me poking fun at Shantal. I won't have her in harm's way.

'You showed me around,' she persists. 'And besides, you do owe me this. For the massive lie you fed me.'

Okay, so that's true. I probably do owe her. Just not this. Still, I don't want to tell her point-blank that the activities I am referring to are the perfect way to land one's ass either in hospital or behind bars, whichever gets to you first. But she's adamant, standing toe to toe with me, determination all over her face. She won't hear an argument. She keeps her arms crossed and gets comfortable, like she'd stay here the entire day if she had to. A tingling creeps into my chest as I realize just how close we are, just like when we were arguing over her vision for pre-season and testing. My line of sight sweeps over her subtle curves, perfectly tanned legs. If someone pushed me from behind, it wouldn't take much for our bodies to collide, and honestly, part of me wants that more than anything right now. *Dude*. I shove that part into a box and duct-tape it twice around. There's no way we're doing that right now. Not at work.

'Being in that car is a threat to your life,' I amend my warning, fighting off an embarrassing crack of my voice to boot. 'Driving the way I learned to drive. You could die.'

'What, are we drag racing?' Shantal prods.

I just continue to look at her with as much warning and/or pity as possible.

'Stop.' Her expression contorts into a semblance of what people look like when they see a car crash in real time. 'No.'

'You said you wanted to go!' I protest. 'And it's not a straight shot or a race. I'd just take you through a favela, how I used to practise.'

'I'm sorry – you took a car around corners through the favela, as in the neighbourhood that's relying entirely on a hill to remain *intact*?' Shantal gasps. That did it. She's singing a

73

whole different tune now. 'Darien – forget me. *You* absolutely cannot be allowed to do that. We cannot have *any* injuries before this season.'

'We won't if you back out of this.'

'Funny, I recall even your trainer saying human error can happen,' snaps Shantal, turning away.

I grit my teeth. *Insufferable*. 'You know what? We're both going. Tonight.'

She holds her hands up. 'I never would have asked if I'd known what the hell this was!'

'Oh, so now you *don't* want to find out how "all three of us could be absolutely deadly"?' I throw on an especially whiny voice to parrot hers.

'Ugh!' Now it's her turn to become so frazzled that she gives in. 'Fine! Is there another set of gear I can wear or something?'

'Gear?'

Shantal's mouth falls open. 'You have to be *kidding* me.'

'Who wears gear driving a damn passenger vehicle?'

'Darien!' she yelps. 'Tell me now what the horsepower is on that passenger vehicle and then try to convince me we don't need gear!'

'You'll find out,' I reply plainly. 'Meet me at the gym doors at ten tonight.'

Chapter Twelve

Shantal

My hands literally shake as I wait by the stupid doors. I can't believe this. I've bickered too close to the sun this time. Even Sonia would never have taken part in something so dangerous. I wonder if she'd endorse my actions right now. At the very least, I'm sure she'd appreciate my wardrobe, most of which are pieces I bought with her years ago and chucked into my suitcase without thinking. I've put on a pair of obnoxiously tiny, ripped denim shorts, and a white tank top with an unbuttoned baby blue linen shirt over it, complete with my trusty Converse. It's not the comfiest but will blend in decently anywhere in Rio.

Darien turns up soon enough, dressed as he usually is – as he was when I first met him-slash-André – in football shorts and an old GP2 shirt.

'All right.' A quick, if not sheepish, flick of his eyes in my direction doesn't escape my notice. I feel my neck start to heat up and, even though I'm darker-skinned, I'm praying it isn't a reaction he can see. 'I've brought the car.'

'The AMG?'

He shakes his head with a smile. 'We can't use that. But we very much can and will use *this*.'

With the click of a button on the keys in his hand, a vehicle in the dimly lit lot chirps, and its headlights flash. It's a Chevrolet Corvette: canary yellow, accented with dark blue stripes. The colour combination makes for a violent war waged on the optic nerves. The rear of the car sports an understated spoiler; the interior glints with subtle barring, indicative of some kind of reinforcement.

'This was my dad's,' says Darien, with notes of both admiration and melancholy in his voice.

'Did he let you bring it out here?'

'Nah.' We cross towards the lot, and when we reach the car, he opens the passenger door for me. I catch sight of an unusual look on Darien's face. He looks almost confused, as if there's something he wants to remember but can't. 'He passed away when I was younger. Accident with a truck. But even after I got my kart, I learned all my strategy in here. First sitting where you are, watching my dad, and then driving with my uncle. Racing.'

I'm not sure what to say, given that I'm now in the very place where Darien Cardoso-Magalhães's motorsport career was born. I let out a deep breath before speaking. 'I'm sorry to hear that. Though this must be a strong car, if it's lasted all those things.'

'Oh, only somewhat. My mom and I have done our fair share of repairs,' he says with a laugh. He starts up the engine, and it purrs loudly, greedily even, as he pulls out of the lot. 'Like, after the first time my uncle let me race for the car. I won, but the Corvette took a good beating. Mãe was *pissed*.'

I manage a laugh, but it comes out strangled.

Darien briefly glances from the road to me. 'What?'

I don't know. It just shakes me that he could do that to what sounds like a family heirloom. 'How could you just . . . put your father's car, the car you became a racer in, on the line so easily? What if you damage it so badly you lose it for ever?'

Darien just cracks a grin. 'That's the thing, Shantal. This car is a beast. You think my dad would want me keeping it chained up in the garage all day?'

'I think maybe that's what I'd want to do.'

'Interesting.' His smirk is amused but not condescending, judging from that crinkling of his eyes that betrays his genuine reaction. 'You do know what happens to a car you keep in the garage, never drive?'

'Well, it stays in good shape,' I answer slowly, though I'm wary this may not be the reply he wants.

'Nope. It stops working. It . . . forgets how.'

My expression has got to be vacant, because he lets out a chuckle. 'Cars were made to be driven, you know.'

Darien drives us well into the city, to the beach where we'd come on that first day earlier in the week. Ipanema – I can tell from the patterns on the sidewalk. In the distance, I see that same hill stacked with colourful houses illuminated by blinding streetlights. Cantagalo, Darien called it. It's even more beautiful at night, something you could only find on a canvas. But then I notice little things that strip away at the façade. Things like the narrowness of the streets, or a particularly unstable building.

'Little gift just for you,' says Darien once he parks. He produces a helmet from the space at his feet. It's emblazoned with the number sixty-seven and *Nico* in glittering silver on the back, with a picture of two blue macaws forming a heart with their beaks on the top. The Brazilian flag is encapsulated within the shape of the heart. It's absolutely adorable. 'My race helmet. You can put this on.'

'I can . . . but this is yours . . .' I trail off in disbelief. Darien nods his permission. *Go ahead*.

I gingerly take the helmet. Our hands brush just slightly, but it's the kind of touch that is both too much and not enough for me to handle when he passes it to me. It's heavier than I'd expected, and it hits me abruptly that I will wear the same helmet a Formula 1 driver uses in races. I just look at it with an air of shock for a moment.

'You put it on.' Darien's tone conceals humour as he helps me slide it over my head. His fingers skim my neck as he concentrates on fastening the belt beneath my chin. I feel like I'm sharing something incredibly intimate with him, which is ironic given we've not even been able to stand in the same room without bickering for the past few days. The helmet smells like him: his sandalwood cologne, a hint of cardamom, and then the minty scent of gum. I'm glad he can't see how flustered I am. I've got no words left to argue with.

'I'm technically not supposed to be out around Rio at night without some kind of chaperone or whatever, because people can get out of control, but it's worth the hassle for these things,' he explains as he flips down my visor. It's like everything gets a shade darker, unhelpful in the pre-existing dark. He tugs at the seatbelt that mimics where backpack straps would normally sit, on either side of my chest, checking to make sure it's secure. 'Like I said, these are my summers, my childhood.'

I'm shaking in my Converse as Darien changes gears, and we begin to drive towards the hill. Okay. We're just going to go up. It could be worse. I distract myself by taking my GoPro camera out from my backpack and securing it to the dashboard, where it'll video the view out in front so I can refer to it in programming the sims later on. I repeat a little mantra in my head. *We need this to win. We need this to win.*

'You can take a deep breath, we're gonna make it through this alive,' jokes Darien, but I think he finds it more of a joke than I do.

'Death isn't funny,' I reply, more sharply than I intend. 'And you have me wearing this thing. When people put on helmets, it's usually to protect themselves from some sort of grave danger.'

'Oh, really?' Darien laughs. 'I put that thing on you so I don't have to hear you complaining about the lack of safety measures before I bring us down.'

'Sorry, *bring us down?*'

'Yeah. What, you think learning this stuff is as easy as controlling a car on even land?' He doesn't quite meet my gaze. 'We're going down the hill.'

I think this is my cue to begin to shut down so that I will actually survive the ride down the hill. I stare at the dashboard, my only thought being that we are *so* dead.

'You good?' tries Darien. I can tell that this is not him actually asking if I'm okay but him hiding 'you put us in this situation' behind sympathy.

I nod, this weird little jerk of my neck that is definitely not good. 'This is. A lot.'

'Told you.'

'Of course you did.' I sigh, pressing my hands to my knees. I just cannot leave well enough alone, and this is the consequence. I remind myself this is what I need to help our program, but that notion became moot ages ago. We are clearly here because two stubborn people could not shut the hell up.

'Hey.' Darien flicks his eyes my way. 'Give me your hand.'

My eyebrows scrunch in surprise beneath the helmet. I'm

too flabbergasted and nervous to protest. I extend my hand, and he grabs it firmly in his strong, warm one. 'You're not in some unforeseeable future right now, Shantal. You're with me. In this very well-reinforced car that has survived a billion things much worse than this, and you're about to get some logical insight into why I drive how I do, just like you wanted.'

'Okay,' I say. 'Okay.' My breathing quickens as I take in the fact that we've stopped at the top of the hill. The entire beach sparkles below us, and we are level with a handful of other favelas that still buzz with activity. There's a lot to see, but Darien and I are concentrated on one another, the only things that matter in here. I can hear him breathe, quiet inhales and exhales that are much more controlled than mine. 'I'm just . . . scared.'

'I know.' He squeezes my hand, and a rush of reassurance fills me up, slowing my panic. Even through the tint of the visor, I see the rawness in his eyes, a part of him that is completely and utterly true. 'I still get scared, too. But that's what makes me careful.'

I can't do much except watch him as he turns the car around at a narrow plaza atop this hill, Cantagalo. He revs the engine on the Corvette hard so that the whole thing shakes loudly. A couple of people in the plaza are gathering around, murmuring excitedly as they take out their phones and turn on flash.

Darien shoots me a grin. 'You ready to hang on?'

I immediately grip whatever I can find in my vicinity, including the little handle above the door. I'll probably be needing it.

I've scarcely got a second to prepare myself before we shoot forward and drop off down the hill. There's a strangled yelp that apparently comes from me. Darien veers to the side to make sure we don't flatten someone's dog, and then to the other side to avoid a popsicle stand. My stomach has plummeted right to the floor of this car. I severely underestimated the steepness of this hill.

'*SHIIITTT!*' I yell as we take a particularly nasty turn. We go over a hump that makes our car jump before it hits the ground again with all four wheels. I think my ass flies right off the seat.

'You wanna see how I learned?' Darien shouts over the engine.

'I don't know!' I squeak.

On the next curve, he yanks the wheel, grits his teeth. My breath refuses to leave my lungs as the car drifts around a building of treacherously constructed flats, clearing a row of vendor stands and forcing us to slingshot out the other side. I have moved to cling to the reinforcement bar now. The handle was not enough.

We skid around the next few turns, and what Darien does next is vaguely familiar. He uses his racing line to let the tug on the car pull us right through. A quick swerve here and there to avoid some more dogs – is that a lizard? – and then a lurching stop as we reach a hill-free street. I'm jolted into Darien's side and, instinctively, I latch on to him, like he's the reinforcement bar. He's all muscle: muscle that I feel tense and relax with every movement.

'You made it,' he laughs, knocking my visor up. I don't let go just yet. My entire body is shuddering, probably from way too much adrenaline. My eyes flutter dizzily, but they lock on to his.

'We,' I struggle for breath, 'are a long way . . . from London.'

'Yep. Rio.' He pops open his door with a smile. 'You can let go, Shantal. It's okay.'

I give Darien's arm an awkward little pat before disentangling myself from him. Oh, my god. I must have looked like an idiot. I move slowly towards my door and creep out of the car; the flat ground does not feel real. I catch Darien watching me with a grin. At first, I think he's just tickled by my naïveté again, but there's a hint of admiration there. For what, I don't know. Nevertheless, I return his expression with my own tiny smile.

A crowd quickly begins to form around us, locals chattering in excited Portuguese like the ones at the top of the hill, phones out and at the ready. Before I can lose Darien among the wave of oncoming fans, though, I reach out for his hand. And just as I do, he also holds out his arm in search of mine. Our fingers meet in the middle, and we hang on to each other for dear life.

'You look good,' he says, 'in my helmet.'

One minute, Shantal. You get one minute to be an emotional teenage girl over this. That's it.

I pick a stray curl out from the hinge of the visor. My face is warm with a combination of embarrassment and something completely different.

'Thanks. *Darien.*'

Chapter Thirteen

Darien

'Explosive movements are something—'

'*Explosive movements?*'

Shantal turns to Henri, who looks absolutely appalled. The rest of us can't hold it in. We burst out laughing. Miguel is slapping his knee while I lean against him. I'm pretty sure even our trainers can hear us from the conference room in the Heidelberg building, despite the fact that we're all the way out on the track for a second walkthrough.

'Oh, god,' groans Shantal. She reaches over and pokes Henri in the ribs, making him jump. 'Is it any better if I say "explosive motions"?'

'Not really,' I tease her, 'but go ahead.'

She rolls her eyes at me with a generous helping of disdain as we all finally pull ourselves together and continue our early Monday morning track walk, down the main straight and towards the first corner. 'Well, *explosive motions* are something we worked on a lot with Crystal Palace,' she tells us. 'From some . . . first-hand observations, I've determined that can benefit our team, too.' We share a knowing glance.

Maybe I'm genuinely hallucinating, but I could have sworn we formed a *shred* of a rapport up there on Cantagalo last week, and even a shred would be enough to move on from Shantal's frosty, all-business demeanour. Unfortunately, it looks as if we're back to square one. In fact, it feels like we're behind square one. The wall between us crumbled for a minute, but now it's back up, and it's sturdier than ever.

'So that's what I'd like to begin with on Conquest's sim systems,' she finishes.

'But Shantal, what *are* explosive motions?' Miguel echoes all our thoughts. 'Other than the uncontrollable shits.'

Now even Shantal can't hold it in. She laughs this big, beautiful laugh with this weird little hiccup in the middle. 'Beautiful' almost seems like a criminal word to use for the woman who's been gradually picking away at my brain, but I guess it's accurate. Especially considering yesterday. Everything about yesterday.

Man, I need that wall to fall apart for good.

'Okay, I give in, it sounds funny,' admits Shantal. 'But in football, we train explosive motions to allow our players to change direction, move faster, react quicker. I want us to target that. Improve our adaptability, give us an edge on the sharp curves and overtakes. Catch the things the other teams might not?'

'That I can agree with,' says Miguel in approval. 'Turn times were a little slow in the old data, right?'

Shantal nods. 'Just slightly. So your trainers will work with you on the individual components of the performance plan they got together this morning. We decided to start by running a slightly modified version of this very track on the sim, so we can figure out exactly where we stand.'

'Is this the Coach Shantal part?' Henri asks with his usual childlike curiosity.

'I guess you could say that.' She's not being obvious about it, but I can tell that little compliment bolsters Shantal's confidence. And seeing that, seeing the way she holds herself becomes surer, something in my chest goes warm.

'This could be the leg-up Heidelberg needs to take the Championship. Coach Shantal,' I remark with a smile.

It seems to take Shantal aback. I've seen people preen before – pretending they know everything about our team's engines, asking for a hot lap to impress us with their ability to stomach it; I've seen it all from people in Shantal's position. Yet she still doesn't care about appearances or fame; she just plods along like a kid figuring out a little more about the world with each step.

And for the record, she did look *really* good in my helmet.

We pack up shop for the day after a weight-training session. Celina has me doing a new exercise on Conquest's programmable Iron Neck rather than the usual slower stuff: a small but quick turn that leaves my neck and shoulders hellishly sore by the end of it. The trainers show us how to turn Gs up and down, how to switch up the abruptness of a turn, link up our data so the machine knows what setting we need to practise on every session. It's different. We're definitely struggling. But struggles, at least in practice, are wins.

Instead of being on track for the remainder of the week, we spend it introducing more motions that will increase our team's response, using equipment smarter than anything I've ever seen in my life (even at that one weird-ass gym in Montreal). Shantal, to her credit, is adapting well to a sport she has so little experience of. It's got to be the seventh ring of hell, but she does her best to come back the next morning with a coffee and a yawn. She is as persistent as she was about going to Cantagalo, and I'm coming to admire that.

Friday rolls around fast, hot and sunny. No one's in the frame of mind to work out with the weather so nice. It almost feels like a sin. So it's a relief when the trainers let us all out for a much-needed off-day.

I watch Miguel and Henri chatter excitedly, gym bags and suitcases on their arms as they head off into the atrium for the weekend, not a care in the world. I'm pretty sure Miguel's already buzzing with excitement about seeing Diana again for winter testing weekend – they're suffering through a forced exile from one another while their respective teams prepare for the season. Henri's just starstruck by the thought of actually meeting 'the Diana "Danger" Zahrani'. Henri, as young and new to me as he is, seems to allow absolutely *nothing* to knock him down, and when it does, he gets back up right away. We still joke with the kid, because there's an obvious opening there – I mean, he's barely allowed to drink – but both Miguel and I have earned a new respect for him over the past two weeks.

'Hey, Dar!' Miguel calls, waving me over. 'You know a guy, right?'

'Depends on what you need.' I grin and sling my bag over my shoulder. 'But odds are, I know someone for it.'

'Do you have a good pitch around here?' Henri cuts in eagerly.

'Oh. *Oh*, are you *asking* me that?' I feign extravagant insult. 'There's a turf in Leblon, someone's uncle has a membership . . . and I can absolutely get us in. *Plus* I know a couple of guys who wouldn't mind joining us.'

Henri is in complete awe, and Miguel's just about ready to

burst with anticipation, until his attention abruptly shifts . . . to Shantal Mangal and her iced coffee.

She's just on her way out through the atrium when Miguel, the fool, shouts, 'Hey, Shantal!'

She turns and doubles back to join us, slightly warily. 'Uh-oh. What's going on over here?'

'Nothing, don't worry. Well, except football . . . what? Tomorrow?' Miguel glances at each of us in turn, and Henri and I both nod.

'Tomorrow,' I echo, and I'm not sure what kind of spirit has possessed me, but I'm pulling out all the stops in prayer that she'll say yes. I swallow hard. Shantal, a head and a half shorter than me with a voice like a Disney princess's, has me off my game. 'You should come. I know we've been busy since last week, but I just wanted to apologize for the Cantagalo chaos – the car and everything—'

'Darien.' Shantal looks exceptionally guilty as she holds out a hand to stop me. 'No, it's okay. I made you take me. It's my bad.'

Henri and Miguel watch us with eyes ping-ponging back and forth between the two of us. I clear my throat and shake off the fact that glimpsing the momentary chink in Shantal's armour has just completely fazed me. 'Really?' I raise an eyebrow. 'So this means we can stop rehashing the whole André thing?'

Her expression quickly morphs right back to a scowl. Ah, how easily she freezes me out. 'Never.'

'*Anyway*,' Miguel cuts in. 'He's an idiot, but he's right about the fact that you *should* come. You'll enjoy it, we're just playing for fun. It's nothing serious at all, right?'

Shantal gives Miguel an apologetic smile. *He's* getting smiles? Definitely on her good side. 'I'd love to. But I have work to do on the numbers I picked up with Darien.'

'Maybe just pop in for like, an hour. Please?' I try anyway. I meet her eyes while waiting for a response. Please, please, please.

'Okay,' she finally gives in. 'I used to play, but that was a while ago. And you are all scary good at football here.'

I wave a dismissive hand, even though she's right, because most kids in Brazil who have a penchant for the sport practically learn to dribble and walk at the same time. 'You'll be just fine.'

I hide the relief I feel immediately after the word 'okay' leaves her lips. And I try not to think about why I'm already so obsessed with the specialist who's going to leave in just a few months' time.

Chapter Fourteen

Shantal

I didn't lie. I haven't played football for ages.

Part of me wonders if Darien intends to truly humiliate me in the presence of all these football pros, so I enter the Leblon indoor field gingerly. It's a welcome change from my room in the Ring, though, where I've now brought all my things with the intention of staying week-round. In the coming days, I've got to finish with all my work and simulation programs, so we'll be ready for the first run on the modified practice track next week. I set the room up like some sort of MI6 headquarters, with monitors surrounding my laptop on my desk and wires every which way. It's all I've been stressing over since we got here. A bit of physical activity outside my roost won't hurt. Just not physical activity with the guy who is currently the biggest distraction in my life.

I decide to focus on the familiarity of the synthetic grass beneath my feet. I've put on a pair of studs for the first time since university; it's just a pair I picked up that morning, but like my original club studs, they're neon orange and black. My teammates would call them my 'tiger claws', not only because of the colour, but also because of the cruel scratches and bruises their plastic spikes would leave on other girls' legs. I was far too hot-headed and stupid back then. I will never disclose how many red cards I earned, but it's not a number I am proud of.

'Saturday football!' Darien's excited voice breaks through my bubble. A bag is thrown to the benches behind me. He comes from my left, bobbing his head to whatever he's listening to through his black headphones. For once, his T-shirt and football shorts match the occasion. 'Shantal, you came!'

'Well, it'd be rude to stand you all up,' I reply with a smile, adding that little *all* to make for a slight stab – I'm not just here because he asked. My wary response also hides any excitement at being on the field again that might be woven into my voice.

He grins. 'All right, chivalry. Nice cleats, too.'

'Thanks.'

'No, like, actually. Those are club-level.' He gestures to my studs. 'I'm definitely invested now. Don't tell me, I want a surprise.'

'I see.' It's almost frustrating how *easy* he is with everyone. He looks so at home on the turf, too.

The others flood in soon enough, toting their own bags and strapping on their boots. Alongside Miguel and Henri, Darien introduces me to a few of his friends from around here: Luciano, Tomas, Paulo Ricardo, and Giovanni, all of whom are exceptionally fit and exceptionally good-looking. What are they drinking in Brazil? This is going to be the most difficult scrimmage I've ever played.

'So I assume you all like football?' are my first words once Darien has acquainted me with the group.

'Love,' Darien corrects me.

'Love football.'

Tomas nods. 'We do this every week. It'll be fun to play with some new faces this Saturday. Luce, actually, has just gotten some good news for us. Go ahead, *irmão*.'

Luciano could probably pass for some sort of Greek god with his bronze tan, green eyes and dark brown hair held in waves so effortless I can't tell if they're the product of a perm. He beams brightly, glancing around at all of us. 'The *Seleção* came calling. *Finally*. Scouts want to watch me play in the next round of try-outs.'

This incites whoops and cheers, hugs and back-thumping. I do join in the cheering – it's obvious just what an *enormous* deal it is to be in the running for a country's national team. It's the biggest step to the global stage: Copa America, Olympics, and, above all, the World Cup. This may not be such good news for me, though, as I'm about to attempt to play with or against a national-level footballer, and no one else in the group seems perturbed.

We go through a cycle of warm-ups before doing any playing, just a few stretches to loosen up the muscles and whatnot. When I sit down to join, though, I get a couple of looks of confusion from the new guys.

'So, Shantal,' Giovanni asks me with a hint of scepticism, 'what brings you to Saturday football? Joining us to play?'

'Sure.' I reach out and touch my toe in a runner's stretch. 'It's been a minute. I was on this small club team during uni, but you know how those things go.'

'How do they go?' Henri is predictably confused.

'Well, it's just that not all parents think it's worth spending time and money on their daughter trying out for a big sports club. They always have other futures in mind for her. *Better* futures.' I smile wryly. 'Especially true for immigrant parents, perhaps.'

The memory is fleeting but strong. I remember my parents putting me and Sonia in Bharatanatyam lessons with a guru one of the local aunties had suggested to them. We were just kids – I was three, Sonia five. Sonia grew to become a graceful dancer, every move of her limbs like watching water flow, her *abhinaya* – her expressions – bringing grown adults to tears. That wasn't my thing at all. I was all about football. My parents were content to drop a few grand on Sonia's *arangetram*, her extravagant graduation ceremony constituting a four-hour solo recital, but to spend the same on sending me to play across Europe with my club was a completely different matter.

'Well . . .' Paulo clears his throat awkwardly. 'Women's football is a . . . rough terrain, is it not? Maybe a career with security is better.'

Luciano shoots Paulo a look before cutting in. 'It's never too late.' He sneaks a wink my way, a wink complete with more than just friendly encouragement. 'I see those boots, I think you're gonna bring it. What do you play?'

I'm trying not to go pink in the face as I answer. 'Winger, mostly the left.'

'Winger?' I can't tell if Tomas is trying to hold back a laugh or not. 'You suppose you'll be able to keep up?'

Oh? The winger position is arguably the one that's got to do the fastest running in a match. I'd rather not debate my abilities, even if I'm a little rusty, but it was bound to happen. I've met – and had to win over – enough male footballers in my career at Conquest that I know they value 'show' more than they do 'tell'. 'We'll find out, then?' I reply stonily.

'We will,' Luciano confirms, turning his warning glance to Tomas. 'Let's play, Shantal?'

I return the warm smile he reserves for me with one of my own. 'Let's.'

Darien seems to quietly take note of this entire exchange. He slowly approaches me with a slightly raised eyebrow when we gather on the field to sort out our teams.

'What are you doing with your face?' I crouch and give the laces of my right boot a good tug to get them tighter before wrapping them round my ankle. I've been told it's bad for the feet, but I've done that since I was a kid.

'You're getting awfully close with Luce.' He squints against the sun coming through the window panels on the ceiling to look at me. 'You two are, like, footy-flirting. Your cleats, your position, all that.'

I almost choke out a laugh. *What?* This would be funny if it wasn't causing my heart to stutter in retaliation, noting that little sting of something in Darien's voice. Was that . . . jealousy?

I bite back a smile and reply, 'Oh. I suppose I didn't realize.'

'What . . . but . . .'

I can't hold it any longer. I snort, and the sound opens up a flood of my humiliating, hiccupping laughter. 'Look at your face! Darien!'

He's just barely managing a confused smile. 'What the *fuck?*'

I shake my head, my ponytail bouncing. 'Darien, what does it matter what I choose to do? I'm not *footy-flirting*, and even if I am, I'm just messing about. Luciano is *stunning*. He's a serious contender for the national team, for crying out loud.'

'Yeah.' He nods, almost resignedly. His studs still hang from his fingers where they swish, to and fro. 'Yeah . . .'

He trails off as he sits down in the grass to lace up. I allow myself one glance before returning to tightening my own boot, tongue clamped in a vice. What was he going to say? And then . . . why the hell did I want to know so badly?

* * *

The moment the boys call kick-off, I'm at university again.

I remember playing like it was my oxygen. The first touch is instinctive; I catch the pass cleanly. From here, I decide the only way is through. I stop, feint to the left, and nudge the ball right past Tomas and to a waiting Paulo. He keeps it safe till we can connect once more, and that's all we need. I blast it into the net, past Henri in defence.

'GOAALLL!' I bump knuckles with Paulo, whooping. 'Show' rather than 'tell'. Works every time.

While I'm smaller and carry less muscle on my frame than the guys – not to mention being years out of practice – I play strategically, staying in positions where I can pass, score, or make a connection that helps our side. I know I can't best the likes of Luciano head-to-head, so I avoid the direct fights, working to get the ball around instead of through.

Tomas shakes his head in disbelief when we call the game after an hour (7 –3) and begin to pick up our things.

'Holy crap.' He stops and regards me in some wonderment. 'How?'

'We all dream.' I shrug between guzzles of water. 'For me, it was always this. I wanted to be where you are. I played with these high hopes of, like, Crystal Palace Women's, but the way my family is, even if I got offers . . .'

'Leaving home, huh.' Luciano nods. 'I get that. I guess I'm lucky my chance is so close by, you know.'

'You are.'

'You play like a new Marta, *mina*.' He holds out a hand. 'I'll give you that.'

'Honoured, coming from you.' I smile and shake it.

'Be back next Saturday.'

'I'll certainly try.'

I sweep a curl from my face with a chuckle as Luciano heads

94

on his way. Miguel puts on a whiny little mimicry voice. '*You play like a new Marta. I love you, Shantal.*' He makes about five different obnoxious kissy faces, at which I roll my eyes.

'You wanted to play for Crystal Palace?' asks Darien as he piles his own stuff into his bag beside me. I can tell he's resisting adding to Miguel's quips, which is at least to his credit.

'I did. But football doesn't pay the bills,' I hum as I start to unlace my boots. 'I went and studied athletic training and comp sci instead, then interned with Conquest . . . so here I am. Quite a way from my initial intent,' I add, almost a jab at myself.

Darien just sits with that for a moment. Perhaps he's thinking.

Then he drops his bag and water bottle. 'Let's do a one-on-one. Please.' He actually clasps his hands together, as if in prayer. '*Please.*'

I look around, picking up the ball. We're the only ones left. 'Why?' I gesture towards the others, disappearing towards the car park.

'Because. It's better than playing with computers.'

I laugh, slightly snidely. 'Aha! Well, I'm quite good at playing with computers, I'll have you know.'

'It's not as fun as football.'

Without warning, he slaps the ball from my hands, and runs down the pitch with it, dribbling it deftly.

I watch Darien, immature as he is, grinning at me, his curls falling out of place, his eyes creasing with genuine happiness. Ugh, I want to hate him so badly. I really do. He's got his head in the clouds all the time, whereas I have my entire company's fate riding on my performance here. I don't have the room in my head to take up another source of stress, nor in my heart to hold someone else dear, only to lose them in the end. I have no other options. I can't, I can't, I can't.

I sigh. *Just football*, I tell myself. *This is just football.*

Chapter Fifteen

Darien

Shantal is in deep thought, I can tell. Her little ponytail swishes as she jogs over, already plotting her path to the ball.

'Just us,' I tease her, dribbling back towards the net. 'No one to connect with.'

'No need,' she replies.

In one swift move, hooks her foot round mine and steals the ball. The way she crosses me so effortlessly is pretty damn amazing. Her ball control is insane. I'm trying to catch her, but she's a winger – she's got to be fast, too. I've never played on a team or in any particular position, just kicked the ball around till I grasped the sport, like most kids growing up here. Shantal, though, is serious.

Once I compose myself, I'm able to get around her to stick out my leg, and the ball slips my way, letting me gain possession. Unfortunately, I'm now darting around an aggressive Shantal.

She hops back a few steps and flaps her T-shirt, trying to keep cool. My eyes unconsciously travel to her exposed midriff, the waistband of her Nike Pros peeking out over her football shorts, as she wipes her face with the hem of the shirt. I'm not sure how I didn't notice it before, because she's clearly built like a footballer. Strong, sculpted legs, toned arms and abs: she is literally knock-me-out *wow*.

Meu Deus. This is unexpected.

Something warm floods my chest and creeps lower than that, even though I try to concentrate on getting this ball past her, you know, just your average football one-on-one.

So naturally, collision is inevitable when Shantal swoops in and fights me for possession. She brings her leg over mine and tosses the ball behind us with the tap of a cleated foot whose spikes are maybe an inch from leaving scratches on my skin. Even when I fight back and succeed in stealing it at such close quarters that my back is almost against her chest, she keeps chipping away at me. She is merciless and takes no breaks for 'are you good' and 'you okay'. She is a little too good at this. She has beautiful footwork. She has a beautiful body.

Shantal takes advantage of my distraction, sweeping the ball from beside my foot. She smacks an absolute cannon into the top right of the net. I'm shocked to the point where I can barely tell my own legs to move. Well, either shocked or in complete and utter awe. Why isn't this chick playing club football?

'Fuckin' hell, Shantal,' I manage when she returns to centre pitch with a dimpled grin and the ball at her feet.

'Keep up,' she quips, executing a flawless drag-back. She uses her size as an advantage rather than a drawback, darting away quickly. I'm still in the fight, but as I snatch away the ball and dribble around her, she tries her level best to keep me from getting away with it. If I nudge her arm away, she nudges mine back. We go shoulder-to-shoulder, the proximity marked enough to make out the baby hairs on her forehead. I couldn't care less if I won or lost. At this point, I'm just making excuses to so much as breathe the same air as her. I can't do much else other than admire this woman.

It's my slide tackle to step in and rein in a slightly long ball that ends the frantic scramble for control of the game. All of a sudden, we're lying in the turf, laughing both at and with one another. I'm so close to Shantal now that I can count the barely discernible freckles on her nose, that I can feel her breath on my cheek as she loses her composure with her eyes squeezed shut, burying her head into my shoulder. She snatches my voice away so even when I try to laugh, I can't get a sound out. I feel like it's ridiculous. Yeah, it's ridiculous.

It's immaculate. It's a moment that ends as soon as it had begun. 'Hey! Dar!'

Shit. It's Celina's voice, and not too far away, either. Shantal pulls away with a gasp as we scramble to our feet in an attempt to amend the situation, but coming our way with a smirk on her face, my trusty trainer's seen it all.

She stops before us, cocking her head, interrogating us in turn as if she can glean some information from our very demeanours. 'Hmm. Well, Darien, I'm here to let you know the mayor called. You *do* recall you've got civic duties today?'

'Wha . . . civic duty?' I groan, grateful at least for a distraction on which to focus all my emotion. 'Noooo!'

'Sorry, but you know these things. You've got to go talk to him, shake hands, other niceties,' says Celina with a shrug. 'You have fifteen minutes, and I,' she holds up a backpack, 'have good clothes. Go look pretty.'

She shoots a wink and a smile at Shantal, but our steady technology genius just looks slightly more irritated than usual.

Forget that happened. Her eyes throw a silent piercing glare at me.

I nod her way. *Okay*, I imply with a widening of my own eyes.

'See you guys,' I actually blurt, before grabbing the backpack, turning, and nearly bolting to the locker rooms.

My heart is beating double time. I'm grinning stupidly. But that's for no one to see or know except myself.

Chapter Sixteen

Shantal

'Turn hard, turn hard, more, a little more . . .'

Jack Lyons chants his encouragement as I watch Henri take his trainer's suggestion and lurch to the side on the sim, gritting his teeth against the weight of the steering. As the development driver, he is essentially next in line to either of the two seats, Darien's and Miguel's, whichever might require filling at some point. So we've been working him up the walls just as much as the other two, and now I'm throwing the brand-new Ring simulation track I tailored with mods picked out from the Cantagalo drive into the regimen. It has all three drivers just as nervous as I'd intended. It's a fair reaction; it's been a good two weeks since the football game, and they've not got so much as a look at the new system. This is a surprise for all of us, which is what makes it so perfect.

'Whoa!' Miguel yelps, physically recoiling from the screen. 'Guys, Turn Seven, there's some weird . . . is that a chicane on elevation? Dude, what'd I just experience?' he calls out to the other two.

'Warning would have helped about ten seconds ago,' Darien grumbles with an exhausted air. 'What'd you put in this sim?'

Knowing I'm making men who are supposed to be at the top of their sport struggle gives me a wicked burst of satisfaction. I have to hold back a slightly evil smile as Darien tugs his car around yet another hairpin turn. They've not even encountered the worst of it yet – the very reason this sim was so highly sought after by Heidelberg.

As the guys each come to the end of their first few practice laps, the screens display a rest prompt, and I get to work on my end. I run the new program on my control computer. 'Okay, and now I'm going to throw a couple of things in there for the next few laps,' I warn them.

'You're throwing in more than whatever the hell we just *did*?' exclaims Miguel incredulously.

I just shrug and bring my cursor over the button that will push the program to the simulators. 'Have fun.'

With a click of my mouse, the real Conquest simulation starts to run on all three set-ups. It looks fairly normal at first, with a rolling start when the drivers guide the car through and out onto the track. This time, I've enabled opponents, with nineteen other cars on each simulator.

The sims themselves are well-crafted pieces of technology, essentially a chassis with a screen set-up that wraps all the way around, so the driver, suited in their helmet and strapped into the seat, feels as if they're in the actual car. Conquest's physical set-up is a tad different from most of the existing technology, integrating statistics obtained from the wind tunnel tests we've received so far from Heidelberg HQ in Germany to create a level of resistance, porpoising – bouncing of the car – and handling that mimics the real thing as closely as possible. But the jewel in the crown of the new simulators is in the program and its ability to *learn* – to use the sensors in the seat, in the pedals, all throughout the chassis to scope out the driver's style. And then, it does something magical with that learning.

About one lap in, the changes start to kick in.

'Wait, what the hell? That turn wasn't there before, Shantal!' Miguel sounds like he's just seen a ghost. It almost makes me burst out laughing.

'It's *changing!*' Darien yelps in horror.

'That's the point,' Celina chides him, although she looks as entertained as I do. She gives me a satisfied nod.

To be honest, out of everyone, Henri handles the new program with the most grace. I think it's because his ego has yet to grow to the size of the average Formula 1 driver's (something I'm learning more and more about as I spend time around hotshots Miguel and Darien). He's still willing to be humbled, and at the end of the practice run, once the sim displays the rest screen again and all three drivers lean back with heavy sighs, I'm fairly confident that even if his turn speeds aren't as fast as those of the other two, it's his driving that will have been the most consistent through all the adaptive track shifts.

We round everyone up for a debrief once the guys have grabbed water and talked with their trainers. Darien, still toting a water bottle, has the first question.

'Bro. What in the Labyrinth was that?' he asks in disbelief, throwing his hands in the air and almost flinging his water bottle at Miguel in the process.

'Well, the goal of this new technology is to target your soft spots,' I offer. 'Trying to take the things you all have the lowest times on and make them faster. And as I discovered, that's your explosive motions. Your response times, your times around fast turns, when you're looking to take a gap, those can be faster. And since you, Darien, had the fastest times around sharp turns, I've used footage from the kind of driving *you* learned that helps you react faster on the track to create a modded version of the Heidelberg Hybridge Ring. What you just saw is essentially what happens when you take the Heidelberg Ring and lay it over the Cantagalo favela.'

'You did that?' I'm not sure if the look on Darien's face is one of fear any more, but his arms have lowered, and his brows furrow together. 'That's *unbelievable*.'

'And the way it kept changing . . .' Henri trails off with a shudder. 'What was that?'

'The simulator is capable of learning from the way you drive. So every move you made in it, literally, was stored and analyzed to change the track on the next lap according to where you were weakest. Where you needed reps, so to speak,' I tell him.

'Reps?' echoes Darien with a raised eyebrow.

'For the record,' I shoot back, 'you'd be shocked at all the places *you* need work.'

Miguel purses his lips, but I can tell he's holding back a laugh when he meets my eyes with a poorly concealed grin. As he and Henri head off to hit the showers, Darien hauls himself onto the edge of the desk where the computer sits before turning to look my way. 'You gotta take a compliment, Shantal. This is really amazing.'

'Flattery's not going to get me to change my opinion of you, you know.' I close out the computer program before locking eyes with Darien. It shouldn't affect me that his gaze is so big and bold, always with the aura of someone who's about to tell the funniest joke you've heard in your life. This man has caused me nothing but grief since I got here.

'Oh, I know that.' He leans in with a mischievous smile that makes my limbs tingle. *Stop it, Shantal.* 'But I kinda thought you were rethinking said impression on that turf, what, two weekends back?'

I roll my eyes. That moment was a brief lapse in judgement, and I'm determined to put it behind me. 'You're so *unserious*. I'm here to get a job done, Darien.'

'Doesn't mean you can't have some fun while you're at it!' he insists. 'The season is a snowballing pile of stress. If you don't cut loose, you're never going to survive it.'

'Is that all you wanted to share with me, then?'

'I mean, kind of, yeah.' He shrugs, but my nonchalant attitude hasn't caused the honest glimmer in his eyes to fade at all. 'You can stay upset at me if you want. I'm not here to change your mind. You just strike me as someone who does a lot of really, really phenomenal things and doesn't get the flowers she deserves for it. So I'm giving you flowers. Take them.'

Darien hops down from the desk and leaves the room with a wave goodbye, but his voice doesn't leave with him. *Giving you flowers.*

I think of Sonia, my parents' perfect child. All the stress of this assignment. The fact that maybe Raya should have had this opportunity to work in Brazil. And then I think of Darien, who knows nothing of the weight I've been shouldering since I was old enough to realize it. And he says to me, he will give me flowers.

Flowers.

I allow myself the smallest chuckle before I grab my backpack and walk out.

Chapter Seventeen

Darien

The days begin to fly by, and suddenly we're in high gear preparing for winter testing. It won't be our first look at the cars – we get a peek when we do the livery reveal on Valentine's Day – but it will be our first time driving them, and we've been told the overhaul is huge. Fortunately, as information has come in on our newest models, Shantal and the engineers have worked to make sure the sims are as identical as possible to the cars. It's been a learning curve, but the trainers are pleased with the improvement, and the rest of us are just hoping it'll be enough.

I can feel it in my shoulders, though – my entire body is full of stress. As much as I try not to let on in practice, I have to get along with this new car – *speak* to it, even – if I want to fulfil the conditions of keeping this centre alive. It's all that's been on my mind since we started creeping up on livery reveal, so I've decided to find something else to focus on.

It's Carnaval, and that means all of Rio is only play, no work. Of course, our family celebrated every year, but I remember how it was after Pai passed away. I used to sit on his shoulders, the same way I'd sit on my mom's at the parades, and he'd point out every float to me, sing to every song. As I got older, it became pretty easy to put the memories aside each Carnaval and, if I'm being totally honest, it was definitely the alcohol that made it so easy.

So granted that *no one* on this team has ever been to Carnaval before, I decided to take on a couple of responsibilities. The first? The pre-game.

We order bottles and bottles of Brazilian rum, whisky, the works. We load up my room in the Ring, but it's not long till the drinks are flowing. This will only last so long, of course, what with tomorrow marking exactly one week till the pre-season test. And yeah, we can't have any of the good stuff in our bodies after this last hurrah. Alcohol, as Celina likes to say, is nothing but reward for exceptional performance once the season starts. Either you do well and you get to drink, or you suck and you have to go dry for months.

'Who the hell bought this?' I raise a can of Smirnoff that I *definitely* hadn't ordered.

'Me,' Miguel offers, shrugging carelessly. 'Remember that extra duffel bag? The one with my spare crash helmets?'

'Ah, the helmets,' I recall. I nod in acknowledgement. 'That was definitely way too heavy to be helmets, dude.'

Our fourth and final guest to arrive, Shantal, tentatively walks through the open door and into my room full of liquor with a smile and a roll of her eyes as she takes stock of everything we've procured. 'This looks like a uni fresher's room.'

We all turn to Henri immediately.

For all his childishness, he's absolutely slamming back a red

Solo cup of *something* that will undoubtedly come back to get him tomorrow. I lean in and take a whiff. '*Bro*. What is that?'

He just looks at me, totally clueless. 'Some of Miguel's stuff and then, like, Pepsi? Or the Brazilian version?'

'I have to ask again.' My eye twitches as I regard Henri with as much deep thought as I'm capable of in the moment. 'Can you even *drive*?'

'Well . . . I just graduated high school last June,' he says with a tipsy smile. 'I've never even been to college.'

'Oh, he's a baby!' Miguel whines, ruffling Henri's pale brown curls before popping the tab on the nearest Smirnoff and taking a swig.

In a move swifter than I'd have anticipated, Shantal grabs a bottle of rum and uncorks it, filling herself a cup. She catches my watching gaze and meets it with a raised eyebrow. 'What?'

'What?' I shake my head for a little extra emphasis, even though it's definitely not working. I could say I'm staring because she has these goofy blue and gold tinsel clip-ons all up in her hair, or because she's wearing nothing but a bright green bikini top and booty shorts, and she never fails to shock me with all these parts of her personality (not to mention she's drop-dead *gorgeous*) but I decide to tell a little white lie. 'I didn't know you liked rum.'

'We love rum in the Mangal family,' she retorts with a scrunch of her nose that makes her gold hoops swish. If I were a man with less impulse control, I think I'd pass out, although the impulse control isn't keeping me from going hard as we speak. I have to do an awkward little cough and turn towards my makeshift bar to pour myself another drink so she doesn't notice.

Many, many drinks in, we're all decidedly loose enough to head out to Ipanema – without the usual security entourage, to my excitement. I'm not exactly sure what strings Katrina and Demir might have pulled, but I'm relieved we get to enjoy the holiday without additional attention. It's just the beginning of the festival, the first day, and midday at that, but the first day is all we'll have. We're on the grind tomorrow – which means we have to soak in whatever we can now.

The boardwalk is already crammed shoulder to shoulder with people dressed in bright colours and as little as conveniently possible. I've tried my best to get us all to blend in as well as possible en route to the parade. The three of us drivers are nowhere near identifiable, with sunglasses, bandanas tied around our heads, and the most common T-shirts and board shorts I could find. Either way, everyone's way too plastered and occupied to notice anything which, in my opinion, is the beauty of going out at Carnaval.

'Parade's not till way later.' Miguel lowers his sunglasses and waggles his eyebrows at us as we walk. 'How we feeling about hitting a bar or two, dancing? We all dancers here?'

I clear my throat. 'Yeah, actually, I think we should go for it.' I sneak a covert little tip of my head at Shantal as if to say, 'Dance, right?' She just lets out a laugh.

'Oh . . .' She throws her head back, looking up at the sky with a groan. 'Give me one reason this will be a good idea.'

'You'll be so drunk later,' suggests Miguel, 'that you won't even remember this!'

Shantal gives that a moment's thought, but eventually she sighs. 'Probably true. *Just. This. Once.*' She wags a finger my way with each word.

Henri, Smirnoff in hand, raises it eagerly. 'Let's go, guys!'

It's only half an hour before we've found ourselves at the first outdoor bar of the day on the beach. It's clearly makeshift, with the enormous dance floor coming off the bar area itself, but it is *packed*. Shantal bobs her head to the beat as I return from the bar with a margarita for each of us.

'Thanks.' The guarded look on her face starts to fall away, making way for curiosity as she glances at the floor full of tourists and locals who are mingling over the blaring tones of modernized samba. She sips at her drink. 'Ooh, this is good stuff.'

'As it should be.' I raise an eyebrow at her waist swishing ever so slightly side to side. 'Did you wanna go dance? I don't know how much good I'd do you, though.'

'I couldn't,' she shoots back immediately. Looks like I've found the defensiveness. 'Why don't you go for it?' she suggests. 'No shortage of dance partners around here.'

She's making a valid point, I guess. There are a lot of girls in this club. They're really pretty, but I just shrug impassively. Maybe a month ago I'd have thought about it, but they're not Shantal.

I turn back to her, and I say, 'I won't go for it unless you do.' I take a sip, no, a gulp of my margarita for courage. 'You deserve to have some fun.'

'Fun.' She echoes the word like she's never heard it spoken in her life. 'Well, like Miguel said.'

'We're going to be too slammed to remember anything,' I recite, extending a hand to her. 'So. Dance?'

There's a moment where I think I haven't sold her on it. I'm using everything I've got, puppy-dog eyes included, and it looks as if she's going to say no, straight up. Until her expression breaks into a grin. Shantal is beaming at me, and as she takes my hand, walking backwards towards the dance floor, I can't even compute that something's changed her mind. All I see is that smile.

'Oh, you're gonna tear it up?' I tease her as she takes a spin on the beat.

'Well, Darien, if you're going to know everything else about me, you'd better find out that no one tears it up harder than a girl from Guyana.'

Spoiler alert: she's very much right.

It has to be the alcohol taking over both of our senses, but before I can register it, my hands are on Shantal's waist, and I think an Anitta song is playing, and Shantal moves like it's second nature, tapping my arm as if to say, *Just follow me*. I do, and we're completely in sync with every step we take, as Shantal deftly guides herself beneath my arm and I spin her in towards me so her back is right up against my chest, her butt flush against me, her body warm against mine and my hands pressed to her bare skin.

The sun beats down on us, making the sparkly tinsel in Shantal's hair seem to reflect in the light as she grinds against me, throwing a mischievous smile back my way. I can feel every puff of her breath escape her lips and brush mine.

I take it you like that? her eyes seem to prod me.

A little too much, mine reply.

And I never in my life thought I'd be watching the woman developing simulators for my Formula 1 team absolutely drop it to the floor, but jeez, when Shantal said she'd shake it, she wasn't lying.

With a laugh, she tugs on the back of my bandana, steering me over to her so I don't get lost in the crowd in my daze. She adjusts the thin fabric and tucks a stray lock of my hair back under it, her slim fingers lingering on my forehead for just a second longer. Neither of us can look away. Maybe we are daring one another to hang on, I'm not sure. Playing a game – who gives in first? But I don't think I want it to end.

'Holy *shit*!' Miguel whoops, tugging Henri over so hard he almost somersaults headfirst into Shantal's empty margarita glass. 'Can we talk about that, Miss Mangal?'

'Stop it.' Shantal elbows Miguel with her free hand, laughing as she hides her face in my shoulder. I hold back a smile as I give Miguel a little nod, and we all head off to get more drinks.

The Carnaval parade is put on at night, when the sun has set and lights come on all down the street route. Floats resplendent with massive props, flashbulbs, sparkles, feathers, and, of course, troupes and troupes of dancers begin to make their way down; from the stands, we are able to see every second of it. There's wonder in Henri's eyes as he bounces along to the booming music.

All four of us wrap our arms around each other and cheer and dance like we've been doing this for ages. It's probably because of the incredibly heated dance we shared, and definitely because of the alcohol, but my gaze immediately travels to Shantal. When she's not stressed, not worried, not upset, there's a sense of ease about her. She's donned a bunch of coloured bead necklaces over a Crystal Palace FC hoodie she brought with her, and the smile on her face tells me everything I need to know about how she's faring. She looks so much more carefree than I've ever seen her before.

We eventually take an Uber back to our training quarters, all of us grinning and giggling as we part ways. Shantal gives me a little wave when she slips into her room. That same smile, that same giddiness: it's in that moment that I realize I may just be in too deep. *Way* too deep.

Chapter Eighteen

Darien

Somehow, Shantal is still able to go *right* back to the divisive anti-Darien wall the next morning, as if we didn't just dance without room for so much as a grain of rice between us. But I know I'm not just imagining it now: we absolutely had a vibe going on all night.

I'm convinced she has an evil twin standing in for her between the hours of eight a.m. and five p.m.

'Hey, Shantal.'

I approach her as calmly as I can outside the Ring's conference room, where the entire team is slated to sit for a presentation on our newest car's stats with seven days until the testing sessions. I even get there early to make sure I can catch her, because I don't know what she's had on her mind, but I think I desperately need to debrief.

'Hi.' She throws back a huge gulp of coffee as per usual, training her eyes on me for a few seconds before clearing her throat. 'The meeting isn't for fifteen minutes.'

'Well . . . uh, I actually wanted to talk to you. About last night.'

I think she's going to choke on her coffee for a minute. Her eyes go momentarily wide. 'What . . . oh, the dance?'

'Yeah,' I laugh nervously. 'That. I feel like after something like . . . that, it's only fair of me to ask you . . .'

'What we are,' she finishes. I hear it in her voice for a split second; in fact, I even see it on her face. It's a minuscule hint of the same kind of nerves I have, mirrored in her demeanour. But then, like someone's flipped a switch, it's gone. 'It was just a dance.' Her tone is casual. She busies herself checking the papers in the file folder she holds. 'We were drunk. It happens.'

I'm not going to lie, that one definitely stung.

I agree, we were drunk. But I like to think I was sober enough to have sensed *something*. Right?

Her eyes flit back up to me, and this time, they're full of guilt. It's like watching a prisoner's steely exterior crack to reveal a human being desperate for a minute of freedom, a sliver of sunlight. And that, I'm definitely not imagining.

For the next week, I try to avoid thinking about both what I'd seen on Shantal's face that day, and the fact that the Ring's destiny being in my hands means this season has to go off without a hitch. I push on with training, to take the moments of laughter and chaos I share with the guys in stride, but the night before pre-season testing, none of it does me any good, and I toss and turn in bed.

So naturally, the next morning, when the first of four days of testing dawns on us, I feel like I should've taped my eyes open for it. I'm hoping the double shot of espresso I down on arrival at the Ring's track will hold me over.

Thankfully, once I leave the compound, I realize I didn't

need the espresso. The cameras are everywhere, and all the additional pit-lane and paddock set-ups that had been placed the night before have completely elevated our backyard practice track. The press pack rolls in early on, and the teams follow soon enough, funnelling in around the back of the compound as they look up at it in amazement. Fans have completely flooded the area outside the Ring gates to get photos and autographs as motorsport royalty arrive – they won't be allowed in until the last two days of the testing. I have to sit in the Heidelberg garage for a minute and just take it all in: the bright colours of the nine other multimillion-dollar teams off to my sides as they ready their cars and drivers to compete, right here, mere miles from where I grew up. A swell of pride fills my chest when I see the way it's all come together. Full circle, and I'm praying this is only the beginning.

I pull on the sleeve of my racing suit, the new white livery with ice blue and black racing stripes as well as our sponsors' branding. Conquest is now the next largest logo aside from Heidelberg's own and the Hybridge sector.

Our new livery isn't the only change that's hit the paddock. There's a couple of new drivers down in the smaller teams. Vittore has one rookie. Wilson Nitro has two, *and* a new name – Flashpoint SwipeIn Robinson Racing Team (it's a mouthful).

I catch sight of Diana far across the row of motorhomes, darting in and out of her own garage, helmet in hand. I almost shiver – as much as she's like family to me, she's going to be *terrifying* this season. The Championship, currently kept at our headquarters in Germany, is up for grabs from Miguel, its previous winner, and there's no better motivation than taking the title from your fiancé, of course.

The air of tension isn't helped by the sponsors who – as reward for embellishing our suits – mill about the garage of the practice track. I try to simply smile and say hi. It should be so easy, but this feels like the eerie calm before a real race. It's nothing, just the Formula 1 pre-season testing. It's only life and death.

Celina gives my arm a gentle tap. 'Hang in there. You know the stakes, but you know you've *prepared*. Remember that this is just practice. We're looking at the car more than you. You'll be just fine, yeah?'

Her reassurance goes slightly in vain. I know as much as anyone else that the pre-season test is for the car, which is why we deck it out in ridiculous gear like the massive grates we call aero rakes attached to its front, but it feels like I'm starting over and making a first impression – like a rookie. And on my home turf, no less.

'Just breathe.'

I turn to find the owner of the simple advice: Shantal, armed with a massive bottle of water and sunglasses. She gives me a small nod, brushing a hair from her face. She's wearing it loose today rather than in a little ponytail, and the slight waves brush barely past her shoulders, skimming the fabric of her white team T-shirt, which is tucked loosely into denim shorts. 'Are you panicking right now?'

'No,' I bluff. As much as I've come to trust her on so many levels, fear is pretty strong, and no fear is greater than that of failure.

'We are *all* here if anything happens.' The light lilt of her English accent soothes me like some sort of lullaby. 'And you didn't put in weeks of work just to lose your composure now. Make it count.'

Her advice must be what I need, because I return her nod and finally get moving on prep before hitting the track. My heart thuds hard in my chest as I walk towards my glittering crash helmet. Got to make this count.

I'll be doing the winter testing alongside Miguel, as it will be on-track for the races. Miguel, for his part, is currently out running time, a good half-hour of asphalt to get a bit more car data, mostly. So far, he's been flawless, keeping the sponsors, cameramen and the celebrities scattered through the garage and under VIP awnings happy. There are only a few grandstands crammed into the corners, because a practice track can't accommodate more than that, and this one's totally cordoned off, but aside from those already packing the benches, more clutches of loyal fans have gathered behind the second layer of fencing, far out past the gravel traps, beyond the catch fence, where they can watch safely.

Shantal heads to her spot on the Heidelberg pit wall, where she'll be able to watch us, hear us, and see the data come in. I wait for the car to return. The livery is beginning to take shape. Since Heidelberg has chosen to support Viva Brasil this series, an environmental initiative dedicated to preserving our rainforests and natural diversity, as an ode to the location of our new complex, we've had some changes made to the paint. The car is a beautiful frosty white with sky blue palm fronds and small silver macaws flying across the side. The shimmering silver will stand out well during the night races dotting the Formula 1 calendar.

Soon enough, Miguel pulls into the main garage with his car, clambering out once he's given the go-ahead by mechanics. 'It's really fast, but it's smooth.' He yanks off his balaclava, and his shock of dark hair stands on end. 'If I was okay, you'll be awesome.'

I'm at a loss for words, partially out of nerves, so I hold out a hand. He takes it and pulls me in to clap my back with a small tap. 'Show them,' he says quietly.

I purse my lips as Miguel goes to get some water. I'm rooted

116

to my spot. My first kart race is all I can think of. I'd never told Miguel about that, never told a soul.

Mostre a eles quem somos. Pa' Papai.

Show them who we are.

I don't believe in signs. But if this isn't a sign, I don't know what is.

I take a deep breath as I lower myself into my car, emblazoned with my number sixty-seven, and strap in.

Slowly, I leave the garage and turn into the pit lane. I exit the box onto the main track, and I will the car around me to disappear. I let it turn to nothing but the blue skies and asphalt track beneath my racing boots, until I'm standing there with silence all around me. It's like I'm here on a track walk, but there's no team to prod me about my worst turns or take embarrassing videos. It's tranquil, and it reminds me of why I put myself through the annual hell that's pre-season to begin with. The drive is beautiful.

My car is weightless. I glide around the next turn, soar onto the straight. Just you and your four wheels, the beautiful world flying by at two hundred miles an hour. This was how I fell in love with racing: I got to see Rio de Janeiro every time I looked at the track ahead of me.

I see it now, too. I lap at speeds beyond my usual with a smile on my face. This can't get any more perfect.

Chapter Nineteen

Shantal

'Shantal!' Miguel calls from through his helmet as the furore of car preparation buzzes around us. I can barely hear his voice, but I turn away from my laptop on the counter, heading towards his car, where he's just gotten out, and the mechanics are moving towards Darien's garage with a bucket of brightly coloured, slime-like flow-vis paint. I've been told they can apply it to the front of his chassis when he pulls back in, and so get tabs on wind flow, along with the new Conquest sensors we've been using.

Miguel must be grinning; his eyes are crinkled at the corners. 'This is your first time seeing the cars, right? Are you enjoying the show? Darien's gonna put one on for you. I mean, the way that guy has gone for a toss, looking at you with those puppy eyes.'

I feel an uncontrollable flush rise in my cheeks. As if. I'm not here for puppy eyes. Not for *his* puppy eyes.

Miguel chuckles, patting my hand. 'I'm playing with you. But actually, how's it going?'

'Stressful,' I reply with a nervous laugh. 'You are all so *strange*.'

He just waves the thought away with a goofy little cackle as he joins me on the wall with the engineers. Numbers have been coming in. Afonso explains to me what's strong, what's not so strong. It's different from the older stats we'd checked out way at the beginning.

'Shantal, are we good for Darien?' the lead mechanic yells from Darien's garage.

'Yes, go ahead!' I reply, still focused on the graphs forming on my screen.

Initially, I'm unfazed by the reports Afonso gives me as Darien does his out lap. It's pretty standard, till he goes for a hot lap, as they say, and suddenly, everything changes for us.

Darien's data are absolutely astounding. It should not be possible on a car he's never been in before, a car he's learning as we speak. I can't just watch points on a graph pop up any more. I have to tear my gaze from the monitors and on to the track. This is real, and I can't for the life of me believe it.

My eyes go wide as the number sixty-seven car whizzes past us. It should be a crime to be this fast. The speed traps are reading outrageous statistics that I can scarcely comprehend.

So naturally, it's not long until we get a request from Darien and Afonso: it's time to put him on soft tyres – the fastest compound we have. The man's only been running *medium tyres* so far.

'I can do softs,' his voice crackles over the radio. 'Go ahead and open the box.'

Afonso looks my way. 'We're going to pit him,' he says over

radio to the crew and me. Then, to Darien, 'Good. Box, box next lap. We will change them out.'

Darien comes into his box. 'You said to make it count, Shantal, now it's time,' Darien says into my headset. I can't help but smile, shaking my head as I watch him on the screens. It's easy when he can't see me.

The way the car zooms out of the pit lane sends my pulse bounding. Darien is running at, if not above, the expected speed.

'Traps are reading upwards of three-twenty kilometres an hour on those straights. Three-thirty,' the engineer reports excitedly. 'He's on his way.'

Camera feeds show Darien easily lapping the others, making complex corners look simple. I've never seen anything like this up close.

'We're watching history being made,' says Celina with a broad smile. 'Unbelievable, right?'

Unbelievable. Unbelievable doesn't even begin to cover it.

It's the way Darien drives: a manner as laid-back as everything about him. Each turn looks so simple, each corner a clean shot. On straights, his car looks like it glides into the curve at the end with a sort of ease that no one else has, except maybe Miguel.

This is the miracle. All the training we've done in the past month, all of it spent trying to get Henri and Miguel essentially mimicking Darien's pin-drop turn style, it's paying off. We are running the best times on corners. I let go of the biggest breath as I scroll through side-by-side data for Miguel and Darien. I took a gamble, we all did, and it worked.

'We look good,' remarks Miguel, grinning as he taps his screen. 'We look damn *great*.'

I laugh in relief. He gives me a congratulatory knuckle-bump, and both of us turn towards Darien's car as it soars across the main straight, illuminated by direct sunlight.

And naturally, moments after Miguel's made this proclamation, Darien's car pirouettes right past the pit wall, spinning front over rear wing, sparks spraying every which way.

'OH! OH MY GOD!' I yell as Celina and Miguel wince. Darien almost immediately rights himself and keeps chugging along as if exactly nothing happened. My hands are on my head. I'm hiding behind Celina, for crying out loud. '*Wow*. What? What *was* that?'

'Little spin,' Miguel replies casually. 'Too much push in an unfamiliar car or track can do it sometimes.'

I shake my head. *Little spin?*

Darien gets out of his car after his lap to roars of applause and cheers, his arms held high as he whoops happily. I don't understand how he does it. That spin? That's the only thing that replays in my head. That, to me, is nothing short of a near-death experience.

'How was that?' he hoots, snapping his visor up to reveal smiling eyes that meet mine. He raises a fist, presumably expecting me to return the gesture and bump it, but I must still appear in shock, because he says, 'What? What'd I do?'

'A *spin* like that . . .' I press a hand to my forehead. 'Miguel called that *little*. Do I want to know what *not so little* looks like? Huh?'

'You gotta shake it off,' Darien tells me. 'You don't want to know. And you can't let your imagination take you there. So,' he smiles sunnily, 'how was that?'

I bite back less kind retorts. I don't, and I never will, understand the kind of devil-may-care attitude this man has adopted. Nor, apparently, will I understand why my heart plummeted so quickly and took so long to recover the second he was in any sort of danger.

I choose the safest route of response. 'That was good.'

MARCH 2024

Formula 1 Season

Chapter Twenty

Shantal

Bahrain, first race of the season, dawns on us quickly – like, *really quickly*.

'*Let's go, plane leaves in two hours!*' Miguel yells in his biggest Barça matchday voice, banging on all our doors bright and early on a Monday morning. I think I'm going to cry. I've never been the most chipper of morning people without a coffee (which I realize I need badly), and I can barely figure out how to roll out of bed, a situation that is exponentially harder knowing I'll need to be on a jet in a couple of hours.

I'm an unhappy mess, with tangled hair and eye bags heavier than my luggage. Someone's rented limos that we get to take to the airfield, and it's so bad that I miss the first one with the three trainers, hopping into the second with the drivers. It's all very posh in said limo, except that I couldn't care less, and Henri's bouncy enthusiasm isn't curbing my irritation.

'Whoa, there's champagne!' he yelps, grabbing himself a flute and pulling the entire bottle out of its bucket of ice.

Miguel shoots him a look of slight judgement from where he sits, lounging with a bag of fancy little peanuts.

'Hey there, buddy.' Darien chortles. 'Easy on the bubbly. You'll throw it all up the second the plane leaves the ground.'

'Are you even legal, dude?' Miguel adds with a raised eyebrow.

Henri fumes for all of three seconds before giddily getting back to his champagne.

'Wake up.' Darien throws a peanut at me. His aim is unfortunately true. It knocks me right in the forehead.

'Hey!' I whine around a great big gulp of my coffee. 'I *am* awake, thank you very much.'

'You're not a morning person,' remarks Darien.

'Oh, he'd love to know.' The snort that escapes Miguel's mouth is ridiculously loud. Even the limo driver glances at his rear-view mirror with disdain. 'Sorry, Hen, but I think your girl's been looking for a guy who could grow a beard the entire time.'

'I can grow a beard!' Henri tries, but the laughter in the limousine almost drowns him out.

'I believe you,' I tell him with a tired drawl and a defensive clearing of my throat. 'But I'm not looking for beards, no beards, any kind of beards.'

'Yet she's all eyes for another man.' Miguel clucks his tongue dramatically, shaking his head for that little extra sting.

I almost fling my coffee cup his way at that, but Darien glows pink. It's quite funny to see how he gets. Regardless of the flair and the murals and the dances and the funk songs to his name, he's really not hard to fluster.

Seeing him off his game like that definitely wakes me up, if not the barrage of peanuts.

I chug the last couple of sips from my coffee with a contented hum, rubbing at my eyes. Darien's shoulder nudges mine, and I look up to see the most precious smile on his face. He's as tired as I am, but rather than bleary, his eyes are full of admiration. For what, I am not totally sure, but he says to me, 'You ever realized something?'

'I've not got enough brain power for that right now,' I tell him with a yawn. 'What did you realize?'

'I dunno.' He shrugs, gesturing to my almost-empty cup. 'Just that we need to get you bigger coffees.'

'Tell me about it,' I groan into the depths of my depleted caffeine supply. 'I need more. I need to start drinking those Jolt Simply Strawberry things.'

'Don't do it.' Darien shivers so obviously that I feel his entire body do a funny little wiggle beside mine. 'Jeez. It gives me the goosebumps just to think about it. You know how much sugar is in those things? You think they end up all pink like that 'cause of nature?'

'That's kind of the *reason* I need those things.'

'Oh, yeah. I heard if you drink an entire case, it'll give you a heart attack.'

'Heart attacks are not funny, Darien.' I elbow him in the ribs, and he makes this obnoxious wind-knocked-out sound.

'I didn't say they were!'

'Maybe you didn't.' I set my jaw. 'But when you put bad energy like that out into the world, it tends to come right back to you.'

The second we arrive in Bahrain, fresh from the airport in a new limousine, it's like Darien's done a shot of espresso. He hops down from the limo with raised arms, both hands waving wildly, a huge grin on his face. He's so genuine with his fans. He jumps across the line of barricades and officers to grab phones and take pictures, sign shirts and posters. Miguel is much the

127

same way, and Henri mimics the two of them, his eyes wide in awe at the sheer number of people here calling his name, waving his photo around on massive boards. With a chuckle, I grab my suitcase to follow the rest of the team into the hotel, but then I hear Darien's voice.

'Shantal!' he calls.

I tentatively head over to where he stands with a family that's talking to him in rapid, excited Portuguese. He has the dopiest smile as he interacts with them, pulling the hat off his head and fitting it on the youngest of their kids' heads.

'What's up?'

He shouldn't be able to hear me over the clamour of the crowd, but he turns around immediately, a silver Sharpie marker and a photo in hand.

'Please,' he says.

It's a photo of the two of us on the pit wall together at the Heidelberg Hybridge Ring, across from the practice track, and it appears we are each giving the other a fairly dirty look. I remember this one clearly because it had been taken when we were first reviewing the drivers' stats from last season, just before I pulled Darien aside to talk about the Cantagalo fiasco. Before things between us started to change in the strangest of ways.

'Come on,' begs Darien. '*Please* do me this little favour. You're a part of team Heidelberg now. You're gonna get asked for autographs. And besides, I'm a Shantal fan. Would you turn down a fan who just wants you to sign a photo?'

I accept the Sharpie and photo from him with a heavy roll of my eyes. 'Oh, my god.' I'm using all the energy I have to keep a straight face, but I feel my cheeks going pink. After all the antics I had to put up with at practice and everything riding on this race, I should still be upset at him, but I can't be. It's *adorable*.

128

I scrawl my name across the bottom of the photo in flyaway cursive with the *S* as a big swoosh and the remaining letters crowded up against it.

Darien gives the photo a big, tacky pat. 'Thank you, Shantal.' He catches my eye, and his smile only broadens.

Chapter Twenty-One

Darien

Qualifying is no small affair in Bahrain. It does, however, end up yielding results incredibly similar to our winter testing line-up. The hourlong session determines start order for race day, and in this case, Miguel, king of the Saturday affair, ends up sitting on pole – first – for the weekend, with me on second position, making for a Heidelberg front-row lockout. Diana's on third behind us, Nic fourth, Alex in fifth. It's a fun little arrangement we have going on as we storm into Sunday: first race of the season, and my first race back. This won't be like quali, with sessions that offer us relief in the form of intermittent breaks or out laps. This is a straight two-hour marathon, and I've got to pray my nerves will hold up through it all.

The chassis of my HH-08 shudders around me as I pull into my spot on the grid: second. It's always an uncomfortable place to be. Either you get ahead, or you don't – there's no in-between here. People watch your car with even more intent than they do the pole-sitter's; you have the say in how this race is going to go. I've never loved it.

My engine growls greedily as I glance over at Miguel across from me. This isn't my first rodeo with him as my teammate. Miguel absolutely thrashed me last season, finishing almost every race ahead of me, except a chance poor performance and one DNF. I don't know if it was driving so much as what was in my head. I shook when my car just neared his. Now, my hands are steady on the steering. It's Heidelberg's legacy on the line; Heidelberg's legacy in my home country. It's do or die.

The red lights overhead go on one by one. My heart pounds, and my vision tunnels with each light. By five, I can't see anything except the track ahead of me.

And when the lights go out, it's instinct.

I slam the throttle and surge forward, picking up speed going down the straight. All the while, I'm praying I've got enough of a jump on Miguel, but it's not quite enough. I stay on the inside, eking out my ground and turning with just a feather of the brakes. It does the job. I slip through the gap, swiping in front of Miguel going into the second turn of the track. It's sure to cause some chaos around the field, but that's not my concern now. I'm leading the Bahrain Grand Prix.

'You are P1 at the moment, Darien, P1,' confirms Afonso through my radio. That's all I need to get me through the rest of this race. The heat is scorching, the conditions abysmal, but in that moment, I'm the highest I've been in a long, long time.

'Let's get it,' I reply.

We do. I'm taking turns even faster than last year in this car. It's like I'm driving in the Corvette with my dad, the only thing I've ever wanted, the only thing I never got to experience. The track morphs into the streets of Cantagalo, the turns into winding paths down hills dotted with vendors and houses and stray dogs. It's going as well as it could until the second pit stop of our race looms before us, and just ahead of me, a yellow flag comes out. Moments after I've slowed for the flag, it's inevitable: *SAFETY CAR* flashes across my steering display, coupled with the arrival of a new car to the track just ahead of me, a Hybridge 250 with flashing yellow lights.

'Car,' I groan over the radio. 'There's a car. Dude, I had such a delta!'

'I know,' Afonso returns my sentiment. 'Let's just stay ready to box. Box on next lap, box.'

I bring the car into the pit lane the next time I pass the exit, and my team gets us all set up in good time. We're back out, back behind the car, and back in place before we know it.

'Miguel out behind you, also on new tyres,' says Afonso.

'Shit.' I keep my eyes on my line, but that signature numb feeling in my hands is starting to creep in. Crumbling at the wheel is every driver's worst nightmare, because every driver has once crumbled at the wheel. It's embarrassing to lose control on the track, lose form, but the part about it that remains a long time after is the shame. It's the weight of knowing that you were expected to perform, and when that moment came, you just . . . couldn't.

I take a deep breath. *Get a grip on yourself, dude. Come on. You were leading. You are leading. You can do this.*

'We'll try to get ground when the flag goes up. Darien, listen to me, he is going to fight you.'

'Okay. Okay, yeah. What scenario?'

Afonso pauses for a moment. 'Scenario B. We fight back.'

I swallow. Fighting back is a gamble. I'm not suffering tyre degradation right now, going this slowly, but if I go in for the fight and he fazes me enough, it's possible.

I think of the indoor turf in Leblon, and I picture Shantal on the field as I darted around her with the ball. I remember the way she saved her movements for the moment when she knew they'd hold value – when she knew she could take advantage of my exhaustion, sneaking an orange-cleated foot around mine and towards the ball. Explosive motions, or whatever she'd called it.

I chuckle quietly. Time to say a little prayer.

'Car going in on the next lap.'

With a careful exhale, I adjust my grip in preparation for the fight. He's right up behind me. When we restart, we'll get in easily – his medium compound tyres are brand-new, same as mine.

In front of me, the safety car moves aside, and it's up into the ramp. Green flags wave clear ahead.

I just slightly accelerate into the next gear, turning to close a potential gap when Miguel lurches forward behind me. The fight is on, and Miguel is pushing with as much aggression as he has. No order from the team means open season.

Miguel is the most terrifying son of a bitch anyone would want to see in their mirror, and when he darts into the barest of gaps on the next laps, I'm too rattled to catch it. He's slipping into it, and the only thing that saves me from obliteration is the end of the turn, when we straighten up, and I'm still slightly ahead. *Crap*.

It's a hunt for the next few laps. I up my pace just enough to keep him from closing in. He's got DRS – he's pushing harder than I am. I need Miguel's tyres to have suffered just enough to slow him down, preferably within the next few minutes.

'Delta closing. One point five. One point three. One one five. He is about point three faster. Point five faster,' Afonso reports to me as we log lap after lap. *Faster?* How is this guy going *faster*?

All I can do is push. I push until we have three laps. I hold him off, defending like my life depends on it – which it might. *No gap. No gap.*

My tyres are the first to cross the line on the last lap.

I'm practically dizzy, light-headed with shock when it hits me that I *did it*. We've won the first race of the year, which is exactly what Afonso is yelling as I yell with him.

'FIRST RACE, DARIEN!'

'YO! WE DID THIS!'

'WE DID THIS!'

I pump a fist in the air as I slow my car down close to the fence along the straight where our pit crew have climbed up on the gates and lean over the top with huge grins that I return, even though they can't see my face. And among the throngs of crew members, hands gripping the fencing, is Shantal.

I'm not completely sure what's gotten into the woman, owner of *the* most upset scowl under the sun, but she's grinning like nuts right now, and I'm not mad about it. Sure, that's in part because it's her technical genius that helped me in this race. But there's something else under the surface. Seeing her smile – seeing *her* – is a dream come true.

My visor is still down, but I like to think that our gazes meet for just a moment when I take the flag from my mechanics and hoist it in the air, waving it over my head as I run my victory lap before pulling up to the P1 marker at the end of the line. It's unreal, the front of my car touching that board as I stand on my chassis and raise the flag.

Screw the ultimatum. Screw the stakes. I'm here to stay.

Chapter Twenty-Two

Shantal

My heart flutters when Darien drives by the fences, and it doesn't stop all the way to the podium, beneath which our team stands as the national anthems are played: first that of Brazil, and then Germany, Heidelberg's mother country. It doesn't stop when Darien lifts the first trophy of the season, the first win of the season, when he sprays Miguel and Diana with champagne – a predictable top three, I am being told. Even when he gets down from the podium and runs straight to the team with his arms wide, it keeps on fluttering.

I head towards my room in the hotel at the end of it all. But prior to so much as opening my door, I realize I've got a guest. Someone new is sitting outside my door in a basket filled with chocolates and tinsel.

I slowly approach the doorframe, where my intruder has made himself comfortable by the threshold. He is a fuzzy white teddy bear with happy eyes and a little smile, sitting in a wicker basket. He holds a plastic heart full of Jolly Rancher sweets in a rainbow of colours. Written across the heart in white cursive are three words: 'Thank you, Shantal.'

I pick up a little card that sits beside the bear. Written inside in messy but bubbly handwriting is a short explanation for my visitor.

> Shantal,
> Like I said. I hope you remember. You deserve your flowers. This isn't nearly enough but this was the best bear I could find. I hope you like him, and give him a good name.
> Yours,
> Darien

It is a silly, naïve gift from a silly, naïve boy. But it is the kind of thing no one does any more. I love the bear the minute I see him.

I reach over and lift him up. I have to do a quick glance down the halls to make sure no one gets to see me in my moment of weakness before I bring the basket into my room. Like a total idiot, I grin stupidly and hug the bear tight. My heart skips a beat as I take in the smell, a hint of Darien's sandalwood imbued in the teddy's fur.

What name will I give him?

Oh, of course. *André*.

'I haven't been *completely* truthful. My marks slipped last session, Ma found out, and then it was all . . .'

Anjali goes on talking on the screen of my phone, gesturing wildly as she recounts the entire saga of her feud with her parents. She's still a Year 12 – she hasn't even got to university yet, and in the grand scheme of things, her parents will not care what she's done with her marks in a couple of years. But she's also my cousin, which means that her brown family, like mine, puts a bit too much emphasis on our performance in school. Just a bit.

'. . . said I'd have to get *married* if I don't get my grades up! I'm *never* getting married, *didi*,' she goes on. 'Not ever, now. Look at my parents! They're so mad all the time, all snippy and shi . . . stuff.'

I laugh at her momentary correction, a slip-up she's only got to cover because her mum and dad are somewhere in the house. If it were just me, she'd have nothing to hide. Anjali may be my cousin, but she, Sonia, and I were all brought up together, in a joint household in Clapham, before Ma and Babu got the money to move out, all of five minutes away. Anjali would call both of us *didi*, the Hindi term of endearment for an elder sister, owing to her Indian father – our uncle. We've been thick as thieves all my life, which is why seeing her back to normal like this, back to her usual endless rants and five-paragraph-essays of chatter, is almost disconcerting to me. She bounced back so quickly after Sonia. But she also didn't see what I did – hear what I did.

'You're off somewhere else,' Anjali jabs me mid-conversation (one-sided as it is).

That gets me out of my own head. 'What?' I jerk back to life.

'You're somewhere else,' she repeats. A smile creeps into her eyes and onto her face as she pokes at the camera. 'You little troublemaker, what are you doing over there in Bahrain?'

'Nothing,' I say far too quickly and far too defensively. Anjali is five years younger than me – she'll never know anything unless I crack. The problem? I tend to crack easily.

My cousin just cocks her head, giving me an uncannily well-honed 'disappointed aunty' glare. She holds it for all of five seconds before a mischievous grin takes over. 'Who is he?'

'Who is *who?*' I try, but she points an accusing finger my way.

I furrow my eyebrows.

'Behind you, *didi.*'

I do a quick turn, and the sigh that leaves my lips is one of resignation. My keen-eyed cousin has caught me red-handed. I'm sitting on my bed in the hotel room, and behind me, on the dresser, is André the bear.

'Someone bought you that.' She beams, all proud of her detective skills. 'Someone bought you that bear. Tell me *everything.*'

The wave of delusion that sweeps over me at those words is stronger than what I'd thought was possible. I want to. More than anything, I want to tell her everything. I want to be a carefree young woman like I should be. It only lasts a second. The thoughts return in a wall that crashes over me as hard as a ton of bricks.

'You know I can't.' I'm not sure if my voice is emotionally detached or ashamed. 'I don't think I can.'

'God, *didi!*' Anjali flops backward onto her own bed with a groan, bringing her phone with her so I can see just how disappointed she is. 'Don't you ever dream, huh? Before it happened, of all the things you could have had? You can still *have* them. You're the only person keeping those things from yourself.'

I can't help but smile sadly at the amount of optimism my cousin exudes, all the time. Even now, even in this situation. 'Anjali . . . doing whatever I want . . . that would wreck your aunty and uncle. I'm their only daughter, I have to stay close to them. I have to . . .'

Anjali is quiet for a moment. I don't love the lack of sound coming from her end of the call – it's exceedingly unnatural. The guilt in my chest is immediate.

Then she says, 'Tell me about him anyway.'

I break.

I tell her about how it's as if I have to hold my hand over a lit candle every time I so much as interact with him.

I tell her how much I cannot stand him.

And then that turns into something else.

Chapter Twenty-Three

Shantal

Despite the team's best efforts, Diana is in perfect form for the next race, Jeddah weekend, and she takes the win at the Saudi Arabian Grand Prix. We can't be too mad since Miguel ends up in second on podium, while Darien swings a P4, but I know he can't be taking it too well; he knows he's got to establish consistency to stay in the running for the Championship, especially with Miguel so close to him.

And that brings us to Melbourne, Australia. Albert Park appears to be one of the prettier races on the calendar and it's Peter Albrecht's home race, but the heat this year is especially brutal, and I'm not loving the idea of the drivers cooking faster than an egg on the street when they get on the track.

'The inside of the cockpit might hit, what, one-twenty Fahrenheit once we get rolling?' Darien is telling Celina as he exhales a heavy breath, raking back his curls. The sleeves of his Nomex fireproofs are rolled back, tattoos snaking out from under the hem of the fabric. One hundred and twenty degrees

Fahrenheit is quite hot, but when I step towards the pit wall to grab a water bottle, it's not the heat I'm trying to distract myself from.

Darien and Miguel qualified P3 and P4 respectively, which puts them both in a tough position for today. It'll be a long two hours. I've begun to wish I'd brought a hand-fan.

'BATH TIME!' I hear Miguel proclaim from somewhere in the garage.

'Hey, Shantal.' Celina hurries up to me. 'The kids want their baths, but Louie and I have got to head to the motorhome for a trainers' meeting. Can I ask you a favour? Can you quickly grab those big bins from the back closet and start the baths in the physio room? I just need those at eight Celsius. I am so sorry, I'll literally pay you—'

'No need to pay me,' I stop her with a laugh. The poor woman's been running around all weekend getting Darien his cold vest, towels, drinks; everything to make sure his core temperatures don't shoot straight up. 'I'll take care of it.'

'Thank you.' She presses her hands together and shoots me a look of desperate gratitude before nearly running down the hall towards the conference rooms.

Back closet. Okay.

It takes me a minute to orientate myself to the space, but I eventually weave past the drivers' rooms to the closet, where the two tubs, big plastic things that look like they could hold kids' toys, sit one inside the other, with two thermometers and rubber ducks – god, children, I tell you – in the top bin. I heft them out and set them up in the PT room. The massive ice chest in the room already holds the bags of ice, so I dump a healthy amount into each of the baths, set up the thermometers, and start filling them with cold water.

'Did you find the ducks?'

The sudden introduction of a voice into my otherwise silent

environment makes me jerk the hose so hard that water ends up all over the floor around the second tub I'm filling.

'What in the name of . . .' I turn around, ready to riot, but the words fizzle out the second I see who's at the door.

Darien leans against the doorframe, and I honestly wish someone had issued some kind of warning, because he's wearing nothing but a pair of navy-blue board shorts. And I'm here. And he's here. *Lord*.

He's got tattoos up both arms and over onto his chest. Doves, cursive words, flowers, stars. He has one on his right thigh, too – a falling Icarus. He hasn't removed his jewellery yet, so his gold cross still hangs around his neck, small diamonds still in his ears. He's absolutely built, absolutely beautiful. Darien: six feet of well-defined muscle and smarminess that have decided, for some reason, to focus on me. His eyes meet mine, and he's evidently smirking, definitely poking fun. I feel my cheeks flush. *Traitors*.

'Did you find 'em?' he asks again, searching my face for an answer with a gaze that sends my stomach fluttering like I've just gone down the steep drop of a roller coaster. He tilts his head inquisitively, and a stray curl falls over his brow.

Mutely, I point to a side table where I isolated the ducks, each labelled with a number in permanent marker: 88 and 67.

Darien ambles over to the table and grabs his duck, grinning at me once he's holding it up. 'Can't have a bath without your duck.'

I think I'm going to pass out. *Concentrate, Shantal, concentrate, deep breath, deep breath.*

He waves a hand in front of my face. 'Yo. Shantal. Earth to Shantal.'

'Yes! Yes.' I'm not completely there yet, but if I make direct eye contact with Darien for another second, I fear I might not make it to race start. With a tight smile, I reach around him, avoiding any physical contact that could cause me to collapse on the spot, and turn off the valve for the hose, gesturing vaguely to the tub. 'All set.'

'Cool, thanks.' Without so much as a moment's pause, he steps straight into the tub with a little wince before sitting right down inside and coming up completely drenched, hair slicked back by the water. It is exceptionally hard not to watch the way the muscles of his back move, the lines of the tattoos moving with them, as he hoists himself to a comfortable position. The rubber duck, damn the thing, pops up and looks straight at me as Darien shoots me a happy little thumbs-up.

I feel like I've just had one too many glasses of wine, when I match his gesture. Miguel, who enters the room seconds later, gives me a look like, *Oh, I see*, and hops on into his own ice bath. Of course, Miguel is also easy on the eyes, but I don't happen to be having heart palpitations around anyone other than Darien. Darien, who has already made my life difficult enough by being a pain in the ass and is apparently hell-bent on making it even worse.

I leave the room with the quickest not-so-subtle glance back, and even as the two of them exchange some talk about orchestrating a pit barbecue behind the crash fencing because it's *that hot* and they get *that hungry*, I could swear that man manages to catch my gaze. I slam the door shut behind me with shaky hands, and for a moment, I can't do anything but stand with my back to it, trying to regain my composure and my breath.

Chapter Twenty-Four

Shantal

Australia suits Darien much better than Saudi Arabia did, and he lands a P2 in the race, bringing him to a total of fifty-five points and second in the Championship, with Diana Zahrani for Revello in first. In fact, the only unfortunate thing about the race is that Miguel, Peter and Darien attempt a pit barbecue in the back of the track to cook brisket, and the stewards dig it up a whole six hours early, condemning not only a ton of meat but also a ton of coal.

Nevertheless, the team is immensely impressed with race performances; it looks as if the new training facility is holding up insanely well against expectations. Darien's aim – to at least make P3 in the Championship – is looking achievable, as is Heidelberg's in the Constructors' title fight. It's Miami up next – one of two 'home' races for Darien.

'And there's Turn Fourteen.'

We're all gathered in Darien's Heidelberg garage on the Miami track prior to the first free practice of the weekend. The garage should be saving us from the brutal sun but, although I have on a cap and sunglasses, my head still feels like it's cooking. Miguel shields his eyes and points to the furthest end of the racetrack from us, which is . . .

'Is that section of the track under . . . under a—'

'Turnpike,' Darien answers with lips so tight he has to be struggling to keep a straight face. 'Whoever built this probably went on a *serious* trip while they were making the plans.'

'Driving under a highway in an F1 car definitely wasn't on my lifelong bingo card,' adds Miguel. 'But you get your pick of the bunch in this sport. Pretty much everyone's a little bit . . . out there. It's what gets us fans, to be honest.' He squints at someone taking a photo by one of the other teams' cars – Jolt, I believe. 'And Kardashians, apparently. At least I think that's a Kardashian. Might be a Jenner.'

'Being "out there" earns fans?'

'Being *bold* earns fans.' Darien smirks as he corrects me, exchanging a grin with Miguel.

'Cowboys,' they proclaim together, which is just slightly freaky.

'Okay, cowboys.' Celina hustles up to us with a hefty clap of Darien's back. 'Time to put on the cooling vests and get fluids in you both. Let's get a move on. No one wants to bake outside without defences.'

'Agreed.' I take a generous swig of water from my tumbler. 'It's scorching out here.'

'God, the cockpit will be a nightmare,' Miguel says as he cranes his neck to continue surveillance. 'Is that the president?'

His trainer, Louie, appears before us with a tall bottle of electrolyte-rich hydration drink. 'You can go find out after you've downed this.'

While the trainers sort out the vests, I get to watch the

mechanic crew prepare Darien's car. The goal of a practice session is essentially to gather track data, figure out how the car and driver can make tweaks to shave off seconds, and that requires change after change to the car, potentially major ones mid-session. The mechanics have to be prepared for anything.

Darien, sitting off towards the pit wall with his vest and electrolyte drink, hops down off his chair and nods towards the car. 'I see 'em do this all the time, but this never gets old. One of my best buddies from her garage *loves* screwing with the engine and stuff. This is his idea of paradise.'

I couldn't exactly see how, but I'm also the sort of person who struggles with the instruction manuals for Lego sets. 'I suppose that could be.'

He cracks a smile. 'Do you want to sit in it?'

'Do I . . .?' I look up at Darien in shock. 'Do I *what?*'

'Go ahead.' Darien tips his head at one of the mechanics, and he returns the gesture, calling out to the guys to stop work for a moment. The crew kicks back on the chairs lined up to the right of the garage to take a break, and Darien gives the car a little pat that screams *pride and joy*. 'I'll be right here. Just don't press anything.'

That's a quite vague warning but, eyes wide, I tentatively step in the cockpit of the *Formula 1 car*, a beautiful white and ice blue machine that makes my work car look like a lawnmower, one foot at a time.

'Hold the halo and lower yourself,' instructs Darien, crouching down beside the car, his arms resting casually on the edge of the cockpit. He's so close I can make out every shade of brown in his irises, and as I follow his directions, bringing myself down to the seat that's moulded specifically to his body, I struggle to look away from him. *Look away*.

'And the belt. Is it all right if I . . .' He gestures to the straps hanging to the sides.

'Sure.'

Gently, he brings the seat belts over my shoulders and buckles down, giving the straps a good tug. His arms brush mine, his curls tickling my forehead as they fall forward.

'Just in case,' he says, and I can feel the breath that he lets out with every word on my skin. He grins. The dimples, those are the next thing I notice, tiny valleys that etch themselves into his cheeks as his eyes crease happily. The rest of the garage fades out, and it's just Darien in front of me as he fiddles with the seat belt, his eyebrows knitting in concentration. He grabs the steering wheel off the tool chest to his right and tells me, 'I'm gonna reach in front of you, Shantal. Sorry . . .'

He does, he reaches in front of me, and he fits the steering wheel to the dashboard – do they call it that? – in the front of the cockpit. This time, it's not like Carnaval. I'm very much sober, and I very much take note of every single possible sensation in the moment. His cheek is centimetres from mine, his chin right over my shoulder. He smells of sandalwood and mint, and his body is cold, owing to the vest he's got on.

'Okay, and now,' he messes with the steering, 'hold on to this at three and nine o' clock.'

I bring my hands up to the steering wheel, right beneath his, and he turns to me so abruptly that my heart hitches in my chest.

'Can I show you what the paddles do?' Darien asks.

I can't do anything other than nod yes in the moment. My brain is so overcome by his proximity, my senses totally awash in his presence. I feel like my emotions are short-circuiting. I've had such a tight grip on myself and now I'm suddenly out of control.

Why do I *want* to be out of control?

'Move your finger here.' His voice is quiet but deep. *This is a harmless little tutorial,* I remind myself. *Don't make it mean anything.* Even though we are sharing air right now. Even though the way he speaks to me is intimate without a semblance of touch. Even though I can't take my eyes off him.

His hands work deftly with mine, taking my fingers and moving them from the steering to the paddles behind it.

'If you push this one . . .' his index fingers brush mine, 'you can get DRS. And if you push this . . .' He moves my fingers down a paddle. 'Upshift and downshift gears. Then this one . . .'

His eyes drag themselves away from the steering wheel and up to mine as he guides my fingers down to the last paddle of the steering wheel. 'Clutch,' he murmurs, a deadly kind of huskiness lacing his voice.

'Clutch,' I echo.

I think I melt a little bit on the spot. I like to tell myself it's just the raging Miami heat, but I know better. I'm holding my hand over that dumb burning candle again, except this time, there's something blissful about the way it stings my palm.

It's a fun little secret to keep, you know, that you're losing your mind over a fleeting moment like that.

It stops being fun around the time the cars go out on track. Because that's the point where I remember that no part of that fleeting moment can mean anything to me.

Even an obnoxiously long shower after the day's two practice sessions does nothing.

It still feels like there will be some kind of evidence of my transgressions there, of Darien's touch, no matter how hard I try to erase it.

I lie back on my bed and watch the high-end fan in my hotel room spin round and round. If I close my eyes, his breath caresses my cheek. If I open my eyes, I see the smile in his deep brown ones.

Darien Cardoso-Magalhães, what are you made of?

Despite the implicit obligation I took up after we lost Sonia – the obligation of the good child, the child who will marry a good, stable guy and work a good, stable job – my soul still pulses like a caged bird yearning for freedom. I feel as if I'm a young girl running along the beach back home again, on top of the world for a few glorious seconds. I don't quite know if I've been feeling that way since Darien smiled his smile with the damned football in his arms at the pitch back in Rio, daring me to accept his challenge, but all it took was the reality of the way he sends my mind and body into overdrive to remind me that something is *certainly* going on.

I press my face into a pillow, hoping it will dispel my thoughts of him, this high I don't want to ride. But it doesn't do a thing. I still feel his strong hands covering mine as he guides me from paddle to paddle on the steering wheel.

I throw the stupid pillow to the side, and it's all gone, except for me. I'm alone in this room. My only companion is my denial, and maybe the shadow of Darien that I can't stop seeing. I should hate him. Our lives are vastly different. Our responsibilities are a world apart.

'We can't do this,' I whisper quietly. 'Don't waste your time on me. Leave.'

I remember sitting on the floor in our living room with a photo of Sonia, large, framed, at the mantel, garlanded in jasmine flowers. Her picture, the same one that is on my nightstand – smiling broadly, not a care in the world – watched us all cry as the *pandit* led us in prayers. Sonia's *shraddh*, her wake, brought family and friends from far and wide, people from the other side of the globe; that's how loved she was.

We mourned for thirteen days, during which I contemplated what purpose I had without Sonia. During which my parents watched me eat, sleep, come up and down the stairs once or twice, not a single word uttered to anyone.

On the thirteenth day, I realized.

Ma and Babu wanted happiness again. But I didn't. I had felt it all leave my body, and I knew that – henceforth – I would be incapable of it. Incapable of love.

I should have felt more remorse or realized how much I was hurting myself, but I didn't. Neither I nor my parents did. I regretted nothing. There was no other way for me to mend my life than close the doors. So when I sat down to talk to them after the *terahvin*, the rituals we performed on that thirteenth day to grant Sonia's soul peace, I told them point-blank that I was beginning to think I wanted an arranged marriage, in an attempt to offer my parents the happiness they so badly craved. I'm not sure they'd seen it coming – they had never so much as suggested arranging something for me. Sonia's was a love marriage, after all. They were shocked, but they agreed, perhaps because they were as shaken as I was. Over the weeks, they warmed to the idea. A long-absent spark began to fill them both again as they talked about the logistics of finding a potential husband. I figured that would be that.

Yet now, this blissfully ignorant, innocent-eyed but mischievous face fills my thoughts and occupies a gap I never asked to have occupied. This face *makes* me regret, stirring up a dull throbbing in the back of my head.

I finally stand up and take my phone off my dresser. Maybe a walk will do it if lying here won't, I decide.

But as I approach the door, piling my hair into a knotty bun, someone else beats me to it. There's a loud knocking.

Hesitantly, I crack the door open, though when I see it's just Miguel, I open it all the way. I'm about to question what he's doing here until I realize that there is a look on his face, a look that sends my heart sinking into my trainers: raised eyebrows, wide eyes. Fear, confusion, and above all, shock.

'Shantal.' He's out of breath, scared – an expression I haven't come to associate with Miguel. 'It's Darien.'

Formula 1 drivers train to resist the forces of their own cars, as well as to resist the forces of another. Although some things can't be resisted at all.

Celina gestures desperately to a nurse, her forehead creased with worry like I've never seen before. It's evident to me, even though they're all the way down the hall from the family room, where the rest of us wait.

Miguel and I each have an arm around a rattled Henri, who just looks at me, scared out of his mind. I am no different. I'm learning a new fear right now. I thought the only danger was *racing* in a car. I forgot about the everyday counterpart that is just as treacherous.

'I hear he was just driving on the road,' Henri whispers. 'That it happened on that dumb turnpike right over the track. It was an exports truck.'

My breath seizes up. 'A truck?'

Miguel just nods.

I cover my mouth with my hands and pray it will silence the sound of my resolve shattering. I remember what Darien told me about his father: he'd been in a car crash with a truck, too. It is so rare that lightning strikes twice like this, but here we are. My nerve endings still remember the feeling of his skin

151

on mine mere hours ago, of his fingers guiding mine over the paddles of the steering. What happens now?

We are in intensive care. This place is the limbo state between *yes* and *no*.

Nevertheless, all our heads turn when we see someone come out from the red-marked double doors at the end of that long hall: a doctor, by the look of the white coat. He speaks to Celina, nodding and explaining. She exhales wearily, and I can feel our combined hope that it's an exhale of relief.

They make their way back through the doors. Celina comes our way, her gaze downcast, a stark counterpoint to her bright pink hair.

She stops just before our row of chairs. 'He is stable,' she tells us.

'Oh.' The sound escapes me abruptly, more whimper than anything else, prompting Miguel to rub my back. When I look at him, I see the same tentative optimism on his face.

'But . . . it's not simple.' Celina swallows hard. 'It's the right arm.'

The pressure in my chest is immediate: a fear I do not have to learn. The guys process this statement. I ask, 'How bad?'

'Bad enough that they're hesitant to wake him because he'll be inconsolable when he finds out. They'll likely do that tomorrow.' Celina gestures to me, a small beckoning motion. 'Shantal.'

I follow her to the coffee machine in the corner on trembling legs. She shakes her head grimly, slightly guiltily. 'Shantal, I . . . he won't race.'

My throat feels like it's closing in on itself. Darien has committed so much to this team. They're counting on him to carry the expectations of this enormous complex through to the Championship, and he knows that. To not race . . .

The scattered handful of things he told me about his childhood floods back to me. And god, forget the implications for the team. He will have to live with this for ever. A loss of opportunity, a loss of redemption for his father. 'No. He's got to.'

'His entire right arm, it's shattered.' Celina's voice is so low she's almost mouthing words. 'They had to insert multiple pins. He broke three ribs, Shantal, suffered a concussion, we're lucky his legs . . .'

The mere implication stops my heart.

I press a hand to my chest. I've always been the kind of person who is there for the players' highs and lows, come what may. But this isn't the same. My own bones seem to break with each injury Celina describes, and I cannot even completely understand *why*.

'Shantal, are you all right?' She peers at me with concern, and says, 'He's fine, love. He's okay.'

I bite my tongue to hold back any more sounds of pain, hear a sigh leave my body instead.

'I know,' I finally tell Celina. I don't know if I will be able to watch the toll this takes on him. I almost say that. Instead, I continue, 'It's instinct. You hurt when your players do, right?'

Chapter Twenty-Five

Darien

'Let's wake slowly. Let's just open our eyes. There we go.'
The voice is monotone, fading in and out like it's coming through a broken speaker. I try to obey it. Light flickers in my frame of vision, and then a face.

The face is bearded and slightly wrinkled. It belongs to a tall man in a white coat. He holds a pen flashlight. 'Good,' he says.

Well, that's got to mean something. I can only manage a groan in reply, and when I do, a sharp pain stabs my right side.

'Do you know where you are?'

My eyes begin to adjust to the sterile white lighting. Hospital, probably. I croak out the single-word response.

'Good,' the doctor repeats.

Wait . . . what the hell?

I start to make out cords. Cables connected to the ceiling on my right, holding something up, maybe. I follow the cables to a big white hunk of plaster and gauze. A cast. *My* cast.

My arm.

Oh, *shit*.

My pulse pounds in my ears as I shift my gaze further to the right. Casted to the elbow; all I can see are my fingers. My right arm is unmoving.

'No,' I choke out. 'No, no, this . . .'

'Magalinho.'

A new sound. My mom's voice.

Mãe steps in front of me, her brow knitted, her eyes red. It looks as if she's aged years on worry alone. If I'm in the hospital, in America . . . how long's it been? Long enough for her to fly over? 'You were in the car on the . . . on the way to the club, they said. You were driving, but you did not do anything wrong. And a truck – it came from your right, it . . .' My mother purses her lips. It hits me as she turns away that this is causing her immeasurable pain because this is how we lost Pai. My stomach sinks even deeper. *God*.

'Dr Lopez,' my mom says.

'Darien.' The tall doctor comes back into view. He's balding, bespectacled, and stressed. 'Darien, your right arm was—'

'How long?'

'I'm sorry?' He leans in.

'How. Long,' I say again through gritted teeth. The beeping of some excessive machinery beside me quickens in pace. It feels as if my entire body is shaking.

'How long . . .' Dr Lopez clears his throat. He looks away from me. Is he embarrassed? Why is he embarrassed?

'Six months. The least. It's possible that . . . your arm may not function the same, even after a full recovery.'

Six months.

Six months is a lifetime. Six months is the rest of my season gone. Six months is I let down this team, and I let down Brazil.

That's not even accounting for the possibility of being forced into an early retirement. Of losing the only thing I have left from my Pai.

I want to throw things around and have a complete meltdown, like a little kid; but I can't even do that, I'm so fucking immobilized. All I can do is look up at the ceiling and fight off hot tears that pour down my face anyway. 'Leave,' I whisper, my voice rough. 'Can everyone please leave?'

Mãe is torn. But she leaves, and the doctor follows. I don't know what to do right now. All I know is that I don't want any of them to witness what I'm going through.

It's about half an hour later that someone else enters the room. I've already told the doctors I don't want visitors, but someone has flagrantly disregarded that. I get ready to lash out, until I realize who it is, and everything makes much more sense.

Diana Zahrani looks as bedraggled as my mom, and seeing me doesn't help. Her eyes squint in pain, even though her face remains unchanging. She's clearly just wrapped up a race session, maybe the qualifier: I can tell because she's still wearing her fireproofs and race suit, the arms tied around her waist.

'I wanted to *wreck* you on the track this weekend.' She bites her lip nervously. 'But Darien, you idiot, I didn't know someone else would beat me to the punch.'

'I'm sorry,' I manage, but she just shakes her head, her curls bouncing in their ponytail.

'I talked to Celina.' Her voice is a murmur lost to the sounds of the machines. 'None of us like this.'

'I can't just sit here,' I whisper. 'I can't.'

Diana looks up at the ceiling, exhales. 'I know you can't.'

I'm lost. I don't want to sacrifice racing. Not this last shred of Pai that I've clung to for so long.

'I need this, Diana.' I lock eyes with her, my pupils full of hurt. 'I need to be on the grid again. Soon.'

She clasps her wrist, the adjustable bracelet around it sliding down towards her palm. 'That's what everyone thought you'd say. I talked to Shantal, too.'

Crap. Shantal.

I wonder if she's as wounded as I am. In the end, part of her job relies on my performance. She needs Heidelberg to show up this season, to win the title and, like she had said, there is a degree of responsibility that she assumes for us. There's also the strange new tension growing between the two of us, which I suddenly resent when I realize that tension may only be hurting her further.

'What'd she say?'

'Not much. She's freaked out. What did you do to take up this much real estate in her head, Darien?' Diana's tone is just slightly teasing, an attempt at lifting the mood. I try for a smile, but all I can think about is 'freaked out'. About the state she's got to be in right now. She didn't bargain for all this drama when she chose to come to Brazil.

'Exactly what do you need from me?' Diana finally asks, pressing a reassuring hand to my covered leg. 'I want to help, wherever I can, okay? But the way back from something like this . . .'

'I want to race. I'll do whatever it takes.'

'Yeah.' The sound of the word doesn't even come out of her mouth. She lowers her gaze.

'Just tell me you know of some way, something I can do. Please.'

She looks back up at me.

'Listen, Darien, no one wants to take options from you.' She sucks in a breath. 'But you have to consider the position Celina is in, as your trainer and as your friend. She's got to be terrified. To push you to the limits you want to be pushed, that's a risk for everyone involved. You're going to be in *extreme* pain.'

'It's a risk I need to take, Diana. You know I need to take it.' I look up at the cables, exhale hard. 'What about Shantal?'

'Well, she's shocked, like I said.' Diana gives me a matter-of-fact look. 'But bless that girl's heart, she doesn't seem like she's willing to settle on you just "not racing", either.'

I let that sink in. I've always thought there wasn't a soul in the world who sympathized with the fact that I didn't have any other option beside the race. I never have, not even as a kid. Driving is my only direction. If I don't drive, I could lose this entire training facility and the partnership, the chance to give kids like me a way into the sport. I could lose my shot to make my father proud.

But I think Shantal understands it all, even though she has fears. I've never told anyone everything about my dad, about how my mother recuperated, to anyone. Never even told her, and yet, she seems to *know*. So maybe I won't have to say anything to her about why I need to race. Maybe she requires no explanation as to my adamance. Somehow, she's already gotten it.

Diana closes her eyes. She sits down on the side of the bed and gives my good hand a squeeze. There is a deep guilt in my chest when I realize that as much as Diana being here helps, I want it to be Shantal. I wish it were as easy as touching her. Stroking her hair, her face, holding her to me.

'I know,' Diana says quietly. 'Take the risk. That's all you can do. This kind of recovery will be hell, but push. And Darien, you had better know that for reasons *far* beyond my comprehension, that woman standing outside is willing to take your side through all of it.'

Chapter Twenty-Six

Shantal

Afshin Demir is of the unfortunate yet firm belief that Darien will not recover to finish out his season, meaning that Henri will drive the rest of it.

'You are *young*,' Demir said to Henri. 'I know it seems daunting, but you can adapt. It's your time.'

'My time?' Henri was still reeling, but this sentiment had him in awe nonetheless.

'Your time,' repeated Demir, almost proud. He'd probably have been fully proud if not for the situation.

I just worry, you know, as I watch Henri. We're back in Rio for a week, putting him on the sim to try and do the best we can so he's ready to race. Darien's recovering in Miami, with the doctors insistent on not moving him until they're sure he'll be stable. On this front, we're readying our Plan B, and on another, Darien is still fighting for Plan A. I've heard the rumours, that he's not going to sit with the six-month recovery time. Diana had been the first to get to Miami Dade Medical the day after the accident,

159

when Darien woke up mid-quali, and I heard even her mention something about trying to push the timeline. It worries me.

'Shantal?'

'Hmm?' I snap back to the current situation.

Henri looks up at me, concerned, gripping the steering wheel, screen paused. 'I asked if you thought I took that corner a little faster than our last try.'

I want to tell him he did, because it's probably true; he's been doing so well on the simulator over the past week, so well that you can tell he's already improved in a matter of days. But that would be a lie. I'm not paying enough attention to know if he's gone faster or slower. I can't bear to lie. He deserves so much better. My mind is just elsewhere.

'You took that *hella* fast,' Miguel answers for me from the next simulator. He takes his eyes off the road for just a moment to flick a grin Henri's way, and it means all the more to me. 'It's a brilliant corner you did.'

Henri beams. 'Thanks, mate.'

I shoot Miguel a smile full of gratitude before turning back to our youngest driver with a sigh of disappointment in myself. 'I'm sorry, Henri. I'm just shook. Things are moving fast here. I don't know what to focus on.'

He reaches out and rests a reassuring hand on my arm. 'It's okay. I get it. I feel a bit turned round as well. I guess we can only do our best, right?'

I nod. He's wise well beyond any of our years.

Behind him, Miguel stands up from his simulator, eyes wide and fixated on the door on the other side of the sim room. Henri follows his gaze, to equal surprise.

'Look,' Henri says, gesturing to the door.

I turn around, and I inhale, but the air doesn't want to come back out.

Darien is back.

Diana was the only one who had been able to get into the room to talk to Miguel immediately after he regained consciousness. She'd come out of there looking rattled, and walked over to Celina and me.

'Shantal.' She looked me dead in the eye, despite knowing nothing about me save for that much – my name, and that only because Celina must have introduced me when she arrived. She'd barely been in the waiting room a second before making the determined march down the hall to where Darien was resting. A part of me was bewildered by her, but the other part could pick out the warmth in her eyes, the kind of amity you only found in very specific people.

I had just stood there, silent, wide-eyed, until she spoke.

'He's desperate. He's said he'll do anything to be back for the season. Will you?'

When he said he would do anything, I was not too sure of what that would entail. He'd undergone surgery, with pins in the wrist and stitches. It was a lot for anyone to handle.

And the fact that he is here now means that he was in hospital for less than a week. The physicians must have been livid when he wanted to get out. He wears a hoodie, but I can see his cast still peeking out from beneath the right sleeve. His hair is wet, freshly washed. His face still bears evidence of scratches and bruises, cruel mementos of the crash that we hope has not ended his career.

I don't know quite how to feel.

My emotions were already a minefield before the accident. But now, this decision Darien has made – and the force that compelled me to agree to it, to tell Diana I'd help him get back to driving form in a mere month and a half – causes me almost more pain than seeing him hurt to begin with. This is such a gruelling path. I can barely face the struggle, even though it's Darien who has already taken the first step by breaking out of hospital in half the time he was supposed to.

'Hi,' he says.

I'm unable to move from my spot. The guys immediately rush over to him, checking to make sure he's okay, giving him hugs filled with relief and brotherly care, but it takes me a moment to remember how to walk.

When it comes my turn to speak to Darien, I search for words that don't come to mind. I'm able to do little except wrap my arms around him and let the touch convey what I can't say. I feel him hold me tight with his good hand, his palm against my back.

'I'm glad you're back,' I tell him. 'But—'

'I chose this.' His breath is warm on my ear. 'It's okay. I'm okay.'

'Go see Celina,' I whisper. 'Go get started.'

'Yeah.' I don't want him to stop holding me the way he does, and I know I should resist it, but after this close a call, after everything that the past week has thrown at us, I can't. I don't have the strength to put up walls, at least not now. 'I'll see you.'

We watch Darien head back down the hall, and Miguel says to me, in a hushed tone, 'He's going to try?'

'You know how he is.' I press a hand to my temple, where a throbbing headache has begun.

Miguel, for the first time, at least to my knowledge, appears somewhat vulnerable. He looks back at the sims, with weary eyes that have known these trials and tribulations before. 'He can't live without the race, can he?'

Chapter Twenty-Seven

Darien

'Grab the ball, Darien. Come on. You can do this.'

Celina leans forward as if anticipating something. What she thinks will happen, I don't know. I've been trying for almost ten minutes. And this is the third day I've been back. The team gets on the road tomorrow, and I'll be joining them, for no good reason other than I think I'd disintegrate if I had to stay here any longer, wallowing in self-pity. My arm can barely extend itself. The stupid ball is all the way at the other end of the table.

'Reach out.'

'I'm trying!'

Cel is one of the most patient physios I've met, but even her fuse is shortening. She looks like she's going to smack the ball off the table any minute now.

I manage to get my arm up at table level. That's it for me. I let it go limp with a groan, already exhausted and in pain.

'Okay. See? That was good, Darien! That was progress,' she assures me.

I keep trying to reach across the dumb table and take the ball. It should be so easy. But it's soon ten p.m., and I still haven't gotten it.

Fuck.

How will I drive a car? I need my hand for the steering, the paddles. I don't know what I was thinking, because I can't even move. If I can't even move, there's no way in hell I'll be able to drive. I wonder if my father would be so proud of me now.

I decide to call it a day. Apparently, my window is open, so I try to close it with my good hand, which I can't do properly, it being my non-dominant. I leave it, grumbling curses before flopping backwards onto my bed and taking the TV remote. Whatever.

And then I hear something from outside. The slightest sound, but the kind that makes your stomach turn. Crying.

I get up, clamber to my feet, over to the window. I don't think she notices, but I see Shantal outside on the bench in the little courtyard below. Her shoulders shake as she presses a hand to her cheek.

I take the stairs down to the back door, and silently slip out. Shantal has always been so outspoken, so snappy. I've seen glances of sadness, like that day at the beach, but never like this.

'Shantal?'

She startles, her eyes wide but puffy and red. Her face is without makeup. She's got her pyjamas on, a T-shirt and sweats. I don't think I've ever seen her so . . . out of it.

'Hi.' She blots away all the tears she can and plasters on a smile. It's not the sort of genuine smile she lets slip every once in a while. It twists my throat so that swallowing becomes agony. 'You're still up.'

'Are you all right? Why don't you come in, I—'

'I'm okay, Darien.'

I would usually just let her be, but something is different

this time. 'Come inside, Shantal, I don't wanna leave you here like this.'

She nods and stands up, and together we walk back up to my drivers' quarters room, where that damn table is still front and centre, with the fucking ball there, of course.

I scoff just looking at it, and pull out the chair that Celina had sat in for Shantal. I take my seat across from her with a mumbled, 'Screw that thing.'

'Is she having you . . .' Shantal gestures to the ball.

'Yeah. Yeah, it's just I . . . it's harder than I thought,' I reply with a sarcastic chuckle. 'Everything's harder than I thought. But listen, what about you, Shantal? *Are* you okay?'

She focuses on a tiny knot in the wood of the table for a moment before looking back up at me, and this time, I don't see anything held back in her eyes. She shakes her head. 'I don't think I am.'

'Hey.' My eyebrows knit together as I absorb all this from Shantal's perspective. The accident, the weird middle ground that it put the two of us in, being far away from her family when everything is so chaotic. 'There's nothing wrong with that.'

'It's just . . . something has turned my world on its head, Darien.' Her gaze flickers towards my wrapped hand. 'In so many ways, good and bad.'

'Bad?'

I almost don't want to know. I want to stay in this blissfully ignorant pocket where I get to fall for her a little more with each breath she takes.

She buries her face in her hands. 'I don't know why, but everything changed when I saw you hurt like that. I was suddenly experiencing all these unfamiliar feelings, trying to sort everything out, and then you getting in the accident, it's terrifying, after . . .'

Her hanging words leave a blank I'm unsure how to fill in. A heavy blank, loaded with something that is clearly hitting home.

'Shantal,' I whisper. I don't quite know what to offer her, so I let her decide. 'What do you want me to do right now? What can I do for you?'

'You don't have to do anything.' She lowers her hands, and she bites her lip nervously. 'I just . . .' She looks up at me. 'I can't stand it,' she says, her voice so quiet I can barely make it out. 'Watching someone I care about suffer like that.'

Maybe I should be smart and gather something intelligent from that statement, but instead, all that comes out is, 'Yo, you care about me?'

Now she can't help but laugh, an entire, full laugh. The sound is respite and relief from hospitals and physical therapy, sombre spaces where no one enjoys themselves. I wish I had the ability to freeze her every laugh and smile, no matter how small, and file them away in my memory for ever. If watching her so much as breathe drives my emotions for her an inch, then hearing her laugh drives them forward a thousand miles. I want her to let herself feel, want her to realize that this is so much to me, but I hate myself for that. I don't want to make her do anything or think anything.

Her laugh stops abruptly, forming a short gasp. Her eyes open in shock as they meet mine, and then as they travel down to the table.

'Darien.'

I look down just as she does, and I gasp the same gasp as she has. 'Oh . . . wow.'

My hand, across the table, grips hers, my thumb brushing her knuckles.

Across the table.

'Holy *crap*. Shantal!' I squeeze her hand in mine, look up at her and grin like a happy-go-lucky idiot. 'Shantal, you're seeing this, right?'

'I'm seeing every second of it,' she smiles at me. It's a much more welcome emotion than the tears.

There's even a layer of something new beneath the simple smile: pride.

Shantal Mangal is proud of me, and in that instant, it doesn't matter how horrific this recovery will be. I'd do it all to see that look on her face again and again.

Chapter Twenty-Eight

Shantal

Day after day, even when we travel to Singapore, Celina and I devote extra time to getting Darien back to a steering wheel. Celina runs him through the crucial motions he needs to be able to pilot the car: pull, push, extend, bend, pronate and supinate. I modify the sim set-up that we bring with us so that the steering weight is turned down significantly, and screw around with the program till I end up with something gentler than the beast that is the modded Heidelberg Hybridge Ring. It's not exactly where I saw this system going, but the flexibility of the set-up is unbelievable. Even with Darien's injury, we think the sim will be able to fully accommodate and re-learn with him. The brilliance of it all has cost me multiple sleepless nights and taken the team hours of video calls to perfect tweaks, but it's going to be worth it. I know it will be.

The only issue is that I have no idea if Darien will ever so much as touch the sim set-up we've prepared. He's struggling. I wonder if his reaching out and taking my hand that night, what felt to me like a miracle, was only a fluke, but I know I cannot afford to think like that. Not when this season hangs in the balance for Darien. I watch the frustration creep into his face in the form of a grimace, when he's on the verge of tears trying to lift a weight or do something as simple as grip the handle of the rowing machine. Things that were so easy for him mere weeks ago, and now take much more than a modicum of effort to even begin doing.

And so at the end of the week, closing in on the first race that Darien won't partake in, I decide that for many reasons, it's time for us to take a break.

'You should come to Chinatown with me,' I tell Darien on Friday morning, as we walk down the hall outside the hotel gym.

'Chinatown?' Darien cocks his head at me like I've lost a handful of screws. I'm almost thankful for the return of some of his sass. 'You gonna drive twenty minutes through race day traffic just for fun?'

'Don't question it. I want you to get out of this place for a minute. Not to mention I have business to take care of.'

He just stops walking and gives me an even more sceptical look. 'In the *traffic*?'

I roll my eyes. 'Will you go?'

Dramatically, he gives me a massive roll of his eyes, although he's smiling. 'Fine.'

True to his word, Darien joins me for the drive out from the hotel and through the city, one we endeavour in my small grey company sedan. 'What are we looking for, exactly?'

'A temple.' I scrunch my nose in concentration, glancing over at the GPS. 'Where the hell is this place?'

He cuts his eyes my way as we get further into the streets, far

169

enough that my car is starting to putter anxiously from the stop and start of the traffic jams. 'Let's start by asking if it exists.'

It does. A sign pops up off to our right side: *Sri Mariamman Temple*, first in English, and below in another language that looks like it might be Tamil. I hang a quick turn down the narrow alley leading in.

We almost immediately end up in a tiny parking area before what looks like a piece of architecture out of a history book. The base of the building itself looks fairly discreet, until you get a look at the massive pyramid-like spire on the top. An array of coloured carvings of figures – so realistic you have to do a double take – forms the spire, with similar figures all around the border of the roof: gods and sacred animals. Gold pillars rise from the very top of the spire, glimmering in the sunlight. It's different from the few *mandirs* I'd seen, but extremely beautiful.

I stop the car. 'You can wait or come,' I offer Darien. 'I just wanted you to get away from the stress for a day. Have you been to a Hindu temple before?'

Now he shakes his head no. 'Never. Why?'

'Do you want to?'

He looks up at the carvings, takes in the massive spire with an air of curiosity. 'Sure.'

We walk side by side up to the wooden door, carved with intricate traditional designs. Inside, a small cloakroom holds a couple of pairs of shoes, sandals and sneakers. I slip off my own and add them to the mix, my tote bag and *dupatta* swinging off my shoulder. The thin scarf is a translucent baby blue complement to my white *kurta*, a long-sleeved tunic top, and matching palazzo pants, loose trousers that flutter slightly in the wind.

'Go on,' I tell Darien.

He gives his freshly shined white Dunks a look of longing that makes me chuckle, but uses his feet to slip them off beside my slippers. I toss my *dupatta* over my head, throwing one loose end beneath my chin and behind me, before pushing the door to the temple itself open.

The *mandir* is generously air-conditioned and an entire section of it open to the outside, making it both a good and bad thing that Darien has a hoodie and sweats on. Maybe it looked different at first, but inside, it's beautiful. The interior pillars and rafters are strung with fresh flower garlands, the high ceilings painted with murals of gods and goddesses amid myths I recall from my childhood.

Ahead of us is an expansive hall, with brightly coloured statues of deities all around us. We cross the hall together to reach the *murtis* at the altar of the temple, ornately dressed idols with delicately painted features standing beneath a gold-gilded awning. Each idol is dripping with orange, yellow and pink cloth and gold jewellery. In the centre is Amman, one of the primary patron goddesses in the south of India. To one side of Amman, a group of three stands beneath an arch of carved wood: Shri Ram, Sita and Lakshman, my family's patron deities. Both Ram and Lakshman hold gold-gilded bows, the weapons with which they fought to win back Sita, wife of Ram, from the demon king Raavan. Far off to the right side of the hall is another altar for Draupadi and the Pandavas from the Mahabharat, with a *murti* for Shri Krishna as well.

There is no lack of lore about the gods, lore that we grew up consuming even as Indo-Guyanese kids raised Hindu. Stories of gargantuan labours and epic battles, good against evil and brother against brother. But my favourites were always the love stories. The gods and goddesses would literally move heaven and earth for one another, the gold standard of the purest kind of love. Ram and Sita, Krishna and Radha, Shiva and Parvati. I liked to think that was not completely myth, at least before last year.

A table at our side is laid out with shiny silver *thaal* plates, fruits and nuts, *diya* candles in clay pots, and flowers. I take a *thaal* for our offering, and arrange the flowers, food and candles around it. I light a match. It sparks up right away, and I touch it to the wick of each *diya*.

'I hate to ask,' whispers Darien, touching my arm lightly, 'but what, exactly, are we doing?'

I pick up the *thaal* and bring it to the altars with care, stopping at the rail separating the devotees from the *murtis*. 'Making our wishes known.'

Darien's brow furrows as he follows my gaze to the idols. 'Our wishes?'

'An offering for healing.' I shield the flickering *diyas*, trying my best to keep their burgeoning flames intact. 'For you.'

As I begin to circle the *thaal* before the altar, mouthing the *aarti* devotional under my breath, my hands shake, and I feel my eyes start to well up. This is the first time I have come to the temple on my own, without Sonia. I remember her making these offerings, doing the *aarti*, and following her motions. I swallow on a throat as rough as asphalt. I know what's compelled me so strongly to return, despite knowing the pain I face whenever I tread on memories of my sister. With every memory, I continue to rip open a partially healed wound, the hole where my heart used to be. But as I offer *aarti*, I project my questions in my prayers. *Why? Why have you brought winds of change into my life now, when I am out of options?*

A near silent sob leaves my lips, bouncing off the ceiling of the *mandir*. The *thaal* tilts dangerously in my unsteady grip, threatens to fall.

But then another hand holds mine, levels the silver platter. Darien.

He meets my eyes wordlessly. And he guides my *thaal* with his right hand, the *diyas* burning like stars in an otherwise dark night sky. I watch his arm make the careful, controlled movement, muscles flexing to hold up the heavy platter. It's like earlier that week – it isn't something he notices. His gaze is only on me, one of concern, brow furrowed, big brown eyes full of worry.

He doesn't probe my grief, asks not a single question. He just stays, until I'm ready to set the *thaal* down at the feet of the Ram-Sita *murti*, and then he turns to me. His fingers skim my arm as he takes the end of my *dupatta* and brings it to my cheek, brushing away my tears.

I keep it together the entire walk out the temple, all the way to the car. I don't have it in me to hold myself up any more than that.

I lean in to Darien, and I squeeze my eyes shut. He wraps his arms around me, smooths down my hair. He keeps me close, his chin resting against my forehead, my cheek to his chest as I release every emotion I have felt since getting here and since before then, and I know he knows what it is like.

He doesn't owe me words. I have everything I need.

Chapter Twenty-Nine

Darien

'He held up a ridiculously heavy plate yesterday with only his bad hand. I think the steering shouldn't be much different at this point. Once we build muscle, we're on the right track,' Shantal says to Celina the day after we return from the temple.

The air between the two of us, Shantal and me, holds a lot more electricity after that. The kind of moment we shared out there at the temple wasn't one that you can fabricate. I didn't have to say anything, do anything. I guess I just . . . felt it. I might not know exactly what's had Shantal so preoccupied, the secrets I can just barely make out dancing behind her eyes when I look them dead-on, but I felt it so, so deeply.

Nevertheless, her big mouth spilling this newest development – the plate, that is – happens to be the cause of all my pain and suffering to come, because Celina doesn't let up once she hears that I'm able to move, not even when we travel to Japan for the next race.

'We're getting that arm back in commission. I don't care if it means I have to pull Shantal from the team and sit her down in front of you for you to *move*,' she grumbles as she brings us dumbbells, picking up one with which to demonstrate the exercise. 'Let's do rows. Keep it easy, just pull up. I want to see those movements before I put you back at the wheel.'

I complain and groan through it all, arm exercises that last the next two weeks with an aim at bringing memory back to my muscles. Shantal comes in and out of my training sessions, and she sits down in front of me without having to be pulled away by Celina. She lies down on her belly across from me, props her chin up on her hands, and meets my eyes as Celina spots me through my first push-ups post-accident. She encourages me, murmurs kind words, acknowledges my struggle at every turn. At the beginning of it, I can barely manage to curl a dumbbell. By the fifth day, I'm somehow starting to bench again, even if it's with Shantal taking part of the weight from above me.

Celina decides I'm finally ready to get into a simulator back in Rio at the end of those two weeks. It's like being a baby learning to walk again, figuring out how to get around. She is permitted to be present, but it's only me behind this wheel. Me, my own trainer and, naturally, Demir overseeing the ordeal.

'You've gotten plenty of low-weight practice in. We're on the most realistic setting on the steering now,' Celina explains. Her brow creases as I tug on my balaclava and helmet. She gives the side of the helmet a double-tap. 'Be smart.'

With her help, I lower myself into the simulator set-up. I know this cockpit like the back of my hand – Shantal tailored it to match the car exactly, and now, so will the weight on the steering. The seat is just like the one on my Heidelberg, designed to fit me exactly. As perfect as it is all meant to be, it feels foreign.

For the first time in way too long, my feet start to seek out pedals, and my hands curl around the steering. It reminds me abruptly of the violence of the accident, the eerie similarity of the entire situation to how we lost my dad. A glare flashes in my frame of vision, and I know it's just light hitting the visor on my helmet, but I see the strobe-like headlights instead. The truck.

'Darien?' calls Celina, resting a hand on the faux chassis. 'You all right?'

I swallow hard and nod. *It's okay. You can't crash on the sim.* 'Yeah.'

I flex the fingers of my right hand, then rotate my wrist as the door to the room opens and Demir walks in. He's way too put together for seven in the morning, and he's beaming. 'Good to see you back, Darien.'

'That's the hope.' I manage a nervous smile in return as the team boss joins Celina behind me.

'Ready?' my trainer asks.

'Let's do this.'

I take a deep breath and grip the wheel tight. A weak thread of pain still creeps up the places in my arm where they put the pins, but I choose to ignore it.

Help me out, Papai.

My heart thuds double time as the practice track right in our backyard loads up on the enormous screens: Heidelberg Hybridge Ring itself, this time without the mods that Shantal used to work me up to the real intensity. This is it, as real as it possibly could be. I have to calm down. I need to prove to Afshin that I'm worthy of a chance to stay in this race and on this team.

I snap down my visor. The path ahead is clear. I know this racing line – we've walked the track so many times, done so

176

many laps on the sim, driven around it endlessly during winter testing days. I've always picked up track layouts fast, that's not what could screw me up. So now, I just have to drive.

The sim has me on a rolling start. I picture Shantal's smile, everything she's been putting into encouraging me and standing by me, every time her eyes met mine as I pushed myself harder than I thought possible, fortifying my mind and my soul in moments of weakness.

My front tyres cross the line, and I floor it.

I cruise down the straight, ease into Turn One a bit clunkily and through Pão de Açúcar, regaining my sea legs with much less struggle. The track is absolutely stunning, and I realize as I coast across it that this is the way that it was meant to be driven. Winning is crucial, yeah. But you realize that what is more crucial, just as my mother told me, is time. Enjoying every second as it comes to you.

Taking the back straight of the sim, I almost feel wind around me. I'm racing outdoors, pushing against the breeze to make my way towards that final turn. I come out of it in a bit of a jerk, though my recovery's slick. I exit onto the finish, gliding right across the track.

It's my first lap back, and maybe it's not perfect, but it's my kind of lap.

I whoop and raise my hands as soon as the screen pauses and displays my time. Celina cheers, her and Afshin applauding. Cel wraps her arms around me in the sim.

'Damn good drive,' she mutters, rare notes of pride in her voice. 'Well done, Dar.'

'What *hope*.' Afshin beams at me with a hand pressed to his heart. 'I suppose all that's left for me to say to you, Darien, is *obrigado*.'

I grin up at him as I rip off my helmet. 'So we're back?'

'Well, hold on, there.' He chuckles. 'You know as well as I do that what you just drove was only the first step.'

Oh. My face falls slightly, but I attempt to keep up the smile, ignoring the fact that this realistic steering weight already has my wrist so stiff I can barely rotate it. 'Oh, yeah. True.'

'As you know, races are races, and I'd like to take a bit of a gamble,' says Afshin primly. His arms are folded now, which lets me know this is very much not a gamble he can afford to mess up. 'Celina has informed me of your desire to get back in the car this season, and as we all know, you have quite a bit hanging on your performance in the remainder of the races. The sponsors have acknowledged the nature of your injury, but you know as well as I do that cash is king here, and they won't be making exceptions. Either you bring them the standings they desire – evidence that you, Heidelberg, and Redenção deserve this – or they'll pass on us.'

'Uh, I . . .' I gulp. The removal of my balaclava is far less frantic. I peel it off almost ashamedly. 'I understand.'

'So with that, Darien, I want to give you a proposition.' He glances at Celina with a curt nod. 'I'd like for you to at least drive the practices in Imola, and if those go well enough, the qualifier and the race. I've run this by Celina. She sees this as a gamble, just as I do, but she is willing to greenlight you as you are. You've made an exceptional recovery in a sixth of the time you were given.'

For a moment, my heart soars. I'm going to be back, I'm going to race again. Imola is in a week. I'll be back behind the wheel in a week. 'Thank you, Mr Demir.' The words tumble out of my mouth as Afshin offers me a hand to shake, and I take it.

Then that same thread of pain shoots through my arm, but this time, it's definitely not weak.

I'm *so* screwed.

But I need to take this risk. This is a lifeline for me. I want this Championship, this title, as badly as the rest of the team, along with the opportunity of a lifetime it'll unlock. I'm not willing to lose what I have left of my dad, either. And for me, this is the only way I can keep that.

Chapter Thirty

Shantal

Since we still have a week in Rio before Imola, I tailor up the simulator to use track input from the Italian race this time. I run Darien through a lap before using the same algorithm I've honestly become quite fond of, to pick out his weak spots and work them on a modified track. I should be feeling fairly reassured – things are going as well as could be expected – but I'm scared instead.

Darien sees through my fear even more easily than my parents would. He drives us out to Santa Teresa the next day. I've only been here once before – that was when I first ran into him, back in January. Now we're back here, where Darien lived as a child, and apparently still lives, judging from the way he sheepishly points out the small house that he proclaims is his as we roll past.

I can't help but smile when he tells me about the places we pass. Everything is unique to the way he sees the world. He skinned both knees there the summer he and his friends tried to climb that tree, took his mum to that cinema to watch *Now You See Me* in Portuguese, had his senior photos snapped next to that marketplace so the Brazilian Football Confederation flags would appear in the picture.

I don't think I can view Darien the way I did before coming to Rio. I remember thinking he was superficial, ignorant, cocky. He'd said he just wanted someone to know him as he was, and here we are.

The last place Darien brings us is the cable-car stop. I've wanted to get on the tram since I saw it going over the arches. So finally, we are afforded the chance, crammed on with the local passengers, at least till Darien helps us push our way to the emptier balcony area in the front.

'What'd I do that hurt you yesterday?' he asks quietly as the canary-coloured tram scrapes and creaks its way along. His immediate concern, for the injury and recovery causing him so much *pain*, is mine.

'You hurt *yourself*.' I bite the inside of my cheek idly. 'Nothing else. I just don't want you suffering any more than you already have.'

'You,' he says with a disbelieving smile, 'have such a strange heart.'

'Strange?' I lift an eyebrow as I turn his way. 'Stranger than yours?'

'Easily,' says Darien. His expression gradually becomes teasing: my favourite look on him.

'Oh, well, at least I'm not tearing myself limb from limb to roast in an open-cockpit car for two hours at a time,' I quip. I fake indifference for all but a moment. The amusement twinkling in Darien's eyes is too captivating. His heart is no stranger than mine. He keeps smiling, even when he knows he's trying to turn water into wine.

The tram quivers as we leave the enormous skyscrapers and crowded housing and cross beneath an area of beautiful palm fronds, lush with vibrant shades of green.

'How do you feel about me driving?' Darien's tone has sobered again when he speaks next. The seriousness throws me for a loop. His brow wrinkles, eyes almost pleading; his asking such a personal question tells me everything I need to know of his head and heart. 'I had one of my *tias* say it was too much once. Risking my life for a slice of speed. The chance to live faster than everyone else. Do you see it as . . .' He gulps, and I feel my own eyebrows knit in worry as he goes on, nervous. 'Do you see it as foolish, too?'

Did I put this thought in his head? I wonder suddenly. And if I did . . . does he care that much about what I think?

I reach out and cover his hand with mine. His skin is warm and, as new as this feeling is, it's familiar. 'Darien . . . nothing about you is foolish.'

He peers at my hand, and then at me, almost sceptically.

'I see your passions as an extension of *you*,' I go on, 'and I could never tell you what to do with a part of yourself,' I tell him with a gentle finality. A tentative smile flutters back to his face.

I want to be as good as my word – to stop worrying about this practice on Friday and trust him. But I also want to do all I can to keep Darien safe, and it's jarring, incomplete in the sense it makes.

'Hey.' I turn to him, and his eyes meet mine. 'Just be careful. All right?'

He nods with an adorable grin full of nothing but innocence. It's so simple with Darien. It requires no thought. 'When have I not been careful?'

I can't help but stifle a laugh. He does these tiny things,

beautiful things. And with them, he fills the void that loss left behind in me, piece by piece. He gives me back my courage and my voice and my smile. He makes me want to end what my mother calls my self-imposed penance and *try*. At least until I remember that there is a whole other component to that penance: my plea to my parents.

'What's that look?' Darien's voice is almost singsong as he snaps his fingers in front of my face.

'Oh . . .' I let out an embarrassed chuckle. He reads me far too well. 'Nothing. Nothing, I just . . . nothing.'

Chapter Thirty-One

Darien

I roll up my sleeve and peer at the aggressive scars marring my right arm. The good thing is that they'll be covered. The bad thing is that covering them won't stop the questions.

We touched down in Emilia-Romagna, Italy, just hours ago, but I haven't even had time to breathe. It's already the hour of the annual Drivers' Dinner, and Heidelberg Hybridge F1 Team has a reputation to uphold.

The dinner itself has been an occurrence since the rise of Revello, who consider Imola their home race. The dinner started out as a Revello tradition, with just their team around the dinner table in Fabrizio Revello's house, but quickly grew to accommodate all the drivers on the grid when the Grand Prix was established in 2020, and then morphed into a full-blown gala featuring the core members of all ten teams. Press wanted to see the teams parade around in formal wear, and principals wanted to get hot gossip fresh out of the oven. The Drivers' Dinner was the perfect opportunity for both.

I grab my suit jacket off the bed and slip it on. The jacket and slacks are a matching navy blue, with the Heidelberg logo over the breast: a coat of arms like the distant cousin to Revello's, the Heidelberg family crest. All three of us drivers will match with the white dress shirts and navy suits to echo Heidelberg's aqua and white colour scheme, although I decide a bit of bling is also required. I pair the suit with small gold hoop earrings to match my cross. The finishing touch: a Patek Philippe I bought last year with my first P1 bonus. Appearances are everything at these events. Heidelberg has the facilities now, but we also need to show that we, as drivers, are on top of our game – classy, professional, put-together.

And maybe, just maybe, I want to look good for another reason.

I leave my room to link up in the lobby of the small hotel, where Celina has announced she will personally vet everyone's gala outfit. Under her watch, no one will be allowed to half-ass – of that much, I'm positive. She's already not too thrilled with the number of sour gummy bears I consumed last night, so I make sure I'm extra put-together to avoid her bad side completely.

When I get down, I can see the chaos out of the window. There are already cars everywhere, pulling up along the front of the itty-bitty hotel building, its lights twinkling against the night sky. My heart thrums like the engine of one of our cars. This gala offers every team the chance to make positive impressions and do a little bit of peacocking, especially with our sponsors. After the practices in Miami, I'm stepping out into the limelight for the first time since my accident. It's a lot of firsts. I'm not sure I'm prepared for all of them.

The moment I reach the lobby, I'm accosted by photographers. The sound is so loud, I can scarcely believe

185

it. The media, for their part, don't waste time with the bright light flares and shouted questions. I try my best to ignore the interrogation on the state of my arm, on whether I'll even drive in the actual race come Sunday, and creep through to a separate hallway closer to the ballroom. I can feel the sweat already beading up on my forehead, my pulse quickening as I think of the night of the crash.

In the hallway, thankfully, the others have followed my game plan to get away from the cameras. I convene with Miguel, Henri, and their respective trainers, Louie and Jack. Celina and Shantal, last to arrive, bustle in soon enough.

Cel gets to work assessing the outfit situation right away, with a curt 'Fine' here and a brusque 'That'll do' there. But my eyes catch sight of Shantal, and they can't look away.

She wears a sleeveless blouse similar to a bralette. It's silver and gold and covered in mirrors and jewels, and leaves her midriff completely exposed. What's got to be yards of shimmering navy blue fabric are wrapped around her as a skirt that falls to her ankles, crossed over the front of her body, and tossed over a shoulder. The gold border of the fabric, lined with more mirrors, stands out perfectly against her deep tan. Her short hair has been half pinned back with tiny little diamonds. It conceals none of the uncovered skin at her collarbones, none of her cleavage. The outfit hugs every one of her curves, accentuating her small stature in all the right places.

I must be staring way too intently for way too long, because Shantal shifts on her silver heels. 'The saree wasn't too risky, was it?'

'Uh . . . no,' I stutter. *Dude. You're so much better than this. Be good.* 'You're just . . . absolutely stunning.'

She tilts her head with a shy smile, not quite meeting my

eye, and sends her big gold earrings swinging. 'Oh . . . thank you.'

'Shantal!' Celina calls. Shantal turns, and *holy shit*, the back of the dress is nonexistent. I don't even know if I'm in my right mind any more. I must look like I've lost it right now, but I can't take my eyes off her. I can feel the front of my stupid slacks tighten as I take in every inch of her, every place I want to touch, to feel my skin against. She's perfect.

Shantal confers with Celina for a moment, and then she spins back towards me, her hair blowing back from her face like she's an angel sent straight from heaven. 'Would you like to sit together at dinner, Darien?'

'Dinner,' I repeat numbly. 'Yes.'

'I'm assigning her to you as your handler,' says Celina. 'Shantal seems to be an excellent medium for keeping fragile male egos in check.'

I scoff. 'What's that mean?'

'I'll help deflect interrogation about your arm before you get up and swing at someone so hard you break the other one,' Shantal replies with a hint of sarcasm. She raises an eyebrow markedly. 'There are, after all, representatives from every team here tonight. We need to stay calm and collected.'

'Oh, sure.' Cool. So I've got to sit by Shantal all night and pretend I'm completely unaffected by her. Totally not suffering a raging boner every time I look at her, and my eyes inevitably trace their way up to her perfectly glossed lips.

'Call me your shield,' she teases with an absolutely killer smile. Her smiles. I don't know if I can do this right now.

'What if I call you my date?' I suggest, before I can help myself.

'You want . . .' Shantal looks as shocked by my sudden words as I am.

But then she holds out her arm.

I just blink and give her a confused glance.

'Well?' She sticks her arm out further, giving it a shake so that the gold bangles on it clink together. Her *right* arm. She's still trying to help me out, even in the slightest ways.

I awkwardly raise my good arm to let her loop her right through my left. 'This once,' she whispers. 'I owe you for the temple.'

We enter the banquet hall together, and even if it's just this once, I've never felt so confident as we descend into a mess of sponsors and motorsport royalty.

Chapter Thirty-Two

Shantal

Darien and I cross the hall, nodding polite 'hellos' every so often, defly avoiding conversation. He puts names to faces for me, but I can't keep them straight in my mind. It's only once we sit down at the massive table reserved for our immediate team that my head stops spinning.

'I know pro sport is a game of connections,' I say, 'but I've never seen it to this extent.'

As he joins us at the table, Miguel just laughs. 'Welcome to auto racing.'

Our table consists of all our drivers, trainers and engineers, along with a few empty seats for friends and family, plus-ones. Demir will sit at the head of the table, after he's concluded his run of the room. He's currently doing the same as the rest of the team principals – talking up sponsors, not to mention covertly turning an ear to other teams.

'Working the room is a superpower in this gig,' adds Louie. He nods to Miguel. 'This dude's fiancée is superb at it. Securing funding is the bulk of the job. I've heard she's the best of the best. Done wonders for Revello.'

'Yeah, where is Miss Diana?' Darien asks. I can't seem to look away as the words leave his mouth. He's . . . handsome. He cleans up nicely. The navy suit complements his tanned complexion and his brown curls perfectly. I wouldn't mind if he tore the saree off me right this minute.

'Working the room,' Miguel says, an air of pride lacing his voice as he points in the general direction of the opposite end of the banquet hall.

My jaw drops.

'Di!' calls Miguel, getting up to meet her. She turns our way with a broad grin, and I am *floored*. She's a goddess. She basically floats up to us in a glittering baby blue and gold kaftan cinched at the waist with a matching gold belt, absolutely *flawless*, lashes perfect, eyeliner wings nothing short of immaculate, lips expertly outlined, curls completely flat-ironed so her hair falls in shining sheets of jet black across her shoulders.

'Hey, everyone,' Diana chirps ever-so-casually, like she's not standing before us all looking totally heavenly.

'You . . . you're . . .' Henri is struggling to find the words.

I think I'm fully starstruck. 'Wow,' I finally finish for him, gesturing to her dress, to her entire self.

'Thanks.' She smiles, nodding at my saree. 'You are *killing* it, Shantal.'

I forget what the appropriate reply is, until a 'thank you' finally emerges way too late.

'Revello's giving you glares, Dar,' Diana tells Darien with a wink. 'They can't stop talking about you, your rumoured return to the sims. They're shocked you're doing so well so soon.'

This simple remark melts some of the tension in Darien's shoulders. 'Me, too,' he replies with a voice full of relief.

Seeing him this comfortable for the first time since the accident sends an unexpected warmth spreading through my chest. Unless that's the way he's been looking at me. The way I'm trying not to look at him.

Diana is in her element, but mid-conversation with our table of team members, she catches me unaware. She gives me this knowing smile and, abruptly, the smile moves to Darien, threaded with a touch of knowledge. In that moment, fleeting as it is, Diana reads us, including everything I'm attempting to hide. It leaves me helpless when Darien turns his eyes to mine. I look away immediately, but his gaze is still on me; I can feel the heat of it on my neck.

Thankfully, we are given an escape in the form of the Revello team principal, ringleader of this entire event, taking a small stage at the front of the hall and giving the mic a quick double-tap. '*Buonasera*, everyone.'

'Cristoforo Montalto,' mouths Miguel from my right side as Diana creeps back to her Revello table. 'Powerful guy.'

The tables go silent, attention turning to the principal, Montalto. Out of the corner of my eye, I scope out Darien again. His hand rests on the table, a habit that looks natural but that we all know helps him stabilize his wrist. He runs a finger up the stem of his champagne flute rather unconsciously, and I catch sight of a stick-and-poke tattoo – happy face, dot eyes and a smile – on the side of his hand. My stomach does a little jump. Those hands. What would it feel like to be touched by such strong, beautiful hands?

I bite my lip and try to refocus on Cristoforo Montalto. Damn it.

The team boss extends an arm towards his table, says some things I barely hear amid the chaos of my mind. I want to give him my attention, but I see nothing but Darien, watch as he laughs when Montalto cracks a bad joke, his eyes narrowing happily. He nudges my arm, and then I feel a slight touch, his hand on my bare back for just a moment. Sparks chase their way across my skin, not chilling me but bringing me warmth, like no man ever has before.

I know I'm not the perfect daughter. I've had boyfriends and flings before this, one of which lasted longer than two years. I was seventeen, and I thought we'd keep going though uni – dumb, I know. I've been introduced to guys at weddings, family friends' sons with whom I had no chemistry whatsoever. Every touch before this was just a touch. It wasn't a feeling.

That brush of Darien's fingers is scarcely enough. I meet his eyes with the hope that they tell him to stay, just for a moment longer.

His own irises glitter with understanding. He sneaks a contented smile before scooting closer to me and looping his arm all the way around, his hand resting on my shoulder.

One little date, one chance for me to leave the pressure and let my heart speak.

I lean against him with a sigh that takes my worries and my responsibilities away in a puff of air. His thumb strokes my skin gently, his thigh brushing against mine.

I want so badly to tell him everything, to tear apart every shackle that holds me back. But I am nothing like Darien. With a smirk, he lied to me the night we met so that he could plant his feet firmly in reality. All I want is to lie to myself so I can continue living this dream.

By the end of the night, we've fielded whispers from Team Jolt, who've been muttering about Darien's arm all the while. I've managed to excel at my post as handler, steering Darien away from the whispers and towards a formidable ally: the champagne.

Both of us are certainly tipsy by the end of it. As the clock strikes midnight, we leave the banquet hall giggling, hanging on to each other's arms.

'And he just looked at you – like, like, *the sim*? He'll use *the sim*?' I mock the journalist who accosted Darien an hour back. 'He was in *despair*. You could have been his front page.'

Darien lets out a cackle. 'The shock on his face, Shantal. That was *satisfying*.' He stops and places his hands on his hips in what I assume is a mediocre impression of me. 'Hit him with the, "Well, can you use the sim? Can you drive any better? Can you?"'

'Can he?' I echo incredulously.

'Nope.'

I shake my head with a laugh. 'That was a rhetorical question.'

'I know.' He grins goofily at me, finally freed from the hordes of guests. 'I just like finding excuses to keep talking to you.'

Maybe it's also the champagne lowering my usual defensive fortress, but I can't help but sneak a smile at that. *Excuses to talk to you*. The sparkly haze of the drinks slowly lifts as I realize that this is not, in fact, just champagne. This is much more real.

When Darien found me in the courtyard after he returned to the Ring complex, I hadn't been able to tell him exactly what I felt. It wasn't that I lacked an answer. I had that answer all along. I was just too scared to admit it.

Now, in the slight chill of the Imola night, as we amble towards the couches on the empty patio outside the hotel, the words slip easily off my tongue. 'Me, too.'

We find a corner couch and sit side by side. Darien's smile is soft as he removes his jacket and drapes it across my shoulders, carefully adjusting a falling pleat of my saree so it sits back on my shoulder. I didn't even realize I was cold till I felt the jacket, cosy as it is. 'You too, huh?' he says quietly.

He lets his hand hover near my neck for just a moment, before civilly backing away. And god, do I hate myself for that. I need to be honest with him because I don't know if I can play keep-away any longer.

For a moment, I fear he can see that stupid look on my face, the stupid look of longing. I look away, but Darien, as if he can read me, gently tips my chin back up so I'm level with him.

His eyes lock onto mine. 'I'm not as dumb an American as I seem,' he whispers with a smirk, and I stifle a laugh. 'I should probably focus more on, like, the Championship, but then I see you, Shantal, and I can't look away. Because I know we're both finding excuses, but . . .'

'GUYS!'

'*Oh*, my . . .' Darien turns around with his hands raised. 'Dude! Henri!'

'Whoa.' Our youngest driver's eyes are comically wide. 'Sorry, sorry, this is clearly a moment. Kind of. But anyway, we need you guys in there. Cristo's absolutely plastered, and he's about to make a toast to you, Darien.'

Darien's ensuing groan is nothing short of hysterical. He gives me an apologetic smile, holding out a hand that I take as he helps me up. 'Time to watch drunk Cristo try to make one of his dad speeches,' he remarks, although his voice has an adorable sort of guilt to it.

We do, in fact, get to witness a drunk-dad speech from Revello's team principal, but even with that entire debacle occurring right before our eyes, mine can't focus on anyone but Darien.

Chapter Thirty-Three

Darien

I shift in my seat next to Peter, who's grinning and waving to audience members and journalists already. I doubt Peter Albrecht has ever had anything negative published about him. The dude lost his seat in Heidelberg in what I firmly believe was the most unfair, wicked twist of fate in 2022, but not before immediately getting an offer from Revello to join Diana on their team for 2023 and onward. Like I said, it's impossible to discount the guy. Not to mention he's already got a Championship under his belt, because of which racing with him as my teammate was like having a caring troublemaker of a big brother. I give Peter brownie points because he could have made this injury an enormous deal, but so far he's been more down-to-earth about it all than I have myself.

'Hey, man!' Peter beams, his brown curls bouncing as he reaches out and daps me up. 'It's *hot* this weekend, huh?'

'Funny. It's roasting,' I correct him with a smirk. 'Guess we gotta be ready to shred rubber.'

The abnormal heatwave sweeping though Imola is the first matter addressed in the conference, the proverbial 'small talk' about the weather that comes before the real stuff. It ends up being me, Peter, Andrea (ex-Revello driver, currently at Jolt Archambeau), and Formula 1 new kid Atticus Demopoulos. Atticus is a baby, only nineteen years old, racing under the Greek flag for Flashpoint, an entry-level team. He's already nabbed points, though. He was P9 in the last race, driving what is essentially comparable to a well-furnished tractor. Naturally, the interviewer, a familiar torturer of souls named Brian Crowberry, picks on Atticus about this first.

I fight the urge to roll my eyes at Crowberry's dumb questions and instead search for Shantal in the crowd. She's still been parsing away at simulation programming, as she is during most of the off-time on the weekends, so I'm not sure she'll have made it, but it only takes me a minute to find her among the reporters.

Immediately, I'm reminded of last night (and of how deeply I wanted nothing more than to give Henri a good shake). Man, I'd thought I was tripping the entire event, completely off my game, left totally speechless by Shantal, wondering if maybe, just maybe, she felt something, too. I'd have gotten an answer if it weren't for Cristo Montalto drinking *way* too much.

'And Darien. We wanted to reach out to you for a bit of a progress check, pop in and see how the arm is looking,' Crowberry finally prods me. Ah, there it is.

'It's well enough that I can drive a two-hundred-mile-an-hour car without crashing into a wall,' I quip with a subtle raise of my eyebrows. I'm not very well media trained. Even when they gave me advisers, I wasn't much good at listening to their directions. It was a slip of the tongue, I'll say, when I'm put on the spot.

196

Crowberry plays it off well with an excessive laugh. 'We're sure! We do have to ask, though, Darien. What's the secret? How did you recover so quickly? Are you concerned with reinjury?'

I want so badly to yell 'NO COMMENT' and end the conversation right now. *Reinjury?* Who asks a person that? Instead, I decide I'm going to be a good kid and answer him (mostly) civilly. 'Secret's surrounding yourself with people who promote recovery. Choosing a circle that will encourage you when you're in pain and you just wanna stop. Maybe keeping away from the kind of folks who try to pull you back when you want to be taking steps forward. Folks who, I don't know, *are* concerned with reinjury.'

I finish off my thought with the world's fakest smile plastered to my face.

That one gets the barest gulp out of Crowberry, and he moves on as quickly as he'd turned my way. We wrap the conference with another brief discussion on weather and tyre deg, and with that, my hour of misery is over. Mostly.

'You know, my hair was pink, like, three years ago.'

Shantal slowly turns to me as if I've just declared I'll be shaving it all off, and she's going to be the one who does it for me. '*Pink?*' she says with such conviction that I'm sure anyone standing in the hall of the motorhome can hear it.

We're in my personal room, the door ajar to the commotion outside. I made it through the practice sessions – I did FP1 and 3 while Henri picked up 2 so I could rest. I showed up for quali, able to push hard enough to get myself into P5. It's not a bad job. None of it was too far off from the sim prep I'd done on the Imola track, and with the new splint Celina has me wearing, I haven't been in much pain at all. I should be completely hell-bent on gearing up for the two-hour marathon that will be my first race back.

But all I can focus on is Shantal, acutely aware of every single detail about her. The way her hair has started to sweep past her shoulders in gentle waves, with two small braids tied up on top, the glimmer of her brown lip gloss, every crease in her team T-shirt falling perfectly across her body, the slight tense of the defined muscles in her legs when she does an about-face to give me a shocked glance.

'It looked *so* good, Shantal,' I argue from where I sit on my training table. 'I made it work *so* well.'

'Whatever you say.' She glances at my hair with concern. 'Next thing I know, you'll have the R9 haircut.'

I burst out laughing at that one. Her eyes are telling me I've certainly lost it, but it's too funny a nod to pass off. 'I asked my mom to get me the R9 – in the sixth grade.'

'Don't tell me she let you!' Shantal yelps around a bite of her banana as she waves it in the air like a sceptre. 'No! Your mum can't be enabling this!'

'She didn't let me,' I grin. 'But maybe she should have, I would've made that work, too.'

'Keep lying to yourself.' She holds the banana out to me. 'Take a bite.'

'I ate, like, five minutes ago—'

'Take a bite,' she insists, and I can't refuse. I reach over and oblige, chewing on the fruit as I hop off the table and to my feet, and we walk towards the garages.

Just outside, in the pit lane, a crowd of sponsors, celebrities and team members are starting to gather, all eyes on the main straight, a good section of track from the finish line, where Revello's *Cavaliere*, their knight – a legitimate man in actual Italian armour, no kidding – has mounted his horse, with

Fabrizio Revello's own family sword in hand. The grandstands roar as the *Cavaliere* trots full pace on his horse before reaching the finish and slicing through a ribbon held up by volunteers at the line to deafening cheers. It's an Imola tradition for Revello, but it strikes me as so American it's funny.

'That's so "college football" of them.'

'You do that in football?' Shantal says in horror.

I shake my head with a laugh when I realize we're a whole pond apart in terms of understanding. 'American football. We're weird. Anyway . . . I have a favour to ask.'

'A favour? Or a bargain?' she teases, tugging the shoulder of my race suit jestingly.

'Maybe.' I meet her eyes dead-on. 'If I win this race – if, man, because Jolt and Revello are *top form* – will you do me a solid?'

'What solid?'

I lean in so close I can count her freckles and smell the peaches from her shampoo. She raises an eyebrow with the kind of sass that makes me grin like an idiot. I gesture towards the Brazilian flag that has been hung above the car.

'I'm going to need you to hand me that flag.'

'For what? For your lap?' She gapes. 'I couldn't. Your crew needs to do that—'

'You are in large part the reason I'm even *driving* today.' I take one of her loose curls in my fingers and brush it from her face, letting my hand – my once-bad hand – stay at her cheek for just a moment. 'If you don't hand me that flag, Shantal, I swear to you, I won't do the victory lap at all. It's you or nothing.'

'Or *nothing*?' She stares at me in disbelief. 'Then do *me* a solid.' She gets up on her tiptoes and plants a kiss on my forehead, her jesting smile turning to one of determination. 'Race so hard that you have no choice but to give me the chance to hand you that flag.'

I nod, acutely aware of how red I must be going, despite having my Mãe's blush-resistant skin tone. Turning pink like a middle-schooler with a fat crush right in front of said crush. I don't have any actual words. She takes them away from me every time, even if she doesn't realize she's doing it.

'You are gonna be *so good*,' is the last thing Shantal says to me before my team sweeps me away, passing me my helmet and ushering me into the car. I can still see her out of the corner of my eye on the pit wall, giving me a little wave that I return with a wiggle of my fingers. I pull on my balaclava and helmet, which now bears a new cursive script on the bottom of the back, right near my neck: *Pressure Makes Diamonds*.

Even as I sit down in my ever-familiar car and get out onto the track, make my slow formation lap before pulling into the grid, I can't get my mind off the way that the hammer could possibly come down before sponsors and bosses and probably God while I pretend to race like I'm in perfect physical shape. I guess that's the thing. I don't need to pretend. I earned my right to come back here the hard way.

It's easier said than done. My breath quickens when the first red light comes on overhead. It's only been seven or eight weeks, but it feels like I've lived an entire lifetime in those weeks. I've been to hell and back. I can viscerally feel again the pain I felt when I pushed my muscles like that, pushed them in ways they didn't want to be pushed.

But as the red lights continue to flicker on, they morph into the truck's headlights on full blast, they get closer and closer till I'm suddenly upside down, till my arm feels like it's been stuffed in a snowblower.

I blink, tensing both of my arms for good measure. *Come on, Darien. Come on.*

All five red lights go out, and I floor it, pushing all other thoughts from my mind as my car surges forward. I need to do this right. Maybe P5 is better than what we'd expected, but it's not good enough for me.

The pack of cars is tight heading into Turn One. I already hear a distant screeching of tyres behind us that I can't pay attention to if I want to stay on the track. I wrench it around the turn and slip past Peter, into P4.

'You're on the move now,' Afonso encourages me over the radio. 'Let's keep it clean, keep it clean, Darien.'

I do . . . I keep it completely clean as I wait for the next advantageous turn to dart around the inside and get past Miguel: P3. We're on podium places now, but that first lap has ended, and deltas between cars are growing as we enter Lap Two.

'Only push for one more lap. Let's just try and catch Romilly ahead,' says Afonso.

Although we try, we can't clear Alex Romilly in the next lap. From here, it's going to be all about endurance as Afonso commands me to stick to Plan A – save the tyres as much as possible so we can pit a few laps after Alex and get the speed boost that comes with brand-new slicks.

Unfortunately, it's around the time we make said pit stop that my arm decides it would like to protest.

I was fine all race, but as I manoeuvre the car out of the pit lane and back onto the track, the glancing pain I'd gotten on the sim that first run starts to streak through my arm. At first, it's a faint throbbing, but soon, it has me gritting my teeth. I can't concentrate like this.

'Closing on Romilly. Delta one-point-five seconds.'

Damn it. If there's an overtake coming, I need to be locked in. Half-ass taking a gap, and you'll be upside down in the wall before you know it.

'Hang on, Dar,' I mutter to myself. 'You got this.'

I let the machinery around me fall away and leave the pain behind me on the track, just like I'd done at winter testing. We're on a track walk, and my two feet are on the ground, nothing but sunny Imola for miles.

Beside me, I see Shantal, her wavy hair dancing around her face as she smiles, dimples creating tiny yet perfect grooves in her cheeks. I picture her the way she was the night of Carnaval: happy, as she deserved to be all the time, comfortable. I draw my energy off the bliss I see in her eyes. I remember feeling that bliss when I got into a kart for the first time, but I also remember feeling that bliss when I saw her for the first time.

She slows my shallow breaths and quells my rapid pulse. Something about her makes me feel like she knows every corner and trapdoor of my heart, even though I'd never met her before January.

Before I can so much as process it, I've darted around Alex. I'm a good four seconds from the race leader, Diana. It's a lot, but I'm not giving up. The opportunity is still there.

Shantal, I think to myself. *She's in the garage. She's there*.

I feel her hand in mine, the way it had been during those awful PTs, her eyes boring into mine with conviction.

I can't sacrifice the chance to see her holding that flag.

Turn One of my third-to-last lap is a dance with disaster. Even though I've caught up to Diana from a healthy couple of doses of DRS, she's sliding around on the inside. I'm boxed out. I need to move. I need to find myself a gap.

The second I'm able to go wheel to wheel with Diana, I cross her car on the turn exit, in perhaps the riskiest cut I've taken in my entire racing career. My heart is thudding in my ears. My breath is hitching. Afonso cheers into my radio, and I keep on the throttle all the way through.

It's a fight to the finish, but none of it rivals that Turn One move.

P1.

The feeling is unreal. I pump my right fist in the air as I cross the line, and I start my victory lap much the same way.

'He's back, ladies and gentlemen,' Demir says over my radio. 'You've made us very, very proud today, Darien. Very proud to call you our driver.'

'YES!' I yell. Tears of relief? Joy? Pain? I can't tell what they are, but they prick my eyes. 'Thank you, thank you, thank you.'

'We have a request for you.' Afshin's voice crackles. 'Could you give us a dance at the finish?'

'I can try,' I laugh. The dance is an age-old joke that's followed me around since I was a kid, and I'd copy the Brazilian footballers' goal celebrations when I won a race. Ever since F3, I've gotten up on my chassis and tried my best to hit one every time I place first.

I'm thinking of which one I'll do this time when I roll up to the fence to get my flag, and I see Shantal, and pretty much every potential dance move sprouts wings and flies straight out of my brain.

She reaches out towards me with the blue, green and yellow banner in hand. Her hair flutters in the wind generated by the cars. The sun reflects off the glittering diamond in her nose. Her cheeks are flushed pink, her eyes full of pride. She stands on her tiptoes, creasing her white Adidas shoes. I watch her shout something I can't completely hear, watch her lips move as she smiles wider than I've ever seen her smile.

I can't tear my eyes from her as she hands over the flag. In the minute that makes up that lap, I think I might be the happiest guy in the world. I'm the walking, talking embodiment of delusion, but that doesn't matter. Her smile is more beautiful than the trophy they'll give me up on the podium, anyway.

Chapter Thirty-Four

Shantal

I've been trying to convince myself I'm not hallucinating for hours.

I handed him the flag – the flag he flew during his victory lap. I've seen photos, which made it feel both more and less real. I've seen videos, which made it feel like an out-of-body experience. I could see his eyes through the tint of the visor. They caught mine and didn't move until he'd taken the flag from me.

Amid all my thoughts, there's a loud thumping knock at my door. I creep over and peep through the hole warily. Speak of the devil: Darien is there.

I take a deep breath and open the door. 'Weren't you . . . supposed to be getting ready for that nightclub thing?'

It's a fair question. The Imola GP afterparty is in an hour, and he doesn't look anywhere near ready to go out. In fact, his curls are as unruly as they'd been when he took off his helmet earlier today, and he's dressed in a grey T-shirt and a pair of pyjama pants with pictures of little cars on them.

He just grins his usual stupid grin, no thoughts behind those deep brown eyes. Dimples etch his cheeks as he glances at my outfit, a similar degree of un-club-like as his. I've got running shorts and an old college football shirt. 'You don't look like you're ready, either.'

'Is that a concern? You're the *winner* of the race,' I point out. Some unexpected burst of confidence bolsters me enough to press an insistent index finger to his muscled chest.

His gaze flicks to my finger, and then back to my face with a raised eyebrow. 'Come with me.'

'Sorry, what?'

'I swear. I'm not being weird. C'mon.'

I'm intrigued, if not slightly lost, but I grab my phone, close the door behind me, and follow Darien as he sets off down the hall. The further we walk, the louder something playing in the distance – someone talking – gets. Eventually, we stop at the source of the noise, room 812. His room?

'Your room?' I echo my thought aloud.

'You'll see.' He presses his key card to the lock, the door pops open, and I walk into a scene that has me in total and utter shock.

I don't even know *how* the logistical parts of this situation fell into place, but somehow there are three queen-size hotel beds in the middle of Darien's enormous sitting room, all pushed together in front of his TV. Now there's no question I've been hallucinating since this morning, because I believe I see Miguel, Henri, Diana, and . . . is that Peter Albrecht? Whatever the case, they're sharing a pizza, sprawled across the span of *bed*. If I'm not mistaken, it's Keanu Reeves in an American football uniform on the television screen (when did that happen?). A full spread of candy, ice cream, fries, burgers, and more fast food has completely overtaken the dining table.

'Henri's not gonna be back with us till mid-season,' says Darien, as if this will explain everything. 'We thought this was an apt send-off.'

'A . . .' I search for the right phrase. 'Slumber party?'

Darien and the others turn to me, waiting for my reaction. I don't expect the laugh that bubbles up in my chest. 'You know what? I've not eaten a really greasy pizza in *ages*.'

The room reverberates to excited cheers. Diana bounds over to me, beaming in her usual radiant way. She's got on the same car pyjama pants as Miguel, Henri and Darien, coupled with an old Jolt shirt. 'We have PJs for you,' she says in a foreboding tone. 'And lots and lots of pizza. We have more than enough pizza.'

'How . . .' I gesture vaguely towards the beds. But never mind the how, I'm pretty sure that has to be against hotel policy.

She presses a finger to her lips with a smirk. 'Shhh.'

Once I've changed into my car pants, Henri, who's downing M&Ms like they're about to be rationed, explains the movie situation. They've got *The Replacements* on ('that's a timeless classic'). He then hands me an entire cheese pizza with a grin, because Darien told him 'Shantal doesn't eat animals' and 'everyone likes cheese.' I confirm that he is, in fact, correct, and cheese pizza is my favourite kind because I have trauma from my parents trying to hide vegetables in my pizza as a kid. A cheese pizza has never pumped so much happiness into my veins.

'Do you guys know the one-bed trope?' Peter pipes up as the credits of the movie roll.

Miguel pauses in the middle of his quest to grab for the

remote. He quirks an eyebrow at Peter. '*One bed?* What, are you reading romance novels?'

'Only good ones,' he says defensively. 'Anyway. To my point, mate. Is it considered the one-bed trope if you have three beds all pushed together? Are we all victims of it, right now?'

'The three-bed trope,' muses Henri, splaying all five feet and ten inches of himself across two of the three beds. 'Put that in your romance novels.'

We all laugh, and Diana pokes Peter in the ribs. 'Send me book recommendations, would you? My Kindle looks empty these days.'

'You have a Kindle too?' he gasps, and that only escalates the laughter all around.

'*That's* what you used to bring into the garage all the time while you waited for the mechanics?' Darien grins as he reaches for the nearest pillow. 'Maybe Miguel let it go, but me, Petey, I'm not stopping till I get to find out what you've been reading.'

Peter shields himself from Darien's pillow with a shriek. With a wave of his arm, Darien mobilizes the army, and soon it's all of us pelting the veteran driver with hotel pillows until he caves at last. 'Cowboy romances,' he yelps. 'I swear on my mum!'

Smirking mischievously, Darien tosses his pillow aside and bounds right off the bed. He tips an imaginary cowboy hat, meeting my eyes slowly. The tension between us is simmering, at least until he cracks a smile, and the silliness of it all takes over. 'Howdy, pardner,' he says in the world's *worst* Southern accent.

'Stop it,' I laugh, and he flops so hard onto the mattress next to me that my entire body is off the bed for a split second. Both of us giggle uncontrollably, and I try to stifle my hiccups in his shoulder, laughing so hard my stomach hurts, and it's as if no one else is in the room, both of us caught up in our own bubble of stupidity. Somewhere in the distance, Diana croons a loving '*Awww,*' and Henri pretends to gag, but it doesn't register for us. When I'm with Darien, nothing else registers; only a part of my heart that I thought had been closed off for ever last year.

This time, the weightlessness lasts much longer than a mere moment.

Chapter Thirty-Five

Darien

For what might be the first time in history, I get up with the sun the day after a race. It's a bright Monday morning in Imola, and I kind of want to sleep in for another hour, but the sun is too startling for that. I hurdle over Henri's legs and pad over to the coffee machine in the kitchen to get myself caffeine. I check the clock – it's seven a.m., but there's no going back once I have coffee in my system.

Once I've brewed my cup, I head out to the balcony, where Shantal and her iced coffee have already beaten me to the punch. She leans against the rail and sips from her straw, the light breeze tousling the curls peeking out from her two low buns of hair.

'Morning,' she hums around a gulp of coffee.

'Morning,' I reply with a yawn. 'What a weekend.'

She nods, tracing a smiley face in the condensation of her glass, and looks up at me with a twinkle in her eye. 'You did it. Proved everyone wrong. Came back with a win.'

'I . . .' I shake my head with a small chuckle. 'I don't think I could've done it without this team, though. Without you.'

'Me?' Shantal tilts her head as if trying to scope out what's gotten into me. 'I didn't do all that much.'

'Shantal, when I was in the car . . .' I set my mug down on the flat railing, purse my lips as I prepare to recount what was one of the freakiest moments I've ever experienced on a track. 'I could *feel* my arm starting to give out. Like, I was coming up on Alex, I think, to overtake him, and everything was just falling apart. Couldn't feel my hand for a minute. I lost focus, man. It would've been a mess for me if . . .' I almost roll my eyes at myself, at how weird and tacky I probably sound. 'I thought of you, Shantal, I thought of you in the garage, and I don't know . . . you brought my strength back.'

'You thought of me?' she echoes. Her eyes widen like she can't believe the things I'm saying.

'Yeah, I . . . yeah. And when you were there with that flag, Shantal, it . . .' I can't do much other than let out a sigh, try to find the right words. 'I can't even tell you how it felt.'

She places her glass next to mine, and she gazes up at me with those big eyes of hers. 'How did it feel?' she whispers.

'When you win a race once, you just . . . you wanna keep winning more. It's an addiction.' It must be the way she's looking at me that prompts the admission to come on so easily. 'But when I saw you holding the flag, it wasn't just an addiction, Shantal. I wanted to be there for ever, park my car in front of you and . . . and see you *happy*. You make winning more than an addiction for me. You make me want to turn it into a habit, just so I can see you smile like that.'

'Like what?' Shantal's voice is so quiet it's almost as if she's mouthing words, and I have to concentrate on every movement of her lips.

'Like someone's finally given you those damn flowers you deserve.'

She laughs, and this sound isn't quiet at all. It echoes over the balcony. It's so beautiful that a part of me hopes it echoes all through Imola, so everyone can hear the same melody I do. It's in that moment that I realize I've finally, possibly, done it. I've made her forget, even just for a second. I commit every note of that laugh to memory.

'Do you remember . . .' She takes a tentative step closer to me, one that doesn't escape my notice, because my heart is thundering in my chest. 'Before Henri came and told us Cristo Montalto was losing his mind, before that, you said something. About how you should focus on the Championship, and this stress we are under to make this season perfect. Except you can't focus.'

I think back to the moment with a guilty smile. 'Yeah, that Cristo thing didn't help. That wasn't my smoothest of moves.'

'Oh, my god.' I think Shantal actually holds back a laugh. 'Well, the thing is . . . I've tried *so* hard to focus. So hard. And yet I end up here. Completely and utterly distracted by you.'

'*By me?*'

Now it's my turn to go wide-eyed and pleading and *wow*.

Distracted by you.

This is definitely happening.

Chapter Thirty-Six

Shantal

'I'm sorry—'

'I want to do something about it.'

I cut him off so quickly he's almost stunned. Darien is not at all the kind of man to stand in silence and shock, but he's here in front of me, open-mouthed at the raw honesty that seems to have emerged from my previously undecided heart.

The confession is automatic, the way everything is with Darien. I don't even have to try. Around him, there is possibility. There is a chance of regaining the security I have lost over the last year. Maybe there is even a chance of my heart letting someone in again.

'Me, too,' he says, still slightly dumbfounded.

'What if I said I shouldn't want to do something about it?'

'Probably same. One hand doesn't quite work right, you know; it wouldn't be fair to you.'

I bite my lip to hold in my amusement.

'And . . .' I exhale a breath full of raw emotion. 'What if I said I *should* want to?'

'Then *definitely* same.'

In that moment, every barrier between us dissipates. Darien turns to me, moving his hand to tuck an errant curl behind my ear. His touch is warm and careful yet intoxicating.

'Let's do something about it,' I murmur, letting my eyes close as my cheek falls against his palm.

After weeks – months – of suppression, Darien's fingers gently tilt my chin upward. His hand travels to my neck, while both of mine pull him close to me.

He kisses me slowly, and at first, he's tentative. He tastes like coffee, lips soft against mine. I've never felt my soul explode the way it does now, bursting with all these feelings that I have the sudden need to act on. That innocent kiss grows into something more frenzied; his touch is full of the same abandon as his driving. His tongue parts my lips perfectly, and he groans slightly against my mouth as his hand moves to my back, his grip firm yet tender. I turn my head as if beckoning him, and he obliges, brushing his lips across my jaw. I can't help the quiet whimper that escapes me when he finds that perfect spot on the side of my neck that sends a tingle down my spine.

Every touch of his fingers sends part of the wall around my heart crumbling to oblivion. I almost protest when he pulls away with a nervous laugh. 'Well, shit.'

'Shit,' I agree, biting back my smile. I've not smiled like this in ages; I've not been touched like this in ages.

He exhales, presses his forehead to mine. His eyes glitter as they meet mine in a gesture more intimate than any physical contact.

'I think I can go ahead and dump out the rest of my coffee.'

He smiles goofily, innocently. 'You made me feel like I just downed five Monsters.'

I can't help but giggle quietly. I've never met a man so vulnerable and yet resilient, mature and yet naïve. He sees no evil in anyone, not even in me, not even in the fact that – as right as this moment feels – I am still standing at a crossroads.

Chapter Thirty-Seven

Shantal

It's Monaco up next on the calendar, second to last before the summer break. Darien and Miguel have been neck and neck in the tables for the Championship, with Miguel now a mere twelve points ahead, and although the Constructors' title is clearly looking like a lead for Heidelberg, it's everything to play for as we travel to this next destination. Endless thoughts bounce around in my mind the entire flight: the high of the points starting to rack up, the sim working its magic, *everything* that happened in Imola, including that Monday morning. I came into this with shaky hands, and they've finally begun to steady. It's as if someone's thrown my soul into the sky; it's sitting high up in the clouds now.

Needless to say, the Monaco Grand Prix puts me back in my place the second my feet touch the country's soil.

As we drive through the city, I gape at how very put-together everyone is here. The women are clad in Dior and Chanel, some with big, floppy hats and Ray-Bans, others shading their eyes using hands bearing lavishly painted acrylic nails. The men step out from glossy sports cars and adjust their button-down shirts with chins tipped slightly up as if they're royalty. Is that the way I should be carrying myself at this race? I'm not completely sure, and I ask Celina as we make our way through the aisle fenced off from fans and into our hotel, which is a hotbed of the Monegasque wealthy.

'Oh, honey, no,' she replies. 'Don't let them get in your head. But also, don't let them *not* get in your head. Make sure you put your outfits together well for the next couple days.'

I take her advice in stride. For the first race-related event, the press rounds on Thursday, I make sure I've washed my hair and have it in neat waves down to my shoulders. I wear a longer forest green sundress with a tight top and flared bottom that reaches just past my calves, along with small gold hoop earrings and, naturally, my trusty white Hokas. I may need to dress well for Monaco, but I also like to be prepared to walk fast whenever the need arises.

I love listening to Darien – his deep baritone voice is gorgeous, and that slight rasp I've come to love grips the entire audience whenever so much as a word leaves his mouth. But I've glimpsed Monte Carlo and now I'm itching to explore it. When else am I going to get to travel to a place like this?

Darien reads my mind, because the moment the press conference ends and a smattering of polite applause follows the drivers as they step off the panel, he immediately beelines my way with the most massive grin. 'Why don't we get out?' he says over the buzz of the media. 'Go see the car collection. You'll love it.'

'You mean *you'll* love it,' I tease him with a poke of his shoulder.

It's hysterical how flustered he gets. 'Oh, wait, I mean if you don't want to . . . we can always—'

I laugh, pressing a palm to my forehead. 'Yes, I want to see the cars. Let's go.'

The Prince of Monaco's car collection is sheltered in a museum in La Condamine. Inside, everything from the oldest of automobiles to modern Formula 1 cars is on display. What draws our eyes right away is a sleek black F1 model detailed with purple and white, as well as a host of sponsors. I recognize a makeup brand, one of my favourite sustainable choices, and an energy drink logo.

'Diana's 2022 Championship-winning Jolt,' says Darien in total awe. 'Imagine you make history, and then you get to say that your car is on display in the prince's collection.'

I smile when I realize that there's a childlike dreaminess in his expression, one I've come to appreciate deeply. I came to Heidelberg completely clueless, and now I'm determined that this man should see the highest level of success this season.

Once we tear our eyes away from the cars, we decide to walk the city. Darien's been here before, and he navigates it with ease. He points out all the big casinos, located around turns of the racetrack. Monaco itself is small enough that the grand prix spans almost the entire country – a strange thought. His fingers lace themselves through mine, and his thumb runs over the ridges and dips of my knuckles while he shows me a huge painting on the side of a small local restaurant. It's a remnant of last season, a section of track curving down the wall of the building, with Formula 1 cars of different liveries zooming along it so they appear to jump out from the mural.

When the coast comes into view, Darien tells me about all the yachts, massive leisure vessels decorated with flags and glossy gold names on their bows. He picks out the ones he recognizes by their owners, and I laugh when we see Miguel's yacht, with the apt name *Lady Diana*.

'You think he'll notice if we hop on?' I prod Darien with a chuckle.

That devilish look creeps over his face, the kind you might see on a five-year-old plotting to colour all the walls hot pink. 'Well,' he shoots me a smirk, 'what Miguel doesn't know won't hurt him.'

'Oh, my – Darien!' I call as he rushes across the dock dramatically, vaulting over the edge of the boat and landing on the floor with a cheerful little thud. I could scold him, but I'm too amused to do anything but follow. He's happily raiding Miguel's beautiful yacht, popping open cabinets and mini-fridges on the inside till he finally emerges victorious, a bottle of – is that alcohol or water? – raised triumphantly in one hand.

'Drinks all round,' the menace proclaims as he grabs a picnic blanket off one of the benches, spreading it out on the ground. 'He's owed me this ever since I beat him in Bahrain.'

I bite my lip, but a loud laugh escapes anyway. 'Please, Darien, pour some drinks, why don't you?'

Chapter Thirty-Eight

Darien

'I wasn't sure if I should be glad or disappointed that was non-alcoholic, but I think I'm just glad now. *Italian soda.*' Shantal helps herself to another full glass of the carbonated water I'd brought out with a contented sigh, drizzling pineapple syrup on top. 'Rich people, I tell you.'

'We need to get you onto more de la Fuente yachts,' I remark with a sip of my own drink – mango. Can't beat a Guaraná, but it's delicious.

'Without permission,' she adds.

I bring a finger to my lips. 'He doesn't have to know.'

She rolls her eyes, but she laughs that beautiful uncontrolled laugh. I watch her smile, looking out across the rippling water at the yachts beyond. Straight out of a dream. Her toothy grin, the satisfied little sounds she makes with each sip of soda. Indescribable.

'I'm aware alcohol isn't something you drink during the

season, but what if you had to choose a go-to drink?' asks Shantal, swirling her glass idly.

'Probably . . . I think it has to be rum.' I scratch my jaw as a fond memory creeps into the back of my mind. 'Was my *vô*, my grandpa's, favourite, and then my dad's. He'd bring it home for my mom all the time. It's one of those things I remember.'

'When'd you lose him?' she asks, which catches me only slightly off-guard. People like to tiptoe around the topic. I think part of it is just because it used to make me really upset that I didn't recall the important things, what he was like and all of that. All I've got is foods and cars.

'I was about six, maybe. Don't really know too much, just that it was pretty sudden.' I have to struggle to bring back what Tio Julio told me, because it was so freaking long ago. My mom never talks about him, ever. 'It was weird because he raced so much, you know, in the street and stuff. And then he was on the way to an interview – he was gonna get a real job, get us out of the city – and it just . . .' I shrug. 'I don't think I've got any kind of recollection of that. It's all stuff I was told.'

Shantal nods. Her eyes have gone misty. I wonder how we got straight to the most depressing topic in the book like this, but it doesn't seem to be treating her too well. She holds her glass gingerly, no longer too interested in its contents.

'Do you ever just feel bad?' she says. 'For moving on?'

I take a big gulp of my soda to keep myself occupied for a good minute. It's like she knows exactly where to get me, the parts that need healing. Then, 'Every day.'

'Why?'

'I feel bad I didn't know him, mostly.'

'What do you do about it?'

'Nothing, I guess.' I finish off the last of the drink and set the glass aside. 'I've grown up with everyone telling me my dad was my best friend. What *do* I do about that? Can't turn back time and get to know him all over again or something.'

'Would you, though, if you could? Turn back time?' she asks.

I think about that a lot. What would it change, knowing Pai? I want it more than anything. 'Yeah.' And just because the curiosity gets me, 'Would you?'

'Would I . . .' Shantal looks away, towards the coastline. 'I never said I had anyone . . .'

I can feel the melancholy filling the space between us. I *had* to go there. Guilt heavy in my stomach, I lie down, staring directly into the sun, the picnic blanket warm against the back of my perpetually sore neck. Voice soft, I whisper to her, 'I'm sorry.'

Back when I first met her, I remember thinking I wanted nothing more than to *know* about Shantal. To know her reasons, know why she looked at Ipanema that way. As I watch her now, following my motion and lying back on the blanket, I start to very slowly find out why.

For a moment I don't think she's going to say anything. She's gazing up into the sun just as I am. We'll burn our corneas out like this. But she turns to me, and her eyes are heavy with tears. She tucks a curl behind her ear with a sigh. 'I'd give everything I have, Darien. For my sister.'

Her sister.

Someone she grew up with, did everything with. I picture two little girls with matching hairstyles chasing each other around a park or kicking around a football. I always wanted a brother, though I never got one. Would have killed to have somebody to share my life with.

'My mom says the same thing about my dad.' My chest is suddenly tight with grief for her, even though I've experienced none of it, and can scarcely call back my own. 'That's why we moved to America. He's everywhere for her in Rio. She never found anyone else, either. Said if Pai wasn't there by her side, no one else would be.'

'That is just how it feels.' Shantal's hair brushes my cheek as she struggles to put the same damper on her emotions as she has always done. But she can't do it this time.

I watch her eyelashes flutter like the paper-thin wings of a butterfly. 'I was spoiled by Guyana and by my family's love. When we came to England, I lost Guyana. And when Sonia died, she took all the love with her. All of it, every last drop. And so if someone were to shackle themselves to me, Darien, I'm scared I would have no love left to give.'

My heart aches so hard that I can physically feel it. Is this what my beautiful mother went through, what I know nothing of?

I remember something my mom said once, in one of the fleeting moments when she was able to talk about Pai. They were few and far between, but this, I can recall clear as day.

'Once you've felt so much for someone and they leave, all you wanna do is feel that again.'

I don't know what's in my head, but I reach out and wrap an arm around her, and she leans into me. I want to close the distance between us and take away everything that's hurting her. I don't want her to ever, ever feel a shred of pain again. I'd fight off the first person that so much as attempted to cause her the slightest harm. I know we're humans, all of us, breakable by nature, but if anyone deserves to be free from the threat of breaking, it's Shantal. It's always going to be Shantal.

Chapter Thirty-Nine

Darien

Monaco – the jewel in the crown of F1, concealing dangerously sharp turns and narrow tracking – was a race I'd been waiting for during this first half of the season. It tests your mettle to the limit – are you just another kid with fire in his belly, or are you willing to go the extra mile? In an interview after his first win, Miguel called it a siren song: luring you in with its pretty architecture and picturesque streets, and then hitting you with a corner so sharp you can barely see it coming. The quick gear changes and abrupt turns are menacing, but Miguel and I have trained hard to perfect these movements. We leave Monte Carlo with a perfect one-two, and even though I'm P2, I bag an extra point for fastest lap.

Canada, Spain and Hungary, subsequent race weekends, fly by after that, and I bring home one more win and two podiums. It's looking optimistic heading into the halfway point of the season. Miguel and I are tight up in P1 and P2 for the title, which is great, but there's still that little voice in the back of my head greedily growling for more – for the WDC. I'm pushing as hard as I can . . . and I'm trying my best to avoid the growing concern regarding the arm. Celina's aware that it's been bothering me in the car, and I've been trying to ignore it, but she gave me a dire warning after a particularly chaotic race in Hungary.

'Darien, you have to understand.' She looked at me with that disappointed adult look in her eyes that people direct towards misbehaving kids. 'With every second you race, you're worsening an injury that never properly got to recover. Just know that the second the pain gets too much for you, I'm pulling you out of the car.'

It doesn't seem long till we end up in England – Shantal's home – for the final weekend before summer break, and a walk around the track bright and early on a Thursday morning. Silverstone, unlike Monaco, is all about speed. As one of the fastest current circuits, it can be both exciting and disastrous to race around, but I'd prefer to keep it exciting. React and act at the same time. I can do this.

'Isn't this the only race you'd ever watched before you came our way?' Miguel teases an excited Shantal as she walks between us. The default walk is made a bit more special by the fact that today, Shantal has asked to join us. We couldn't say no, and I couldn't resist a chance to do something special for her while she's at *her* home race.

Shantal's hand brushes mine softly, her fingers intertwining themselves in mine. It happens so naturally; I don't even realize it until she squeezes my hand with a smile. 'Yeah, just Silverstone.'

'Oh, you've not seen any of the *Triple Crown races*?' Miguel makes a dramatically appalled face, pausing to turn to Shantal. 'I mean – I take it back, you did see Monaco this year. That's one of three jewels in the Triple Crown. Puts you in the history books for good.'

'Okay, so maybe I'm uninformed on the sport,' admits Shantal, 'but I've tried to do research. The Triple Crown: that's the Indy 500, Le Mans and Monaco – correct? You win it, you join the ranks of legends.'

'You pass on that one.' I tip my head in a challenge. 'Okay, so what about Silverstone? How come drivers love it here?'

'Just look at how the track lets you really push the car.' She grins. 'High speed, high intensity, everything multiple times faster than half the other tracks on the schedule. Absolute insanity, of course, but exactly your thing.'

'You've come to know me too well.'

The trainers give us directions on the turns, Louie addressing Miguel while Celina gets on my case. I remember all the aggressive muscle-control exercises the trainers had us doing for those first couple weeks, the adaptive simulation program we've been doing before each race, the resultant tick-up in our times so far. I'm hoping it'll work its magic on one of the tracks where quick reaction matters most; you only have so much time to respond to threats when you're moving faster than the average race. I'm also hoping that however abrupt these reactions are, my body – my arm – will be able to withstand it. Above all, I need my mind at 100 per cent.

Silverstone is a test of will. On this track, if you're not willing to pull through on any move you make, you're screwed. As fun a race as it is, the turns are quick, the Gs brutal. 'Commit,' Celina would always tell me when I was starting out in Formula 1 at Heidelberg. 'If you're not gonna commit, you fall through, you fall off, and you're done.'

I've had problems at Silverstone before, though. It was all the interviewers could talk about today, and it's all they talk about every year I'm here.

Vittore, my first Formula 1 team, was a year of my life I'd

give much to forget. It was me and a dude six years older than me, Christian Clay. He was the poster child for preferential treatment. An extra tyre-change here, an inversion – swapping cars so he was in front – in his favour there. Our principal, Roche Bernelli, would call me into the office and give me a dressing down for the smallest mistake; Christian would get a light tap on the wrist.

I was *pardo* – mixed – with *pardo* parents, so on this grid, with my mom's honey-coloured skin and my dad's chaotic 3C curls, I stuck out like a sore thumb. I was pretty sure I was already at a disadvantage, I just hadn't expected my own team to make it worse.

It was at my first Silverstone Grand Prix that things escalated. I was called in to pit around the same time as my teammate, and when I got in, nothing was ready for me, not a single tyre. Back on the track, I still managed to stay ahead of Clay, but the team order was inevitable. 'Let him past.' I did. He got overzealous in the chase and spun out with three laps left.

After that, I seemed to be fair game for Clay in press rounds, who blamed me for whatever might have upset his race. He once complained that he couldn't make things work in a situation where he had 'a scrappy kid from the streets' as a teammate. I didn't realize how *bad* the abuse was till I moved on.

I got no offers for the next season because my performances appeared to be so poor, epitomized by the Silverstone incident. If Demir hadn't called me up on Christmas Eve, telling me he saw promise in my driving, that he wanted me on next season, I would have been out of Formula 1 for good.

I've gotten to race two Silverstones since then, and this is the third. It's my shot at redemption, proof that I can bounce back. A P1 here? I imagine my Tia Manuela and Tio Julio watching, the two people who'd helped me through that terrible year at Vittore.

It'd be *unbelievable*.

It's minutes till I get in the car, and I'm not in the same state of mind I usually am. But I don't hate the change.

If I bag this, I bag it for myself, yeah, but I also bag it for Shantal. Learning about everything she's been through has only made me more desperate to make this season worth it for her. She's put so much of herself – what she had left – into this team. It's time for us to carry our end of the bargain. I can't fix all the things that happened to her before, but I can try to weave something beautiful into the future.

Now, in the paddock, she runs her thumb across my cheek before getting on her tiptoes the way she always does and planting a kiss there. Her fingers trace the wings inked on my neck and fall away sooner than I'd like them to. 'Your father is keeping an eye out for you,' she whispers gently, giving me a slight nudge towards my helmet waiting on its pedestal in our garage. 'Go fly.'

This is what I'm good at, I remind myself as she waves to me and hops up on her chair on the pit wall.

As I get in the car, as I leave the garage, and then as I'm on the track and the lights flash on, I repeat the mantra in my mind. *This is how I grew up racing. High speed, low stress. All instinct.*

We're off down the main straight before I can comprehend it. I kick into the same mode I've adopted the past few races, one where I'm just here to drive the only way I know how. I let go of the pressure, and I surge ahead, slipping through a gap between Miguel and Diana to creep ahead of my teammate and towards his fiancée.

Diana puts up one hell of a fight, but this time, I'm ready. My muscles remember every single exercise the trainers drilled into us, those rough turns the sim kept putting me through with its stupid adaptive algorithm, and the next curve is a fight that tips in my favour. I anticipate, brake as late as I can, and zoom over the kerb, surging in front of Diana.

'Up into the lead,' Afonso tells me.

I whoop, wrenching the car around yet another nerve-wracking turn just in time to defend my position. If I give Diana a gap, I know damn well she's going to take it, so I have to deny her the option altogether.

On the track, in that perfect position where I grow my delta with every passing lap, I get so comfortable that I can look around outside and take in the scenery of the iconic Silverstone. Everything else becomes irrelevant. It all fades into the background, which should probably be a red flag, especially on such a dangerous high-speed circuit, but it's nothing less than beautiful to me, all of it.

The deltas start to widen after the first two laps. I get well out of DRS range for Diana, making it even harder for her to chase me down on a straight. We set our sights on holding the defensive and outpacing Peter, who's starting to climb the ranks behind us, managing our tyres well enough to catch him tripping. Every bit of strategy is going just the way it should.

I wonder if it's a sign from Pai, him helping me out in this battle for redemption, not to mention the title. The sun's out in what's been one of the rainiest calendar races; conditions are ideal, strategy is taking, and I'm right where I'm supposed to be.

At least for a moment.

It's twelve laps before I feel my wrist give out. A horrific pain shoots up my arm. I bite my tongue through what feels like a power drill shredding my bones.

I can't do this right now. I steer to the outside and slow down. My tyres screech sloppily against the kerb. Shit. And then there's Peter, arcing around me, claiming that lead. It's like a knife to the gut when I'm already down. It rips away at old scars.

'Darien, come in,' Afonso's voice crackles over the radio. 'Are you all right?'

I shouldn't, but I lie. And I do so knowing full well I'll pay the price at the end of this race.

'Yeah, man. All good.'

The sort of fight I put up for the rest of the British Grand Prix is one that no one will ever find out about. I chase down Peter relentlessly, even as my body yells at me, telling me this is the last thing I should be doing right now. I try to calm myself, but this isn't like last time. The consequences I'm suffering won't have it. My arm explodes in stabbing aches with every turn of the steering wheel, and I push back at the urge to rip my glove off and scream in pain. I finish my race anyway. That was drummed into me at Vittore. Do whatever you need to, but never, *never*, throw away your race.

At the end of it, I'm in second place, and I can't feel my entire right arm. All I can feel is the aftermath of the pressure when you're in the car – the eyes on you, hoping you get through it in one piece, hoping you bring back a trophy.

As I park my car at the P2 board and get out to congratulate Peter and Diana, make my way to the weigh-in station, I wonder that to myself. What would my dad have said if he knew the condition I'd raced in today? It's a million pins to my heart when I realize I can't ask that question. The reason I raced in this condition was his absence. I can't lose my season. I just can't.

Chapter Forty

Shantal

The mass of fans behind us are roaring along with the entire Heidelberg team. 'OHHH, DARIEN CARDOSO,' they sing-shout to the tune of 'Seven Nation Army'. But I know something is wrong. With his helmet still on, Darien clambers out of the cockpit and steps outside, raising his arms in acknowledgement to the fans in the stands. He gives them a quick wave before hurrying towards us, and without so much as a nod at the chaos all around him, the entire team rejoicing, stops in front of me.

'Shantal,' he says, voice strained. 'Can you take off my helmet?'

My eyes travel to his bad arm. He tugs at the sleeve covering it, clutching the wrist, but he stops as soon as he realizes I've noticed.

'Darien—'

'Please,' he pleads.

Though my hands shake, I undo all the clasps and raise the

neck brace. I remove his helmet. He pulls off his balaclava with his left hand, and now the pain in his eyes is clear as day.

He doesn't let me so much as glance at him after that. He disappears into the crowd of team members to say his thank-yous, and the bunch of us begin to make our way to the podium. We watch as he accepts his trophy and raises it high with one hand.

Darien is herded down from the podium to celebrate with the team once more, and from where I stand against the paddock gates, I hear cheers go up from the centre of the clump of Heidelberg staff when Demir lavishes high praise on Darien.

I stay behind after the raucous mob has filtered out of the garages and made its way into the Paddock Club for a bit of an impromptu dinner. There's too much on my mind to want to go there. I'm supposed to know how to fix my players, my drivers, and I don't even know where to begin here. If Darien doesn't tell me what's going on, I can't help him, and for me, that's the hardest part. I want to fix everything. Accepting that I cannot has never come easily to me.

Something *is* wrong. But all I can do is wait.

I end up sitting at my laptop in the hotel scrolling through data.

Darien's data are stunning, as they've always been. You couldn't tell from looking at the charts that he'd ever got into any kind of accident and just now returned. There is a single trough where he had to leave the track mid-race when, I assume, he found himself in some sort of pain. But other than that, it doesn't matter. I wonder what it will take for him to see that, too.

As if on cue, my phone dings with a notification – a text message. And it's from Darien.

I open it desperately. Is he ready to talk? If this is reinjury, we have a week till the next race. Celina will need to move fast and try to fix this.

I need you Shantal

Damn it.

A cacophony of hypotheticals escorts me to Darien's hotel room just a few doors down from mine. The thoughts flood my brain until the stress they cause manifests as a cold sweat breaking out all over my body.

'Darien,' I call through the half-open door, 'it's Shantal. I'm here.'

I slip inside and close the door behind me. He's not in the kitchen or the living room. I check the bedroom – still nothing.

And then the bathroom, and there he is, breaking my heart into a million pieces.

He's sitting in the tub fully clothed, with the shower running on full blast. He leans against the back wall with his eyes squeezed shut, a look of defeat etched across his face, as the water comes down forcefully, drenching his hair, his T-shirt, his jeans. The freezing shower: desensitizing, distracting.

'Oh, Darien.' I crouch down beside him and rest my arms and chin on the edge of the tub. I try not to let my emotions show plainly on my face; it will only make him feel worse, I know. But they slip through. I feel my brow crease and my lips purse. His eyes flutter open, and they're strained, torn.

'Why is this happening?' he whispers, his voice strained, like the plea of a small child still trying to learn how the world works. He grimaces, holding his bad hand back and cradling it the way I've seen so many footballers do. Injuries are awful the first time around, but reinjury is arguably much, much worse for both the body and mind. 'Fuck this, Shantal . . .'

'It's okay. It's okay,' I repeat, as if saying it over and over will make it true.

'What if I can't race, Shantal? What if I lose my dad?'

'I'm here. Don't worry.'

I reach across and squeeze his hand, and then I step into the tub, too. Cold water begins to lap at my feet. The shower immediately soaks through my thin tee and sweatshorts, but I don't care. I lean down and push Darien's wet waves of hair back before pressing a kiss to his forehead.

My eyes are closed; all I feel is his left hand at my cheek. I sit down beside him, and he leans into me, his head to my shoulder as I hold him close. I've never felt this way about anyone; never this defensive, never this protective. A touch is a touch, until it holds so much more than what is skin deep.

'Let's take a shower, love,' I whisper. His breathing is even and yet laden with hurt. I can feel it against my body.

Darien pulls his shirt over his head with my help. I kneel before him, grab the soap bottle off the shelf in the corner of the shower, and pump more than enough into my hands.

When I had taken the Rio job, I had never imagined I would allow myself to become so close to someone. Yet I am here now, drenched in this bathtub as I vow that I would do anything for this man, this man who has done *so* much for me.

Gently, I begin to cover his skin with the soap. My hands are shaky against his body at first, but they steady when I realize that he is familiar. His strong arms, the solid planes of his chest, scars and tattoos I have unwittingly memorized. A name here, the flag of Brazil there, a pair of dice, a cross entangled with a rosary. That stick-and-poke happy face on the side of his right wrist. If there was a detail that I hadn't noticed yet, I take it in now.

His eyes slowly rise from the floor of the tub to meet mine, slightly red-rimmed, as beautiful a deep brown as they've always been. It is a symphony of pain and intimacy and stinging. The shower water pounds down around us and drips down our faces as I reach behind Darien, my chest flush with his, my T-shirt clinging to his skin as I spread the soap across the terrain of his muscles. My breath quickens and catches like a broken record.

I know I should stop. But from here, from this place where my body fits against his like pieces of a puzzle, I don't know if I can so much as move.

'Stay,' Darien murmurs into my wet hair. 'Please stay, Shantal.'

His voice is rough, heavy with desperation. It paralyzes me. It forces me to grow roots that anchor me here.

My legs seem to act of their own volition, positioning me so I can sit with my back to his chest as his thighs press against my hips. I lean back, his mouth finds mine, and what his hands cannot convey to me, his lips do. He kisses me the way someone begs for a miracle. His kiss is a string of words that I don't need to hear to believe.

Thank you.

You're what I've needed.

Every single inch of you.

Even through a layer of wet clothing, the heat of him is palpable on my skin, separated only by the water. I slowly bring his left hand up under my top. I need him closer, and the way he touches me, he needs the same.

'Turn around,' Darien barely whispers, his breath hot on my ear. I do, bracing myself by his shoulders, my shorts and shirt heavy with water. Darien's touch is still stiff, but even as I wrap my legs around him, even with his limitation of movement, his good hand grips my thigh. He lays kisses down my collarbone, making me shiver despite the growing cloud of steam in the shower. His hand moves up, fingers teasing at the waistband of my shorts. I don't think I can take it.

I press my lips to his as if I am starving and will not live

235

another day. My hips jolt forward against him and he groans into my mouth. I stay with him, the only place I can conceive of in this moment.

'I'm sorry.' Darien's voice is husky yet broken as I hold him to me. 'For the way this . . . this injury messed me up . . .'

'I don't care,' I gasp, my voice cracking, 'if you can't . . . can't take off your helmet. I don't even care if you can't race, Darien.'

'No?' The word is almost a whimper.

'No.' I tangle my fingers in his hair, brush water from his cheeks. 'I care that I can still *feel* you.'

Darien buries his head in my shoulder. His hair tickles my jaw. 'I do, too,' he murmurs. 'I do, too, Shanni.'

Shanni.

I cannot tell where water-flow ends and where tears begin. He can't have known, but that name has not felt right coming from anyone else for so long. That name was Sonia's first, until everyone else picked it up, and then, a year ago, it began to sound foreign. Estranged. Yet every syllable fits perfectly on his lips.

He murmurs it into my hair, into my neck, like an incantation, a plea.

Darien peels off my wet shirt and throws it aside, helping me to my feet as I shimmy out of my soaked shorts. Nothing is enough, no amount of proximity sufficient. My back presses against the wall of the shower, and the soap bottle falls to the floor with a loud crash that we both ignore. The softness and the passion of Darien's touch melt me completely. He tears my bra off as I work furiously at the button of his jeans; we are desperate for absolutely nothing to come between us. He moves a hand to my hip while he kisses me, a hand that slowly travels down the inside of my thigh till his fingers brush the edge of my panties, neither giving me what I want nor denying it completely. I hate him all the more for it as his touch creeps beneath the lacy fabric.

I manage a breathy laugh that turns into a moan when he uses just the right amount of pressure in just the right place. He covers my lips with his and catches the next plea that escapes me. My eyes nearly roll back in my head when his fingers shift slightly lower.

'You ready, Shanni?' he whispers, lips skimming the spot beneath my jaw.

I don't know if I can let him tease me a minute more. I hang on to him as if he's a tree in the middle of a storm. I can manage little but his name and my assent. He's left me completely speechless. I've had little to say in the last year, but now, when I could tell him so much, I can only hope he knows.

Even with the hot water from the shower, my skin goes cold when he reaches over to the cabinet below the sink and comes back with a condom that he quickly rolls on before turning his attention back to me. 'How you want me, *mina?*' He presses his forehead to mine and meets my eyes in that way he has, making certain I'm good. 'Just tell me. I'm here.'

'I don't know.' I kiss him, and I kiss him again, and I feel him smiling as I pull myself closer to him. He *is* here, and for me; nothing else matters about this. 'I don't know how. I just want you.'

'Yeah. Yeah.' He exhales hard, a rush of air I can feel on the bridge of my nose. I swear, he shivers a little, and that's all the reassurance I need. He hooks a finger around the side of my panties and slides them off. My entire body quivers with anticipation. His erection presses against my thigh as he holds me to him.

'I just want you,' I murmur again. My thumb traces circles on his back, and I feel his muscles relax slightly. I use my legs to bring myself right up against him, and he moves his hand to hold my waist with the barest squeeze of assurance: *I've got you.*

It's a moment before Darien finally slips inside me, and I lift my hips, gripping his back with so much force that I'm surprised he doesn't flinch. His lips find mine, and mine find his name. 'Dar.'

The first thrust is slow. The pressure it builds in me tears away at any filter I may have had at some point. I gasp, and he groans, moves back slightly before another thrust, this one with much more purpose. Something about us is perfect. It's not like everything else before this; it's effortless. Stars dance before my closed eyelids like Darien's shimmering diamond earrings. Every time he pulls away and comes back to me is a new wave of thrill that fills my abdomen and releases a loud moan from my body.

He replies with a grunted 'Shit, Shanni,' and the rhythm of every beat of my pulse matches our movement. My muscles are shaking with anticipation; I hang on to Darien for dear life. His breathing is heavy and fast against my neck, his arm wrapped around me to leave as little a gap between our bodies as possible. It is absolutely surreal that I thought I could keep suppressing how badly I *needed* him. He does everything right, from the way it feels like we were made for one another, to the way my name is tangled in his gasps, to the way he balances a little bit of passion with a little bit of wild. His hand finds the back of my head, shielding it from the wall, taking the brunt of the impact with his forearm. I kiss him sloppily, my ability to stand on my own two feet waning and the pressure mounting.

'I'm so close, Dar,' I whimper, kissing him again. 'I'm . . .'

'Hang on, *mina*.' He shifts slightly, and then *holy crap*.

People use the term 'toe-curling', but that is what this feeling is. My soul nearly leaves my body as I cry out his name, over and over, squeezing my eyes shut to relish every moment of this.

I have barely enough in me to keep going, but I anchor

myself to Darien and give him the extra push over the edge that it takes for that beautiful sound of bliss to leave him. I feel him quiver with the same ecstasy that still fills me as he gasps for breath. My fingers trace the tattoos that cover his arms. It's a good few moments before we pull apart, making me feel as if I am missing a part of myself when I lean against Darien with a contented sigh.

We clean up, return the fallen soap bottle to its spot in the shower. Darien wraps me in a fluffy white robe, nothing but a towel around his waist so I can still take in his strong form and inhale his fresh scent of sandalwood. Then, both of us completely spent, we curl up in bed, me wearing his pajamas, him enveloping me with his warm arms, his head against my chest. I run my hands through his slightly damp waves of hair, follow the light streaks of blond.

'Shanni, I've never . . .'

His sleepy voice catches me off-guard, halfway between waking and out cold. He pulls away, levelling his eyes with mine. There's a dopey smile on his face and in his half-lidded irises. Maybe he's not fully aware of what he says next, but I will never forget it.

'Never met a woman who . . . gives me goosebumps the way you do. You give me the damn chills, lady.'

'I'd better, the way I'm going to make sure you do your exercises this week,' I mumble with a giggle.

Darien laughs, a low rumble that I can feel in my own chest, as he burrows his head in the crook of my neck. 'I'll take it.'

I think for a brief moment about sleeping in and missing our flight out to the next race, but that's second to the gravity of where we are right now. We forget about leaving. We simply feel one another.

Chapter Forty-One

Shantal

'The numbers from Imola were slightly off in some places, but I believe, given the constraints, there's clearly a trend upward there.'

I nod, maybe a little too vigorously, but I'm relieved. With Conquest, I don't particularly remember having a fear of my boss—he tends to be the conduit rather than the final say. During the Crystal Palace project, it was the team's manager who had the authority to disband our arm of the training division. So it's a weight off my shoulders when Afshin Demir sings my praises to Conquest over this end-of-half-season video call.

My boss, an older middle-aged man named Paul Marchese who'd once (allegedly) shaken hands with the Queen, beams from his little rectangle on my screen beside Demir. 'I've received the data. Shantal, I have to agree with Mr Demir. It's a pleasure to see such improvement. Even after Heidelberg's team fed it through the software to make sure we aren't looking at an increase in lap times due to the car or the drivers – thank you, Mr Demir, for that – it's brilliant data. We see this excellent curve when we look at Darien and Miguel's turn times from last year moving on to this one, and factoring out the handling on the vehicles, their reaction times are beautiful.'

'And those are the little things. We haven't even mentioned the trophies,' points out Demir with a smile. 'This is the most successful season Heidelberg Hybridge has enjoyed in a long time. Mr Marchese and Ms Mangal, I don't believe I can thank your team enough. So Ms Mangal, we would be delighted should you choose to remain with us for the rest of the season. I'm sure our staff and drivers would absolutely appreciate it.'

I peer at Marchese's rectangle to gauge his reaction, and it's a series of excited nods as vigorous as mine.

'Of course, we completely understand if you would like to return to—'

'I'd *love* to stay on,' I blurt suddenly.

For a minute, I think I'm screwed, having cut off the team principal of Heidelberg Hybridge in his own video call, but a grin quickly spreads across his face. 'Oh, *wonderful*.'

The call ends with all kinds of gushing and pleasantries, and when I close my laptop, I can't quite believe what I've done.

I was the one with the least hope when I arrived here. I remember the way my blood seemed to freeze when I thought about doing any of this on my own. But now I have proved myself. The data curves, in true sports-nerd fashion, still flash before my vision. *Brilliant data*. Data we developed the mechanism for.

I get up from my desk chair and push it in, adjusting Sonia's ever-present photo. Her smile seems a little bigger. A little more optimistic.

'I'll get until December now,' I tell her. 'Among the stars. You'd love it. And I guess, maybe . . . you'd love him.'

It almost makes me laugh to myself. It feels like the ground has moved beneath my feet since the events of just a few days back. I wonder if that has to do with how badly my thawing heart seems to want to make room for someone else. And I can't say I don't crave the stolen glances, the minute touches, the air of shared understanding. The feeling of that kiss in Imola.

'Among the stars,' I repeat. Darien's got some recovery to do, but the team is on the rise. I've earned myself approval, and more time here. Time to be *free*.

Perhaps the stars are closer than I ever imagined they could be.

Chapter Forty-Two

Darien

Summer break is my signal to finally breathe for a few weeks. Miguel and Diana head back to Dubai, where they're bound to be entrenched in wedding planning for the break. Henri is here for a week before he goes home to Perth to spend time with his family. As for me, I stay behind in Rio to pay my dues.

Shantal makes it clear she's not even entertaining the notion of returning to London for the second half of the season. She puts me through absolute hell in sims over the next week to restore my arm strength. Her and Celina's combined might is actually pretty terrifying, but it starts to work its magic in the days before the factory shutdown is lifted. Shantal doesn't once let me believe that things can go downhill. She's determined – sometimes more than I am.

And it's a shock to me when the night before we leave Rio for the season restart race at Spa, Belgium, she asks me for the biggest favour.

'I think we should go karting,' insists Shantal after a particularly heinous round of practice on the sim. She sits down in the simulator beside mine and perches her elbows on the steering, her chin atop her hands.

'Karting?'

'You've had too much *edge* this past week. This past season,' she says, her eyes skating over me in concern. 'You know as well as I do what that does to an athlete. I want you to remember what was fun about this sport.'

'I mean . . . it was always a fight for the win,' I try, but Shantal holds out a hand.

'But you had fun fighting for the win, didn't you? As a child, do you remember that? When we were able to enjoy things, no strings attached? No sponsors?' Her voice is gentle, and in it, I hear the personal sentiment. I think about her time in football, the way she laughed and manoeuvred the ball with such little effort, second nature, when we played way back at the beginning of the year. That smile on her face, the love of the sport so plain to see.

'There's a little track,' I finally say. 'Out near Jardim Botânico.'

Shantal smiles, and I see her feet bounce in anticipation. 'I'm so ready.'

It's almost eleven at night when we drive out to the track, just outside the gardens, where the grass is greener than anything you'll ever see in your life, and the stars a brighter silver. I park the car, and we get out. A cloud of humidity still hangs in the air, layered with a slight chill. I'm glad I've got pyjama pants and a T-shirt, plus a sweatshirt in the car just in case.

The small track has long been abandoned. Its narrow turns and simple straights are overgrown with vines and brush that I can make out in the flickering floodlights. But for me, my mom still cheers from the grass. My dad and my uncle still run beside my kart as they give it a push-off, and I drive it down the straight for the first time.

'Maybe you will be on a track much bigger than this someday,' Pai would say, 'but remember where you truly became a racer. On our streets, and here.'

I make my way to the starting line, picking my way through the unruly weeds. I find the faded white dashes before I crouch and sit down on the cracked asphalt. I run my hands over the crevices and gashes of the very place where my passion became determination. I can forget that Pai ever left us when I am here. He still runs alongside my kart and gives my helmet that happy tap after I've done a good lap. Everything I need is right here, where I can be young and free of worry – no career, no races, no team; just a couple of people who loved the way the wind ran through our hair when the top of the car was down.

'You remember this place?' Shantal asks quietly.

I extend a hand her way, and she takes it, sitting down next to me. I hold her close, and her head falls to my shoulder. 'First track I raced on, ever.'

She's silent as we take it all in, the simplicity of it. The track doesn't have stands. There's no room for a crowd. A small shed sits off to one side, where we used to store the karts.

'We don't have to drive,' she whispers with a squeeze of my shoulder. 'It's okay.'

I take a deep breath. I close my eyes and listen to the sputtering of my kart's power unit as it goes round and round: the sound of a kid from the city finding his grip.

'I think we do.' I turn to her with a small smile. 'Let's get the karts.'

We unload our go-karts from the back of the pickup I brought from the Ring. Shantal is racing my number sixty-seven, and my kart bears Pai's old number, forty-two. They're old pieces of machinery, but functional nonetheless. I've been keeping them in my garage in Santa Teresa, and I've only brought mine out on a couple of rare occasions.

I drive his car, but I've never been able to bring myself to drive this kart, to drive with his number. It's always been something I fundamentally associate with *him*. Something that belongs to him, not me. Never me.

I kneel down next to the kart, and Shantal joins me, glancing up at me, pressing a hand to the number plate on its small chassis. 'What do you feel, Dar?'

With a fisted hand to my mouth, I exhale, hoping it will stop the way my bottom lip starts to quiver. 'I've been looking for my dad all my life.'

I close my eyes in thought, and images of a parade of brightly coloured feathered costumes and floats flash before me. A grove of palm trees, my bare feet in the grass, a family dancing together, street football in the winding paths of the streets, the canary-coloured tram weaving around our little town.

'I've always been under this pressure to keep racing. Shanni, if I stopped, I let him go. If I lose him for ever, I'd just . . .'

'Maybe,' she starts, her eyes glistening as they meet mine, 'it's time to stop living within shadows. Maybe it's time to step out from those shadows and choose ourselves.' She takes both my hands in hers and nods at the kart. 'You are more than deserving of this, Darien. Everything you've done, everything you are . . . it's what your father always dreamed of. I know it is.'

I let Shantal wrap me in a gentle hug and bring us to our feet. Her careful embrace slips from around my body as she heads towards my old kart.

'Teach me how to drive,' she says, pulling herself into the seat of the vehicle.

'You gotta hold the steering like this. Give it gas, brake slightly before the turn. Not in, but before, and let the kart carry into the curve. Never use both gas and brakes at the same time . . .'

Shantal grins, gesturing towards kart number forty-two. 'I got this. Are you not going to give it a shot?'

It's time.

It takes more strength than my entire recovery ever did for me to get into that driver's seat. The buckle is still adjusted to fit Pai – he was way taller than me, way stockier, so I have to pull the straps shorter. I click on the belt, and my hands curl around the steering, my feet at the pedals.

'Go, go, go!' Pai laughs from somewhere in the distance.

I floor it, and the start is a little choppy, but the kart still glides easily along the main straight, even after all these years. It picks up speed, and there beside me is my dad, beaming and running, clapping his hands, calling to my mom to take a video with the chunky handheld camcorder as I head into the first turn of the small track.

They say you can hear a heart when it breaks, but I realize today that it's the same for one that's being put back together. As I drive with Shantal, calling out directions, teaching her everything my father taught me, the engines growl loudly, and my heart mends itself.

There on the old racetrack, this time without my parents and my uncle, I start to find my grip once more.

Chapter Forty-Three

Darien

After the break, it's no secret I'd rather be with Shantal the entire weekend than sit in the car and lock in for my drives.

Spa week is a test. Now, Shantal's workload has lightened significantly, and it's mine that's gotten heavier. I dart around doing promos, meetings, briefings on the probability of all kinds of Championship outcomes and what I need to do to get there, interviews, car checks, you name it. The last time we spent more than ten minutes together, alone, was probably at the karting track in Rio. I text her whenever I get a second, feel the tingle of anticipation in my stomach when my phone vibrates in return, hide a smile in whatever meeting I'm sitting through. But it's not comparable to having her by my side during it all.

And then, with less than twenty-four hours till race weekend, I realize that with a little elbow grease and a lot of roping in my mechanics, there may just be a way that's possible.

It takes us a good part of the night before the qualifier in Spa-Francorchamps to get everything together, but we get it

248

done, and at some point I practically pass out from exhaustion. Next morning, I'm up bright and early for practice, shovelling waffles in my mouth at Hospitality before heading down to the track.

I find Shantal on the pit wall as usual, already looking through projections for the weather with Afonso. My hands are literally shaking, I'm so nervous. What if she doesn't like it? What if it's too much? What if I'm—

'Darien!' She turns to me with a bright smile. She looks a lot better than I do: better rested, tribute to her stringent schedule. She's wearing a black skirt and the usual team shirt, her hair pulled into a tiny ponytail at the back of her head. 'Look. The temperature is brilliant today.'

Afonso shifts the monitor my way, and I let out a low whistle. She's right – the numbers look just comfy enough to drive with minimal deg, which means we can allow ourselves a pretty lax tyre strategy for the day.

Okay. I'm distracting myself from the task at hand. *Get it together, Dar*.

I swallow hard. 'Uh, Shantal. I wanted to . . . wanted to show you something?'

She hops out of her chair with a look of curiosity. 'Oh, am I excited. I hope this isn't another pit barbecue, you know. It's far too cold here for that.'

'I promise, it's not.' We walk into my garage, where the car sits on its own, still no crew to be seen. It's fairly early, but I've gotten everything in order.

I reach across her to the tool cabinets and grab my steering from the top of one of them where I've haphazardly perched it. I don't know exactly what to say, so I hand her the entire thing.

'Wha . . .' Shantal's confusion turns to concentration when she turns it around, to the spot on the back of drivers' wheels

249

where there is usually a name and number over the glossy carbon fibre. Here, I've decided to leave out my name. I've written hers. *Shantal* is printed across the steering in easy, loose cursive. Her cursive, ripped from a photo taken back at the start of the season, when she'd signed her name on my copy in shimmering silver Sharpie marker.

She runs a slim finger over the swoops and curls in each letter. Her eyes flick up to mine, full of burgeoning tears. 'What is this?'

'Oh, man, Shantal, I didn't mean to make you . . . don't cry,' I plead, taking her face in my hands. 'I'm sorry, I'm—'

'You do *so much* for me,' she whispers, still clutching my steering wheel. 'No one has ever . . . Why do you do it, Darien?'

'Because you've already done so much for me.' I feel my own eyes starting to go watery, my own chest tightening. 'Listen, Shantal, I want you to know that this is all my cards on the table. You stuck with me through every second of that hellish recovery. I've never met anyone so loyal, so radiant. I've gotten to watch you come out of your shell, to watch you smile again. I've learned just how strong you are. And to tell you the truth, I'm in disbelief. I'm telling you, I can say all these things, but I'm going to pull through. So I want you to drive with me.' I brush my thumb across her cheek to push away an errant droplet, and I tap the cursive script on the steering wheel. 'Every lap.'

I don't know what I expect, but Shantal sets the steering back on the cabinet, leans in and presses her lips to mine. It's all my answers; it's everything I need to know. She pulls away, and she hugs me tight, and I hear every single word when she says quietly, 'That would be my honour.'

Getting into the car, I feel the kind of euphoria I've never, ever felt behind the wheel before. My fingers brush Shantal's name on the steering, and a new kind of motivation, something bigger than myself, fills my body. I drive not because I have something to prove, not because there is a pay cheque at stake, but because this is one of the first things I ever learned to love.

I win at Spa on Sunday.

My fastest lap time, 1:45.348, is an all-time track record.

I've never driven like that in my life.

Chapter Forty-Four

Shantal

Darien stands atop his car, raising his right arm and pointing to it with his left as if to yell, 'WHAT NOW,' followed by what we believe is a famous Brazilian goal celebration dance that sends the crowd roaring. He finally clambers down after his moment of fame, the fool, and jumps right over the fence to embrace the team.

The second I'm close enough to him, I grip his helmet and meet his eyes through the visor. They're full of nothing but love for the race, and I couldn't be prouder.

'You just did that!' I almost scream over the frenzied fans.

And although it's faint, I make out every word Darien laughs through when he replies, '*We* just did that.'

The next couple of races are amazing. Darien drives like his tyres are on fire. He sweeps his other 'home' race in America, the United States Grand Prix in Austin, with another P1 directly after his Spa performance. He struggles and ends up with a P5 in Azerbaijan's difficult street circuit, which I can tell severely hurts him, but he's back fast in Monza, where he steals P3, and heads into Zandvoort to take a P2. By the time we reach the Jaipur Grand Prix, the hottest and most treacherous race on the grid, as well as the last hurdle remaining before we go on summer break, there's nothing but determination on his face.

Jaipur, in the two years it has been run, has been Diana's race. In both 2022 and 2023, I find out, she had got pole, with a podium in 2022 and a P1 in 2023; both years, Darien has struggled here. This only bolsters his motivation to break the streak before Diana makes it three podiums.

And he does. He just barely gets the edge on the third-to-last lap, overtaking Diana to steal P3 and nudge his way onto the podium, not only taking his place among the likes of Peter and – this is a shock – Alex Romilly, but doing so with quite some flair, flair that keeps him in the top spot for the World Championship. I'm on my feet screaming with happiness on the pit wall the second it happens, jumping up and down with the ecstatic engineers. No one can believe it. Darien Cardoso-Magalhães is weaving magic.

I click on the lighter till I get a fierce enough flame that I can light the first candle, and then the next, and then the next. I make it to twenty-six before I give up.

'Why are we Stone Age-ing this again?' asks Darien with a yawn from the hotel room bed.

I just roll my eyes with a little laugh. After several – countless – nights together after Silverstone, I've discovered his deepest, darkest secret: his post-sex slump is dramatic; he turns from a cutthroat Formula 1 pilot to a cuddly, sleepy menace. It's like having an extremely large, extremely tired dog in your bed.

'Load-shedding.' I hum, pulling the thin curtains that

separate the room from the outside air open so the breeze can filter in. This entire room, with the open design and balcony, the gilded architecture of the hotel, feels like something out of a palace, which is one of the things I'm finding I love about this city. 'No lights, no air conditioning, at least for the next couple of hours. Your race has used up all the power for the day.'

A gentle wind flutters my shirt (Darien's, technically) as I make my way back over to him and crouch to plant a kiss on his forehead, taming his curls with my fingers.

'No AC?' he almost whines.

'You'll live.'

'I guess.' A lazy grin lights up his face. 'Maybe it's kind of romantic, right?'

'I did just light twenty-six candles, so you might as well take something away from it.'

Darien glances longingly at the thermostat with its dormant display, and then back at me. 'Yeah, good takeaway. Come here.'

I match his smile and clamber straight into the bed, and he wraps his arms around me, the best big spoon in the history of big spoons, one of his strong legs draped across mine. His nose tickles my cheek as his lips find the heavenly place between my jaw and my neck. His touch creeps lower, lower, until he reaches the hem of the shirt, and when his right hand finally finds the heat between my thighs, I can't help but shiver and let out a contented little noise.

'There's no AC,' he whispers against my skin. 'Don't tell me you're cold, it's about a million degrees.'

'Oh, you stop playing with me, Darien.'

'Only if you. Stop. First.' He punctuates every word with a poke of my ribs, and the effect is immediate. The giggles rush out of me as I curl up to save myself from any more torture.

'Fine, I'm stopping! I'm stopping.' I take his hands and

position them right back around me. 'I am not cold, I am in fact comfortably warm, and it's probably because you're generating enough body heat to melt an igloo right now.'

'*Hey!*'

'How is a person so *warm*, Darien?'

'What do you mean, how? Load-shedding, remember?'

'It shouldn't possibly make you this warm. Not when all the blood in your body is *certainly* not evenly distributed right now.'

'Bro, yes, Shanni, I admit it,' he bursts out laughing, face buried in my hair.

I roll over to face Darien, with his messy bed hair and his eyes screwed shut in amusement, and I take his face in both of my hands. 'Okay, you . . . you heated blanket of a human being – go on, will you?'

I can't even get words out between laughs that threaten to burst my lungs and kisses woven with smiles, and there's something beautiful about that. Yes, we're being babies, but I find that beautiful, too. To be at my happiest like this, it's difficult. It hadn't happened for a long time, until I met Darien, and suddenly, I get to be happy every day. I get to laugh over load-shedding and Dar being needy and horny and dramatic, and never once in all this laughter is there space for sadness. I forget about the pain that wrenches at my chest when I think about stepping out of this dream and dealing with reality.

If only for a moment.

Chapter Forty-Five

Shantal

Given a three-week break between Jaipur and Las Vegas, the season coming to an end far faster than seemed possible, the team returns to Rio for some development and well-needed rest. But Darien and I, it turns out, are on a mission, cleverly disguised as a casual walk through the city that eventually brings us to the town of Santa Teresa, where we had taken the tram before Imola.

'And the last stop,' announces Darien as we near a small home much like the others we've passed on our walk. It's surrounded by open grass and trees, with an old Corvette out front. The house is maybe two floors, and just slightly peeling on the façade, but flags and flower baskets hanging at windows spruce it all up.

'What's this?' I ask with a raise of my eyebrow.

'This,' he says happily, 'is family dinner.'

I gasp as I start to put together pieces. 'Oh, Darien, your mom's house? I can't, I wouldn't be—'

He squeezes my hand and nods. There's so much pride in his eyes that I can feel it radiating like the rays of the sun above us. 'Listen, we want you here. You've done so much for me, you know that? This is the least I can do. Get you to meet the people who stood behind me from day one.'

Just as he's wrapping up his thoughts, there's a shout from one of the windows. A woman stands up there, leaning over with a broad grin on her face – a very Darien grin. It's a completely different expression from the one I recall seeing on her face back at the hospital after Darien's accident. She brushes curls from her face, regarding us cheerily. '*Oy! Magalinho!*' she chirps.

'Hey, Mãe!' he yells back. 'Look who's here!'

She turns to me, waving. I'm not sure if she recognizes me from Miami – we hadn't interacted, and I hadn't yet been close with Darien – but the excitement in her voice fills my chest with the warm sensation of hope. 'Come in, my dear!'

I just laugh, waving back to his mom, but something in her happiness fills me with warmth, almost concealing my nervous tension.

Darien leads me up a narrow driveway and down a weaving sidewalk that brings us to a threshold, beyond which is the bright orange front door. He gives it a firm knock.

'Time for you to meet the family,' Darien teases, giving my shoulder a reassuring squeeze.

The door finally creaks open, and there, with the biggest smile across her face, is the woman herself: Darien's mum.

She pulls the door open and immediately brings both of us into an enormous hug. '*Olá, olá.* Oh, how exciting! Darien and Shantal, hmm?'

'Yep,' Darien manages through his mum's sweater.

Mrs Cardoso-Magalhães holds us back at arm's length, regarding us with pride. 'What a beautiful couple. I've been waiting to finally meet you, *filha*.'

She radiates warmth, with the same bronze tan and chocolate

irises as Darien. Her corkscrew curls fall around her face in piles of brown streaked with the smallest hints of blonde, as well as a faint grey. Smile lines just like Darien's crease the corners of her eyes as she holds the door open for us.

'Come on!' Darien grins, taking my hand. 'Come meet everyone.'

I sigh with a laugh as he herds me inside. It's a symphony of colours. Decorative plates, brightly coloured furniture draped in handmade blankets. And the photos, they're everywhere.

'Mãe loves photos,' says Darien, reading my mind. 'I don't remember some of 'em, but this is my favourite.' He points to one that hangs in the living room, next to the clock, visible straight ahead as you enter the house. It looks like both his parents are in it, all three of them standing on a makeshift football pitch in a park. A toddler Darien holds the ball, and his mum and dad are laughing so hard that their eyes are closed.

'Dar!' a new voice calls from the kitchen.

'My cousin, Karolina,' Darien tells me, grinning.

As we approach the kitchen, I realize that the woman standing there is my age: short with dark waves of hair perched in a bun on her head and a faded blue scarf tied at the top as a headband. She wears a loose white dress and slippers. Her eyes look tired, but they glow when they see Darien, and a smile spreads across her face. She has his clever smirk and expressive eyes.

Darien embraces his cousin with jovial greetings as Karolina beams and says something in Portuguese that sends them both into a riot of laughter. She gestures inside, where four other people are craning their necks to see us from around a dining table. *Hello* and *olá* and *e ai* are in the air, happy sounds of reunion.

Before I can even start to take stock of all the people around the table, someone's hustled me into my own chair and put a plate in front of me. Karolina takes a seat beside someone who I believe is her husband. He holds a very loud, very small bundle in his arms.

'My nephew,' whispers Darien. 'Felipe. Total daddy's boy.'

I watch as Karolina smiles down at her son, offering him a finger to hold with that tiny hand of his. Her husband beams down at them both, plants a kiss in her hair.

Something wiggles its way into my heart as I watch them: sadness? Envy?

But I'm quickly distracted from my moment of pause when the family members eagerly turn their attention my way. A tangle of questions in Portuguese fly towards me, and as chaotic as it is, I can feel the affection practically emanate from them. I don't even try to hide my resulting joy. I've longed to feel this chaos, this affection, for the past year.

'Guys, guys!' Darien waves his hands frantically. It's as humorous as it is sweet. '*Não fala português!*'

A resounding 'ohhh' of understanding echoes around the table. There's a momentary bustle to choose a representative speaker before Darien's mum silences all the overlapping chatter with a flail of her hand and an excited little, 'Shantal, let me introduce you. First . . .' She points to Karolina. 'You've met Karolina. Felipe, the littlest; Cassius, his *pai*; and then this here . . .'

'Tia Manuela, Mãe's sister; and Tio Julio,' Darien finishes happily. 'My aunt and uncle.'

Tia looks like she could be a twin to Mrs Cardoso-Magalhães, except for her striking hazel eyes. Tio, in his straw fedora, smiles contentedly at us both, and then, to Darien, says, 'Took you *this* long?'

His remark makes everyone at the table laugh, and I chuckle. The statement reminds me of my family's embarrassing jokes.

They exchange looks full of mischief and excited smiles before Tio Julio turns to me. 'Oh, *filha*, imagine how relieved we are to find out he's *finally* brought a girl home to meet us.'

A blush reddens Darien's cheeks as I glance his way with a barely concealed grin. I'm the first. There's a certain gravitas to that title.

Chapter Forty-Six

Shantal

Family dinner was everything I'd been missing and more.

I got to listen to all the embarrassing baby Darien stories, met two relatives over video call, heard how Darien got his start karting, and received multiple helpings of dinner while I was at it. They lavished affection and kindness like nothing else I've ever experienced. And it was truly beautiful; when it came time for us to leave with full bellies and hearts about to burst of happiness, I almost didn't want to.

But that same little bit of *something* that had threatened to ruin my night wraps its claws around my heart early the next morning. It is the first thing on my mind when my eyes flutter open to the sun peeking through the slats of the blinds in the bedroom of Darien's house in Santa Teresa.

I don't expect the pain to hit me, and I think that's why it hurts so badly.

I watch Darien's back rise and fall with breaths, his hair tousled against the pillow beside me. After the dinner last night, we'd both returned in high spirits, wine-blush staining our cheeks as we laughed our way through the best of each family member's quips. Now, that feels like a distant memory.

I can't stop thinking about Darien's cousin, Karolina, and her family.

I imagine Sonia playing with her son, holding him as he grabs her hand and she smiles down at him, brushing a hair from her face as she leans down to press her cheek to his. I imagine that he grows up, and she takes him back to 63 Beach, where his tiny feet make grubby footprints in the sand when he walks between his parents. He points to a fish in the water and Sonia laughs, hugging him tight.

My throat closes up. My breathing snags.

I can still see her decorating the nursery, a week before she died. She wore these overalls with plain-coloured shirts under them and made scarves into headbands. She hung blue bunting and whales and sailboats on the walls, compared photos to decide which ones should go on the dresser, folded clothes so small you could fit them in her husband's hand. They'd laughed about that, both of them. Creating that room filled them both with joy.

'Shantal.' Darien's voice, sleepy, sounding as if I am underwater and he's on land. 'Hey, Shanni?'

I swing myself out of the bed on unsteady legs, but I need this. I rush over to the sliding doors that open onto the balcony and push them so that I'm outside.

My shoulders heave as I struggle to breathe. Strangled cries escape me. I allow myself, for the first time, to replay what happened that night.

'*Shanni!*'

Darien's voice is panicked behind me. I hear the balcony door slide open and then feel his arms around me, the warmth

261

of his bare torso against mine. He rubs my back and strokes my hair. His heart thuds in sync with mine as he whispers, 'Breathe, Shanni, breathe. God . . .'

He doesn't push me for answers, even though I can feel how badly he wants them. He exhales and rests his chin on top of my head. I don't dare let go of him. Something about being in the midst of that family so full of warmth and love has suddenly sparked grief in me that I never got the chance to properly process. And for so many reasons, it throws up as much guilt as grief.

'*I* didn't know,' I cry into Darien's shoulder. 'That she was . . . dying.'

'She was . . .' Darien's body goes still with shock for a moment, and then softens again when he holds me even tighter. 'Don't say anything. You don't have to say anything.'

'Darien, I *watched* my sister die.' The once-unspoken words are poison, settling in my throat and shredding my vocal cords. 'She was dying, and . . . we could have treated her, Darien, if we had known. But she did nothing, all so her baby could . . .' I press a hand to my mouth. My fingers quiver, and I shake my head. 'We lost them both.'

'Oh, my god.' The realization gradually enters his eyes as they widen with sympathy. 'Shanni, I'm, I'm beyond sorry, I just . . .'

I know. He lacks the words, but so do I. In the depth of that terrible night, I had heard something crash in the kitchen. When I ran down the stairs, I had found Sonia unconscious on the ground. I was the one who called the ambulance.

We don't want to remember people this way. We want to remember people the way they look in their best portraits: glowing, happy, warm . . . alive. She was already going cold when I found her. Dying. My sister, as always, had planned for everything, but as all of us except Rohit, her late husband, learned that night, the cancer had already decided her fate.

Sonia had been suffering from a grade-four glioblastoma, one of the most aggressive forms of brain cancer, for seven months. With treatment, it was possible, if not probable, that her unborn child would not survive. Rohit sobbed as he recounted trying to convince her that it wasn't worth it, but Sonia wouldn't be swayed. The rest of us were told what had happened by the doctor after they tried to revive her for nearly twenty minutes.

Seven months. My sister quietly endured that hell for *seven months* just so her child could live. I think that was the worst part about it, that everything she put herself through was in vain. Sonia's son – my nephew – didn't survive, either. We tried to stay in touch with Rohit for a time after, but eventually he slipped away, moving on to build a new life for himself. I didn't entirely blame him.

'The night before, Darien, she'd just been sitting with me, just talking and reading, and I remember her saying, "Don't waste your time in making everyone else happy, Shanni. You'll end up walking on hot coals for the rest of your life."' I force the next sentence out, something I've never told anyone about my sister and her decision. 'And that was the first time I heard anything from her, anything like a complaint. Then I found her and . . . and I realized that there was a slight chance that she . . . she didn't do it for herself, that she was just . . . doing what everyone wanted. They wouldn't shut up about kids. Get married, have kids. That's how it goes.'

There's so much I want to tell him. So much I want to come clean about. All those things I've ignored about my own future, about possibly following through on my plea to my parents after this season is over, that I've pushed aside to continue living in this world where none of it matters except the two of us. I am so selfish. It hurts both of us, and he doesn't even know it.

So how do I tell him that? How do I tell him I'm scared I won't be able to *live* again, that everything I promised I would do, just like Sonia, is to make everyone else happy? How do I tell him I'm scared I won't get that happiness for myself? That as much as I've fallen for him so, so hard, I could possibly become my sister, and becoming my sister, of all things, is both my greatest duty and fear?

Chapter Forty-Seven

Darien

'Dar, I just, I can't . . .' Shantal tries, but she can't finish the thought. The burden of it all is so heavy that I feel it weigh on me.

'I hear you.' I do. I hear her almost too well. 'I'm sorry, I'm so, so sorry.'

We stay as we are for a few long moments. My arms circle her as if shielding her from the invisible slings and arrows of stabbing memories. I know exactly what those kinds of wounds do to you, and I'd take them for her in a heartbeat.

'I'm sorry. I woke you up,' Shanni murmurs. 'It's going to be a race weekend, and you need to sleep . . .'

'What do you mean?' I lean back and brush a tear from the corner of Shanni's left eye with total concentration. I've been awake for mere minutes, but I'm completely aware of every detail. 'I don't mind. I'm staying with you, *mina*. There's no other place I want to be right now.'

I know there's nothing I can say or do to fix this for Shantal.

For a human being to carry around that kind of pain for so long is punishment greater than any broken bone or torn tendon.

So I just try to be there. I stand there with her at the balcony door. I'll stand there as long as she needs to.

Her voice cracks as she tells me, 'I just . . . I just don't know what to do any more.'

I trace circles on Shantal's arm with my thumb, worry creasing my brow. 'How come?'

Shantal lifts her head so her eyes meet mine, a curl of her hair sticking to her cheek. 'To a degree, I resent her for it, for keeping that from me. And then I feel terrible when I think that way. Because maybe . . . Sonia did what she did to satisfy everyone else. She never got a chance to love, and now . . . what if I don't either?'

My heart pounds double time as her words sink in. Who expects that kind of sacrifice from a person? It twists my gut just to think about it.

'Love . . .' I swallow hard. The words are difficult, but I try my best to put them together. 'Love isn't a currency, Shanni . . . that's what's so great about it. You don't owe anyone anything to be deserving of love. Loving someone doesn't have to be any harder than we make it.'

Shantal doesn't move her line of sight from me. Only her lower lip quivers slightly. 'Meeting your family last night . . . it was beautiful, Dar. You all show your affection so easily. I wish it were that simple.'

'I do, too.' I don't know, I just want to take away everything that's hurting her and make it mine, so I don't have to watch her fall apart like this. Except that I can't. I've never felt more helpless than when all I can do is reach out and fix that piece of hair that won't let go of her cheek. 'But it's always gonna be your right to *love*, as much as it is anyone else's.'

'And if it isn't?'

Love hard, or not at all, Mãe always told me. Same way she loved my father, even when people told her to get over it, that he wasn't coming back. No matter how hard the world tried to take the right to love Nico Cardoso-Magalhães from her, she never let it.

'You love, anyway.' I smile sadly. 'Can't live without it.'

She hugs me tight, her head finding that place under my chin again, pressed to my chest. Her embrace is fervent, desperate, as if she's clinging to a life preserver, and in it, there's a piece of . . . guilt. Of blame.

I don't question the odd feeling, though. I give her the kind of affection that I was given by my family all my life, the only kind of affection I learned to give: the unconditional kind. I hug her back, and I don't ask why she radiates the emotions she does. I accept them as they are.

That's what you do when you love.

Chapter Forty-Eight

Shantal

Usually, when thoughts of my sister's last moments overtake me, I feel beyond any comfort. I have never felt so held, felt so safe, as I did that morning. My burdens have never been lifted off my shoulders the way that Darien lifted them. I have to remember but, for once, I have been able to feel as well. With Darien, I don't have to be the dutiful Mangal daughter. I can just be Shanni.

And ultimately, I think that's the reason I finally decide to call Ma the next day.

The words are spelled out before I even hit the button to dial the phone. *I've found someone. I think I want to give it a try. That I thought I'd never get to experience that came from a place of grief and hurt. And I think this may be coming from a place of something much more profound.*

My mother beats me to it.

Her name flashes across the screen of my phone, along with the green *accept* and red *reject*. It almost scares me, like she knows what I'm thinking, but it's all the better for me. I don't have to take the daunting first step of calling her myself when I press *accept*.

'Shanni?'

Ma's voice is so excited – more than I've heard it in years, maybe more than when I told her about the Rio job. There's something else there, the likes of which I've only heard at two other points in my life.

'Ma? Ma, what's up?'

'Shanni, I have some really, really good news.' The smile on her face is practically audible over the speaker.

'Good news?' My own voice shakes. I don't even need her to tell me to know what it is and, compounded with all the dread that has built up in my heart over the last few months, the feeling of guilt and anxiety deep in my gut weighs me down like never before.

'News from Navin's family.' A happy laugh escapes her, bubbling over to me through the phone. 'If you agree, Shanni. He likes you, they like you. This December, they've said.'

I've found someone.

The words die before they even make their way to my lips.

There is no complete way to describe the duty you feel as a daughter. The love you have for your parents battles with the love you have for *life*. It's a constant war between balance and responsibility, between mind and heart. When you hear your mother proud, jubilant, when you hear something you haven't heard since the last drop of good news hit the household years ago, you become immobile. You are made helpless by the people you love most.

Chapter Forty-Nine

Darien

The season's been absolutely hellish so far, track temps sweltering and rubber blistering, so it's only natural we go out with a bang before we get a short three-week spacer. The Las Vegas Grand Prix heralds record-high temperatures that shouldn't even be remotely possible. We're using the hardest compounds we have. It's a high-stress race; high stakes, too – the WDC board looks close, with just a few points between me and Miguel. Maybe it's because of all the nerves surrounding this race, chaotic as all those set in America tend to be, and the pressure to perform with Heidelberg Hybridge Ring's future still on the line, that I don't notice something is off with Shantal right away.

She turns down my offer to join us on the track walk with a wan smile and words of reassurance, says she's got data to look at for potential simulator plans with Redenção, when everyone knows she finished those ages ago. She's distant in every sense of the word, seemingly in her own world.

Post-race, amid the throngs of people rejoicing in the garage, I'm still holding both my P1 trophy and my champagne bottle when I catch sight of her heading to the data rooms in the motorhome. I may have just stepped off the podium, but I've got to figure out what's been bothering her.

Miguel notices me before she does, though. He leaves his trophy on a tool cabinet and rushes over. 'Dar. Dar, that might not be such a good idea.'

'What, you haven't noticed she's been off this weekend?' My forehead furrows in confusion. 'I don't know, man, something isn't right.'

'Take your chances. It just . . . it doesn't look good.' Miguel's face is clearly sad. 'We've seen Shantal through a lot of things, but you and I both know we've never seen her this detached. You know how she is with her team, with her "players". I'm afraid it's something that she's not going to crack about. Or that you're not going to like.'

'I gotta try,' I reply with a heavy exhale. Miguel just shrugs resignedly, but I go after Shantal anyway. 'Shantal! Hey!' I call to her before she heads up the stairs.

It takes her a minute to turn, and when she does, her eyes almost look wide, cornered. I can't make that worse by backing her into a quiet corner and pulling the truth from her. So I choose the one option I know never fails either of us.

'Can we go for a drive?'

Shantal wrings her hands the entire time, as we get into my Hybridge Model S and I tear out of the paddock, down towards the exit and all the way through the outside of the track complex, till we're driving along the fringes of the Strip. It's way quieter here, no longer pervaded by race fever or casino fever.

271

I've never seen her this way. Upset, sure. Stressed out, yeah. But this is different.

'Shanni . . .' I grip the steering wheel tight as I spare a glance her way. 'Shanni, what's been goin' on? You're . . . I'm just worried.'

'Worried?' She rolls down her window for more free air. The Nevada heat is no joke, but I get the feeling she's beating around the bush with me, and I want to find out why.

'A little, yeah. It's a race weekend, I know stuff gets chaotic, but . . . I just feel like you haven't completely been with us the past couple days. You know?'

Immediately, I feel the atmosphere in the car grow tenser. Uh-oh.

'I don't . . .' Shantal blows a strand of hair from her face. 'There's a lot I need to explain to you, Darien, but I don't want to do that while you're here, driving—'

'I mean, that's okay,' I say way too quickly. 'There's gotta be a TL;DR version, right? Can you give me that?'

'I cannot really TL;DR this situation.'

'Could you try?' I plead. If this has been eating away at her, it's been gnawing at my composure, too. How are we so close and yet so far from each other? I need answers as much as she does.

With a sigh, she turns to me and says, 'Darien, you've become . . . you've become so dear to me. You went from a pain in my ass to a friend to . . .'

Oh, no.

I wait for more. I can't just let her hit me with 'friend' and leave. But nothing else comes, believe it or not.

'Was that the entire TL;DR version?'

'That was it.'

'Okay.' I try my best to concentrate on the road ahead, one

that winds around the city and back to the Las Vegas sign, where an enormous line of tourists waits to get their photo taken. This car ride has suddenly turned into a tropical excursion from hell. 'So I think I'll need the full version.'

'I told you.'

'Yo. You just friend-zoned me!'

'I'm not—'

'Nah. You friends-with-benefits-zoned me.'

'I don't—'

'You're playing.'

'I am not playing, Darien.'

The remainder of the drive back is dead silent. We get out of the car without a word and walk to the now-empty track. It's probably the best way to diffuse the tension, and possibly whatever is going to come.

'My parents have called,' Shantal blurts once we're at the third turn.

That gets me. I try to keep walking and ignore the distress this is causing me, but it must be evident on my face. 'Your parents?'

'Darien . . . They want me to come back to London.'

'What?'

Is there some reason for her to bolt so quickly? Is it something I've done to her – scared her off, maybe. From the guilt written across Shantal's face, she already knows I'm thinking this.

'I've called Conquest. They had it set up so I was second-half optional for the season, so I'll still be able to deal with most of the sim stuff remotely. I've done the bulk of my job. They'll send someone else if you guys have any outstanding issues. You're familiar with the system. The trainers are familiar with the system. The team just needs to come through. And I'll be doing whatever I can to continue helping with that. I mean, my job depends on it. Yours, too. Our jobs depend on it. I won't just leave you all without any help. I swear to it, I won't.' The words cascade from her lips at breakneck speed.

It's too much for me. I shake my head, trying in vain to comprehend it all. 'Shanni. Shantal, what's going on?'

'I-I just . . . I have to go.' She runs her hands across her face, up into her hair, and only then do I see the suffering hidden behind the guilt in her irises. 'My mum's found a guy. They want to plan the engagement.'

What the fuck?

Now I can't just walk it off. I freeze in my place. I look straight at her. 'You're playing, Shantal,' I repeat.

She just shakes her head, pursing her lips. She's already blinking furiously to hold back her tears. 'Both of them . . . my mother just called me. Just told me.'

It's too much for me to process.

I move to turn away, to head in the opposite direction to Shantal so I don't let all my anger out at her, but it's in vain. I can't leave her when I hear her start to speak.

'My mum said I wasn't the same after Sonia passed.' Shantal brushes away a tear and continues walking at a pace so clipped I can barely keep up. 'I guess I thought this would solve it. I mean, back then, when Sonia had just . . . died, I think they thought it would solve their problems too. Our house used to be full of noise. My parents couldn't stand the silence.'

'Did you know?' I manage.

'No. No, god, no, I had no idea something would come through.' She smiles a forced smile, tries to hold it. 'On the tram that day . . . I guess this was what some part of me wanted so badly to tell you. When I suggested it to my parents, I thought . . . I would do whatever it took to bring some happiness back into the house. But now I've met you. And now . . . Darien . . .' The tears are flowing down her cheeks as she struggles to form

274

words. 'When I heard my mum's voice, Dar, I just, I felt . . . I didn't think I'd hear her so happy again, ever. To be the *reason* for that . . .'

My hands uncurl themselves from fists, all the momentary fire in my gut fizzling out as I take it all in. If I had the chance to make my mother as happy as she'd been before my father died, would I take that? Would I do whatever it took?

'You gave me back so many things that I didn't think I would ever experience again.' This time, it's Shantal's turn to stop walking and face me. 'But Darien, you tore my lies apart. I can't pretend I'm numb any more. Because I'm not. I just, I have no idea what to choose. I don't know how to break their hearts and tell them I want to try to make some space in mine. I don't know if I can.'

I steady her by the shoulders, though I'm struggling to figure out what I'm supposed to say. Something selfless, or something selfish?

'Shantal, tell me you won't—'

As if she's read my mind, she grips my hands tight, presses her lips to my knuckles. 'You gave me back *so* many things,' she repeats, drawing a deep breath. 'I just need time to figure out where I go from here. I'm not going to stop working for Conquest. I just . . . I think I need to go back to London.'

'Shit.'

'Yeah.' Her lower lip quivers just slightly, and that's enough of a sign for me. I bring her close, and I feel her hands press against my back. I try not to focus on the quiet sniffs as she cries. Damn quiet crier, Shanni. Part of me just wants her to sob out loud. The quiet hurts me more.

I know it's no one's fault. It's poor timing, it's fate and destiny, and all the stuff I've never believed in. But when she's falling apart in my arms, it's hard not to feel guilty.

Chapter Fifty

Darien

Iglare at my trophy as I drag it through the door of my dark room, setting it on the island in the small kitchen with a *thump*. Even though it's first place, it's nothing but a consolation prize. One that makes no difference to me after everything I've heard this afternoon. Partying, dancing, all of it felt like an obligation that I couldn't take a shred of delight in, not when my days with Shantal could be numbered, and I still don't know quite who to be upset with about it.

The anger falls away as I see a flicker of something just past the sitting room, beyond the door to the master bedroom and the terrace it leads out to.

The open terrace provides a rush of hot air that isn't combatted by any air-conditioning system, just the chill of seeing her out there on the balcony.

Shantal lights candles just like she did back in Jaipur, tens upon tens of them, maybe a hundred in total. Her eyes glisten with the glow of the lights and something else. She tucks her knees up to her chin, the hem of her flared white pants dancing around her feet as she rests her cheek against her arm and lights yet another candle.

I take a tentative step forward, past the dresser and onto the terrace. It smells of vanilla and cherry blossoms – the candles. Shantal's hair is wet, freshly washed; I can tell from the shadow of damp fabric it has left on the back of her T-shirt.

'Shanni?' I almost whisper.

She turns just slightly, just enough that her eyes can catch mine and hold on.

'You don't need to light this many.' I search her face for any semblance of the happiness I've been so privileged to bring back to her, and all at once, I'm enraged at the fact that someone has been able to snatch that from her in one fell swoop.

'I do.' She cups her hand around the candle she's just lit as it flickers. 'I don't ever want them to go out.' When she looks up at me, the tears in her eyes spill over. 'I've got to go tomorrow.'

'Tomorrow?' My brow furrows as I crouch down, meeting her gaze.

Shantal sets her lighter to the side, and her fingers gently graze my cheek, a touch that's there one moment and gone the very next. My heart threatens to implode, full of so much sadness that I don't think I can take it any longer.

'I'd hate myself for ever if I forgot a single thing about you,' she says, voice quivering. 'I just want to remember everything, everything I can see, everything I can feel, everything about you. And the longer I stay here, now that you know what my future holds, the more it will hurt you.'

'Shanni, no one's to say you're leaving—'

Her finger moves to my lips in a gesture of silence as she shakes her head. 'Don't,' she mouths, brushing a tear from her cheek. 'Don't say anything. I'll have to go home. I can't leave my family waiting for me like that. I just, I don't want to think about the fact that . . . that I don't know what'll happen. I don't want to think about it.'

'Well . . . I guess we gotta think about it. This is our reality, Shanni.'

'Since when have we lived in reality, you and me?'

This is all too true. I live in a world where I can imagine I'm just a normal guy – freed from the pressure of recovery and racing – when I'm with Shantal, and she can imagine she has no reason to return home and leave her dreams behind. So where does that leave us if we aren't together?

Maybe I *should* put my foot down and tell her we can't keep dreaming for ever; that she needs to go home and help her family heal by doing what she needs to do. But I don't. I *can't*. Damn, I'll do whatever it takes, but I'm not going to go anywhere.

I take Shantal's hand in both of mine.

Easy to love, hard to hold on.

Her eyes glow in the light of the candles. 'When I was younger, my mum would tell me we're created with half a heart, destined to find the person with the other half . . .' She shakes her head. 'This isn't fair, Darien.'

My thumb pushes a tear from the corner of her eye. 'It never is.'

I close my own eyes, and I still see dancing flames even where there aren't any, even when I kiss her in the midst of almost a hundred candles that refuse to die out when a dry wind comes our way.

The salt of her tears travels with me, doesn't let up even when I let my lips wander down her neck until her breath catches. Her fingers undo the buttons on my shirt, one by one, her forehead

278

pressed to mine as I push it aside. I memorize the feel of her hands as they trace my arms, my chest.

'Don't leave,' I whisper into the crook of her neck as my own hands find her waist.

She just shakes her head, her lips brushing mine just before she says the words I'm so afraid to hear. 'You know that's not possible.'

'Then what is?'

'You staying with me.' Shanni's eyes are relentlessly pleading when they meet mine. 'One more night.'

And when I lie with her in bed, wide awake as I listen to her gentle breathing, her head on my chest, I think that it might not just be those dumb candles burning, despite every force of nature that wants them put out.

I lie awake all night. I keep asking myself what in the world I'm supposed to do when I realize that the woman in my arms right now, the woman who is going to be gone from here this time tomorrow, holds the other half of my heart.

Chapter Fifty-One

Shantal

It's the day before Darien is due to fly out for the short break in Rio, and we stand in the airport.

We've beaten the rest of the team here, sneaked out of the hotel early in the morning so I can catch my flight. I'll be on the next plane to London.

I struggle to meet Darien's eye when we reach the security checkpoint. I take in every bit of these surroundings, of this humid airport in Vegas that will be the last place I see him. I take in Darien, his big brown eyes holding back tears, his strong arms, the tattoos peeking out from beneath his sleeves and the collar of his T-shirt, stories to which new chapters, new lines will be added. It strikes me suddenly that if this visit home goes the way I think it's going to go, I might never see those new stories. This is the end of the line, and I am nowhere near ready to part ways.

'Be strong, Shanni,' he whispers, brushing a hair from my face.

A sob leaves my mouth before I can control it, but Darien presses his lips to mine, his eyes squeezed tight, and I close mine in the same way. I want to live in this moment for ever, fabricate a reality where we stay like this, together.

'You're going to thrive, no matter what happens.' He is an inch from me, and his words float quietly on shallow breaths that kiss my cheeks. 'You'll thrive, you'll be strong, you'll figure things out. And . . . and if you don't,' he takes a deep breath, '. . . if you don't come back, don't worry. It's okay because you're gonna have a kick-ass job at the very top of the pyramid, a happy family, maybe a kid as mean as you, as awesome as you are, and maybe I'll finally have that WDC title or something, and I'll see you again then. Maybe a lot of stuff will have changed, Shanni. We're gonna be old and tired and all of that, we're gonna be grown-up, but what won't change a bit is how proud I will be of you. I'm gonna be *so proud* of you and I'm still going to think of you. All my life, Shanni, all my life.'

I'm a sobbing mess, but I nod through it, trying to convince myself of what he seems so certain. That our stories are bound together, that we were meant to collide that day at the Lapa Arches, with my fake map and his fake name. He brushes all the tears away, takes my hands, and squeezes them tight as he presses his forehead to mine.

We stay like this for a minute, then more. 'I'm yours,' he mouths. 'No matter what. No matter how far you are. I'll wait around.'

I swallow hard and manage a 'yes'. The past few months are burned into my soul. I know that I am no different: that I'll also be his, no matter how far away he is.

When we pull away, Darien takes my hand, my right, and holds it close to him. He reaches into his pocket and pulls out a bracelet that shimmers so gold it's almost yellow, a simple chain with two tiny macaws linked in the centre, beaks making a heart shape, and he clasps it around my wrist.

'My mom's.' His voice is a quiet caress that just glances past my cheek as his fingers brush mine one last time.

I don't require any explanation as I take in the bird on the bracelet, the macaws. The same as the ones on his helmet. I remember what Joel and Raya had been bickering about way back in January, before I'd left for Rio.

Macaws are resilient.

As much as they might endure, they always summon strength.

I've always envied how hard Darien Cardoso-Magalhães *dreams*. But as I look down at the bracelet he's given me, something tears at the strings of my heart. He said he'll wait. But I worry I will never be able to come back, never see him again. I worry he'll dream so hard that reality will become disappointing.

Before I can look into Darien's eyes and feel regret so deep it hooks onto my feet and holds me in my place, I grab my bag and turn away, hoping he knows that I am doing this for both of us, that a long goodbye would screw us both over. I walk towards the security checkpoint, tears falling down my face as I do and, as much as I tell myself I shouldn't, I turn and glance back at him.

I've never seen him cry this way. The tears form tracks that slide down his cheeks, mirroring mine. He lifts a hand in a little wave, and it feels like I've just been kicked in the chest. He's crushing me, but I purse my lips, shut out the emotion, and wave back as I head for the gate, for the line that separates the dream I want to live in, and the reality I have no choice but to face.

Chapter Fifty-Two

Darien

She leaves as abruptly as she'd entered my life.

I don't want to explain any of it to the guys when I get back, get ready to leave for Rio with Miguel. He's bursting with excitement, since we'll be reuniting with Henri and Peter to spend the lull in races together vacationing in Brazil, after which he'll drop by Spain to see his family, and then it's full circle, with the season picking back up in São Paulo – third to last race. He has so much – *so many people* – to look forward to. Yeah, I'm glad I'll get some time with Mãe, get to catch up and kick back, but I don't know how I can kick back right now.

'Shantal already left?' says Miguel with a yawn as we swing ourselves into the limo that will take us to the airport. 'That early in the morning? God knows the girl can't wake up before ten a.m. and expect to function.'

'Yeah,' I say. Easy, ambiguous. I don't want him to have been right when he told me not to find out what was bothering Shantal after the last race, but he is. Part of me wishes I'd never asked. I

283

grab a bag of those dumb peanuts, popping one in my mouth. The memory of Shantal's grumble when I'd hit her with one on the way to the airport in Rio comes on, harsh and unsolicited.

'Yeah, she's left?'

'Yes, she left, Miguel!' I shoot back with a bit too much force. 'She left, okay? She's *gone*.'

Miguel, normally one to engage in a fight if you pick one with him, doesn't say anything, just lets this new bit of information process. He opens his mouth as if to say something, and then closes it before finally deciding what to say. 'Why?'

'It's a really long story.' I swallow hard, leaning back against the limo seat. 'And it's not mine to tell.'

'She's all right, though, isn't she? Nothing bad happened to her?' Miguel runs a hand through his hair nervously. 'Dude, if something—'

'Nothing happened.' My voice threatens to give out as I hold in torrents of truth that yell at me to let them loose. 'We'd better just leave well enough alone.'

'What?' He's almost gone slack-jawed with surprise now. 'Since when do you not push back?'

The breath I let out is heavier than I intend. 'Since it'll be her who decides if she'll push back or not.'

I spend the days we have in Brazil in a haze. Miguel, Peter, Henri and I are off to Belo Horizonte. I should be taking in all the sights, including the Mineirão, the stadium where we once hosted a World Cup, one of my favourite parts of the country, if anyone were to ask me, but I see her everywhere.

I see her in the pairs of cleats that are displayed in the museum, in the Italian sodas we snag off a street vendor, in the Hokas on the feet of tourists.

Part of me wishes I could be more upset at her for making

that decision so easily, for leaving so quickly; maybe that would make it easier to find somewhere to put my emotions. But I can't. I know exactly what it feels like to have to keep moving forward because if you don't, you could lose someone you hold dear, and for that, I can't manage to push anger in her direction.

'How are you holding up?'

Someone cuts into the moment I'm spending brooding in front of one of the two goals set up on opposite ends of the stadium. They've miraculously let us onto the Mineirão's bright green field, which seems to have delighted Miguel, Peter and Henri, who've been kicking a ball around with cackles and whoops. It's the last person I expect, out of the three of them, to meander over to me. It's Henri, leaving the other two to their own devices at the other goal.

'Holding up? I'm all right.'

'Hmm.' He raises an inquisitive eyebrow. 'Well, our team trainer and *your* lady love did happen to leave a few days ago with little to no warning, and a notice to the entirety of Heidelberg that she's "fulfilled her task" here. You've got to be struggling.'

'Well, the thing is—'

'Did she dump you?' blurts Henri.

God, these kids. Nothing if not straight-shooters. I throw my hands up in disbelief. 'Really, dude?'

'Hey, if you're not going to give Miguel a valid answer, I figure I might as well try. We're all *slightly* concerned. This came about pretty fast,' he points out.

Before I can respond, a stray ball lobbed in our direction cuts off the conversation, and I deflect it with the inside of my foot.

'Pass it back!' calls Peter with a wave of his arm.

Henri gives me a knowing glance. 'Kick it out, dude.'

I do. I kick everything out of my system until the ball hits the back of the net a satisfactory number of times, all the anger evaporating into thin air so thoroughly that by the time I get back home at the end of the day, to the one person I've always been able to open up to with little effort, I'm ready to talk.

I drive over to our Santa Teresa house. It's seen me through my best and worst times, and I need it to see me through this one, too. Small, simple as it always has been, with all my mom's chaotic flowers and bushes surrounding it. I've never minded the size. It holds plenty of love, anyway.

Mãe is out the door the second I've pulled up. With a broad smile and a hug smelling of peaches and mangoes, she's made me a little kid again, running to her after my first karting victory in San Francisco. She ruffles my hair. 'Oh, Magalinho. *Finalmente*.'

My mother sits me down on an eye-popping yellow couch, and before I can even suggest it, arms me with a can of Guaraná, my favourite soda.

'*Diz*,' she demands. 'Last I saw you, you were on, what, summer break? Talk to me.'

It takes a minute to find the words. I pop the tab on my soda, killing time. Pai's always been a sore topic for her. Everything I know about him – *everything* – is a mishmash of my hazy memories and stories from my *tio* and *tia*. But I ask, because maybe I should have done so a long time ago, and because, right now, I think only my mother has what I'm looking for.

'Why'd you never find anyone else after Pai?'

She's been leaning forward intently, but now, it's like her face freezes, a mask of shock.

'Mãe?'

'*Não me diga isso.*' My mother's jaw is stiff, set just the way I do mine. 'I won't have answers for you.'

'But you do, huh?' I insist. '*Por que não?*'

She shakes her head. 'Why you ask me this, Darien? Out of nowhere?'

I'm not actually sure why, and my lack of a response is all she needs to figure it out. Her voice goes soft, her face sad, as her eyebrows lower slowly, her eyes full of concern. 'Darien . . . what happened with Shantal?'

And there it is.

Moms don't really have to probe, they don't have to conduct a thirty-minute interview to get down to the nitty-gritty and extract the information from you. They know you went out that night with your friends to TP Sam Pullman's house, they know that you pregamed senior prom, they know that you suffered your first heartbreak because Cindy Gomez said she did not, in fact, want to go see *John Wick* with you, and they know when you hide something – anything – from them. I've never had to hide anything from Mãe. She always finds out before I can tell her.

I lean back against the couch, looking straight up at the ceiling to avoid letting the tears go. I tell my mom everything, from the very beginning, from how I found out what happened to her, to how we got closer and closer until our paths crashed, and I realized that my life had been divided into 'before Shantal' and 'after Shantal'. I told her about the moment that I really, really fell, when I gave her that steering wheel, and when it all went to hell, Shantal's parents, Shantal's *obligation* to her parents, leaving her with Mãe's bracelet.

'Right girl, right time,' my mom had told me when she gave me that bracelet at the beginning of my F1 career. Right girl, I'd ticked that box, at least. As for the time? It's possible it could be so cruelly wrong.

'So how come you never moved on?' I nearly whisper the last two words. 'How come she can't bring herself to?'

With a heavy sigh, my mom smiles sadly. 'As women, all we're told, all our life, is that we are the centre that has to hold. We undertake responsibilities for others, Magalinho. With every person we care for comes a sacrifice. We hold the centre, even if that means not moving on. Even if that means doing whatever it takes to patch things up, if what you patch up heals someone for whom you care. Especially if what you patch up will fill a hole left behind by grief.'

A hole left behind by grief. My father's death. Is that why she never found anyone else, because she had to look after me? Because I became her responsibility? 'Mãe . . .' My voice cracks. 'I-I'm so sorry, I didn't realize you had to . . . I didn't know, didn't do anything to . . .'

'Magalinho.' Mãe takes my face in her gentle hands. 'Don't you say sorry. Yes, maybe Nico left, maybe Nico took the love with him, but he didn't take it all. He left me *you*. You didn't need to do anything. Even if I was hurting, I still had you. You are reason enough for me to never look for anyone else, anything else, Darien. Hope. *Esperança*.'

Her reassurance is as warm as it's always been, the kind of thing only a mother is capable of, but her words stick in my brain, echoing over and over until they lose meaning, and then regain it.

We hold the centre, even if that means not moving on.

What do I do if Shantal is *my* centre? What do I do if I can't hold without her?

Chapter Fifty-Three

Shantal

'Shanni!'

My mum is calling my name in the airport but my throat tightens as I think of Darien. Of Darien's voice.

I push my bags ahead of me on the trolley and paste a smile on my face. My parents rush towards me with enormous grins, wrapping their arms around me. I can smell the pineapples of Ma's shampoo, feel the wool of Babu's sweater. It's striking how these feelings suddenly hurt me more than they heal me.

It's even harder in person. They are so excited, Ma's got tears in her eyes. I can't believe it – she's not looked this healthy, this effervescent, in months. Babu presses his hands to either side of my face and gently plants a kiss on my forehead. I have to work so hard to stifle the sob that threatens to leave my lips.

This is what I've come here to ruin. All of it.

'How was Rio? How was travelling with the team?' Ma gushes as she attempts to take my trolley. 'Let me get this for you.'

'Oh, no, Ma, don't worry.' I steer it towards me with a knowing glance at Babu, who just chuckles. 'Rio was good. It was pretty, it was a good team. But I'm happy to be home, you know that.'

'You finished your work, though, *na*?' My mum's forehead scrunches with concern, and I immediately fill with guilt. I don't want her to feel bad about this. She hasn't got to feel *good* about something since Sonia.

'I finished everything I needed to finish. It's just tying up loose ends and updating the programs from here,' I assure her, leaning in so I can wrap one arm around her, and the other around Babu. I like to imagine that's where it ends – we walk off to the car happily, never to deal with any strife ever again. But the pit in my stomach won't allow it. The guilt spills over.

On the drive home, I sit in the backseat. I've never been carsick before, but when I get to the house, I drop my luggage in my room and run to the bathroom, fully prepared to be sick. I hate it. I hate that I crouch over the toilet for ten minutes, feel like I could vomit, yet nothing comes.

I've heard of your body rejecting transplanted organs. I've never heard of it rejecting lies.

I go through the motions on my first day back at work with Conquest. The questions about how Formula 1 was, how Heidelberg was. I answer them all robotically, just like I had with my parents. It was good. It was a formative experience. What was Darien like? Wonderful. Great driver. I have my answers planned out. I use the same ones every time someone asks me.

'Up till the three-week gap is a clever way to do it,' points out Raya on my first day back. 'If I'd had the option, I'd have stayed to see the Championship through. You didn't?'

I shake my head and bite my tongue. The undertone to her voice is almost accusatory. *I'd have stayed.* 'Well, my parents called. Family things. And I figured it was time to come back.'

'Hmm.' The snideness almost seems to leave Raya as she looks me up and down, glances around my cubicle and at the photos on my desk. 'The whole team's going to get Abu Dhabi passes, you know. You should come.'

'Why?' I shrug, trying to appear nonchalant. 'I've seen it all already.'

'Right, then.' Raya smiles tightly, glancing once more over my workspace. She nudges a new photo frame by my laptop: it's me with Darien on the pit wall, the same one as the photo I'd signed for him. 'Nice picture.'

'Thanks.' My voice is strained. I'm sure she's not come to my cubicle just to nudge me about why I'm back. 'Anyway. You're . . .'

'Going to be joining them for Brazil,' she confirms, smirking. 'Thought I'd see what all the fuss is about.'

Her eyes flit towards the photo again, and she taps the glass panel right beside Darien's face, her eyebrows rising. 'Is he as good as they say he is, Cardoso-Magalhães?'

'He's phenomenal,' I finally say.

'I can't wait.' With one final grin that doesn't reach her eyes, Raya gives me a nod and turns to trot back towards her desk, her long brown hair swishing behind her.

Later that night, my mum, sensing something is off, takes out her old record player. It hasn't seen the light of day since Sonia last asked her to put on a vinyl.

'Shanni!' she calls from the living room as I wash my hands after dinner. I hear the scratch of the needle, and then the record: 'Mere Sapno Ki Rani' from *Aradhana*. Kishore Kumar's voice echoes off the walls of the room, and when I walk in, Ma's arms are outstretched, a grin on her face. 'Come and dance.'

I take her hands and dance and pretend I won't lie awake all night trying to figure out how I could possibly share my bed with someone who isn't Darien. I know Darien snores, and I know Darien pulls all the blankets over him so that you wake up at two a.m. wondering where the hell the covers went. I don't know if this guy my parents have found snores. I don't know if he takes all the blankets. I wonder if it's true that love comes with time, if it takes a month, a year, ten years, never.

And when I get up in the morning, I make my way downstairs to the family *mandir*, a small set of *murtis* in the downstairs alcove where no one's yet burned the stick of incense sitting in its tray. I take the invitation to do so, lighting a match and igniting the *agarbatti* stick over it. I plant the stick in the tray, fold my hands, close my eyes. I never used to come down here early – that was Sonia's thing – but I started to last year. I started to ask for answers. Now, I have something else to ask for.

Let me be strong enough to take this burden on.
Or let me be strong enough to run from all of this.
Let me be strong enough to love him back.

ONE MONTH LATER

Chapter Fifty-Four

Darien

I pick at the corner of the *H* on the back of my steering wheel, where the white sticker is starting to peel up.

'Hey, Ricky?' I catch one of my mechanics as he's passing by. 'You got some of the adhesive for this? It's coming loose.'

'Sorry, pal, you can't glue that one down.' He almost seems to cringe in sympathy for me. 'We'll have to make a new sticker. Do you wanna remove that for the time being—'

'No,' I reply, way too quickly and way too insistently. 'I don't, I'll keep this one.'

There are two races left in the season, and this, Brazil, is one of them. My steering has weathered overtakes, near-misses, and collisions with the wall of my garage. It's taken until now for the sticker to start to peel. I don't want to replace it. If I do, it won't be the same one Shantal held, her fingers tracing the curves of the letters she'd written herself.

'Everything looking good?' a new voice interrupts my thought.

I nod brusquely, setting the steering wheel to the side so I can address Raya. 'Yeah. Yeah, all good. Hope you're, um, excited to watch the race?'

'Quite.' Raya Almeida is the visiting tech specialist from Conquest. I'd first heard we would get a Conquest drop-in last week, during the last race weekend, and I'd been so sure it would be Shantal. It had to. We had texted here and there, though she'd neatly dodged the matter of what was going on regarding her parents several times. A month had passed. She had to be coming back soon. Right? Instead I heard that it was Raya, a São Paulo-born Brit with deep connections to the Brazilian football team, flying out to observe our team. She'd decided to take up residence in the number sixty-seven garage for the afternoon of the race.

Qualifier had gone poorly for me. At my own home track, some sort of mental block had screwed with my judgement, causing my turns to go wide and my normally late braking to kick in a hair too early. I ended up P6 on the grid, where I'm about to start today. I'm not proud of it, but it's a home crowd. I have to perform.

'Um, Raya, can I have my phone?' I ask her, chewing on the inside of my cheek nervously. 'Just wanna, uh . . .'

She nods, although she's unamused. 'Sure.'

Once she's passed the phone in its royal blue case my way, she speeds off to Miguel's garage, and I jab at my contacts page till I find Shantal under *M*. I press the 'call' button and hold the phone to my ear.

I don't know what I expect, but after a short dial tone I hear: 'The number you are trying to reach is unavailable. Please leave your message after the beep.'

Shit, man. I throw the phone to the side and sit myself down on the chassis of the Heidelberg, burying my face in my hands.

I think of how freeing it was to kart with her, to remember what I loved about the race.

No pressure, I repeat to myself like a mantra. No pressure, no pressure, no pressure, but it's happening, my centre isn't holding and, even with everyone here – my mom, my *tia* and *tio*, my whole family is going to be in the damn paddock – I can't fix myself. Not without my centre.

'Dude, I hope that Raya chick hasn't gone looking for me,' says Miguel with a snort.

I look up, my expression telling him: *Let me be depressed alone, please*.

He doesn't accept it. He sits his insistent ass right down next to me, tips a head towards the steering wheel. 'Her name's peeling.'

'I've been made well aware.'

'Yeah.' He shrugs, giving my arm a wary pat. 'But it's just a sticker. It's not the stuff that really matters.'

I put up the fight of my life in Brazil, the kind of fight that I make sure my home crowd will never forget.

São Paulo is nothing but blue skies and scorching track temps today, the kind of weather that causes sweat to bead up beneath my helmet and soak the collar of my race suit. My pulse is pounding overtime as my gloved fingers find the corner of the H, the chapped corner lifting far too easily for my comfort.

'Let's get on it, Darien, on it,' Afonso's voice urges me over the radio.

I close my eyes, and I search for her until she stands right in front of me, her hands taking my face in their gentle grasp as a faint wind plays with her waves of hair. She nods, a proud smile tracing its way across her full lips, seeping into her deep brown irises.

I can feel my heart rate even as I let my eyelids flutter open. The first red light is just going on. I take the clutch, my composure returning in small waves. She's here, even when she's not. She drives with me, every lap.

And when the five lights go out, I've never been more certain of my motivation than in that moment. Because my father might've left, but his faith endured through the gift he'd given me. Her strength.

I pick my way into fourth, then dart around Peter and Miguel to wind towards a precarious P2 going into the first curve. My start poises me to get close to Diana, up next in P1. The chase is grating, with Afonso calling out modes lap after lap. We drive similar cars, but she has a full trophy case, finesse, a World Championship. That's enough to prolong this endeavour, about ten laps deep as it is before I get even remotely close enough to claim a healthy dose of DRS on the straight. It's exactly what I need for my front wing to skirt closer to Diana's rear one.

'Good gap, go ahead,' Afonso announces.

I bear down on the gas, my car shooting into the curve so abruptly that I come side-by-side with Diana.

Instead of using the straight, I keep level with her down the next stretch of track, and the second we hit the turn, I brake as late as I can, swinging my Heidelberg out in front of her Revello in a ballsy move that'll certainly get me both good and bad press after. It's worth the hassle. It brings me up into P1. I hold on for dear life, taking the race to the very end, defending with everything I've got when Diana creeps up on me two laps before the finish.

When I cross the line for the last time, retrieving my flag for the victory lap, part of me thinks Brazil is happier than I am. The audience is roaring, on their feet in ecstasy, waiting for my celebration, while I raise a hand their way, assuring them I'll do something.

Will she see it? Somehow?

Maybe not.

I take the chance anyway.

Chapter Fifty-Five

Shantal

'Shantal, is the *chai* done?'

I am notoriously awful at making tea. I stand to the side as Anjali's mum, my Janika Aunty, stirs the concoction she's prepared. Janika Aunty widens her eyes at me, as if to say, *Make it convincing.* I nod furiously, even though Ma won't see from where she's standing, waiting at the door for him – Navin. 'It's . . . it's almost there!'

Janika Aunty uses a spoon to bring a bit of the *chai* to her red-outlined lips. She's the polar opposite of my mother, that's for sure. I like to think that the similarities stop at their upbringing in a half-Guyanese, half-Punjabi family. Vaani Mangal is quietly rebellious, traditional yet caring, urging us to take the path our heart yearns for, at least up until Sonia's death. Janika Ramcharan is flamboyant, with the dress sense and taste of a film actress. Her doting Delhiite husband has the kind of patience that you find only once in a blue moon, and her eccentricity is the same kind of rare. They are a match made in heaven. Their chaos is the reason I grew up so close to Anjali – as much as she loves her parents, she loves our calm just as much.

As if on cue, my cousin thunders down the stairs and envelops me in a hug so forceful I almost knock over the saucepan of *chai*. 'Anjali!' I yelp, but she's undeterred by even her mother's squeal. She squeezes me tight, and then pulls back with a gasp.

'You're making *chai*? For a *man*?' she echoes the obvious, her thick black curls bouncing around her face. 'When did this happen?'

'A month ago.' My smile is tight, and I pray that she won't notice it in all the hustle and bustle. 'You know, we'd been waiting for something, and I guess this is it.'

'This is your for ever.' She exhales, the gravity of it all knitting its way through her eyebrows. I know exactly what she's going to say next before she can even open her mouth. 'But then . . . what about the one . . .?'

I shake my head, gritting my teeth, a gesture she quickly catches on to. Her brow wrinkles. 'No,' I say.

The doorbell rings before she can ask me anything else, and my grip on her arms tightens. Anjali tries to give me a reassuring smile, as her mother beams. 'Damn if that boy doesn't love the *chai*, I'll tell you.'

I try to chuckle at Janika Aunty's joke, but Anjali doesn't look amused, leaving me to help set the table. I love Anjali. I'm supposed to be a sort of mentor to her, someone who can guide her now that Sonia isn't there to fill that role for both of us. But I can't help feeling like no matter how much I try to set the example, it is she who truly guides me. There's nothing like seeing the disappointment in her eyes when she leaves for the dining room, nothing like the weight of reality crushing young dreams, to tell you that what you're doing is so wrong.

Navin Kumar, as I and my entire family have known since we moved to Clapham, is straightforward. He is tall, with carefully combed hair, a neatly trimmed beard, and warm eyes. I remember crushing on him when we were younger, before I realized my type was the kind of men I'd never realistically be in a relationship with. Now, he is grown up, sitting between both of his proud parents at the dinner table across from me. We've laid out *chai* and fried *pholourie*, conversation is light, happy. Neither of us meet the other's eyes. I don't know if everyone else thinks I'm just being coy, but I'll let them continue to assume.

'Navin, where are you working now?' asks Ma, her eyes alight with interest.

'Over at St George's. I'm in the foundation programme now, FY2, so almost done . . .'

A glance from Ma: *He's a doctor. He's just perfect. Do you like him?*

I can't quite bring myself to reply.

'That's so wonderful,' I reply once he's explained it all, willing a smile to cross my face.

'And what about you?' he grins, tipping his head towards Ma and Babu. 'I hear you've made an impression in the sports world already.'

'I work for a company called Conquest, with professional teams, mostly football, on weaving new training techniques, new technology into their regimens. It's athletic training meets data analysis, essentially.'

Navin looks genuinely intrigued as he nods. 'That's absolutely excellent.'

He talks so eloquently. So unlike Darien. No overuse of the word 'bro', no cursing under his breath, no terrible jokes. Annoying habits that eventually become lovable. Little things.

And all those little things build up until part of me wants to tear my soul open and tell Navin everything now, before it is too late.

'You will look *wonderful* together at Navin's hospital galas,' Mrs Kumar pops in with a wink later in the afternoon, once all the plates have been cleared and the cups of *chai* emptied. She pulls a large gift bag from beside her, reaching into it to pull out a neatly folded stack of navy blue fabric.

That part of me that wants to resist and be honest and be happy? That part is dumb. This is for more than myself. I watch my parents beaming, tearful for the first *good* reason in months. In almost a year. Ma's eyes are expectant, Babu's eyes proud. I can't say no. I can't turn this down, I can't; I cannot deny them the hope they've been waiting for all this time.

So the larger part of me wins, is compelled to keep lying. I smile the same smile that Navin does, and I pour every ounce of fabricated contentment I have into it to convince everyone that this is where I want to be, that I am willing to do what it takes to support this marriage.

I look down at the silk saree in Mrs Kumar's arms. Navin looks nervous but nods happily nevertheless. Anjali, god, I can't even look, because it will break me. Her parents are both already gleeful.

I squint at the saree, and I realize it's not unfamiliar. It's identical to the one I wore in Imola. It reminds me of a set of constantly humoured eyes that sparkle with all kinds of trouble, the sweetness of his voice when he calls my name. It's been a month since I left. I want to know what he's up to, where he's gone. Yet I'm here, a motion away from sealing this arrangement out of numbness and grief and guilt.

It's like a bad omen. I've always been particularly superstitious. But this time, I've got to get over it.

303

My fingers hover over the silky stack as I accept it and place it on my lap, my heart thundering when I remember the way Darien so gently adjusted the pleats as they threatened to slide off my shoulder. His lips against my skin. Every single second, every way that he has touched me, ways that may be invisible but that will remain for ever.

'Thank you,' I say with a small smile.

From beside his mother, as the parents start chattering excitedly about engagements and parties and going to Dubai – where Navin and his family spend winters – Navin returns my smile: the same size and all. Following one conversation with him, I can tell he is the kind of well-brought-up Guyanese son who's always wanted a well-brought-up wife, one who would attend work parties, hold *poojas* in the house, fast on all the holidays, smile, stay happy through the turmoil that may come her way.

He'll never know I'm not that wife, because I'll spend every minute I can making sure I appear to be that wife. As long as it keeps Ma and Babu glowing the way they do when they watch us together now.

The second the Kumar family has left, I run up to my room in the house. Tears stab at my eyes. I know Darien will be living his own life now, free to do what he likes, because as much as he says he will be mine till the end of time, he deserves to enjoy himself. I wonder if he is out partying before the race like he did before all the others, and if he is, if he has found some other woman there. A part of me hopes he has, that she compels him to move on from what is happening here, but the rest of me knows that would break me.

I crawl into my bed in my dress, reaching across to my nightstand. I pick up the white teddy bear sitting there. It's

André, the one Darien had given me back at the beginning of the season. I still have the note that he'd written with the bear. *You deserve your flowers.*

Maybe Darien is right. It's possible we will find other people and other forms of solace. But none of those will be one another. This is the truth, that I will keep him close to my heart, and, unknowingly, Navin will be burdened with this unspoken secret.

Biting back my emotions, I hold the bear against my chest, hug him so tightly that the charm of my necklace scratches the now-empty heart in his hands, and I can almost feel Darien beside me with his calm smile and happy eyes, smell the hints of his cologne that still linger on André the bear's fur.

'*DIDI!*'

Anjali bursts into my bubble of silence, flying through the door, immediately grabbing the remote from the nightstand. '*DIDI!* Turn on the TV!'

'Anjali!' I yelp, tucking the bear away in a rush of silky dress fabric and flying blankets. 'What the hell!'

'Quick!' My cousin tugs urgently at my arm. 'Come on, see!'

She stabs at buttons, thumb pounding the down arrow and then clicking on the broadcast of the Formula 1 race.

'No,' the word immediately leaves my lips. 'No, no, no, we're not doing—'

'*Didi,*' she says more forcefully. She squeezes my shoulder, meets my eyes directly. 'Just *see* him.'

And there he is.

He's sitting in the car, Darien. He is parked in front of that big P1 board that indicates that he's won the race, and my heart swells with pride at just the notion. He removes his steering wheel from the cockpit before using the halo to haul himself to his feet on the chassis.

I press a hand to my chest, and then over my mouth as I realize what he's doing.

The crowd is roaring around him, the team pumping their fists beyond the fence, and he hoists his steering wheel straight up to the sky, pointing to something written on the back that I don't need to be able to read to know well.

He pushes his visor up, and his eyes are squeezed shut as he holds that wheel up like it's the trophy he hasn't yet received, as tears fill my eyes miles and miles away.

'You left him, Shantal?'

Anjali's voice bears a stab of pain that I had not expected, along with my name leaving her mouth in full. It's always been *didi*, the honorific. This sounds so foreign.

I turn to her, and her lower lip wobbles, her eyebrows furrowing in confusion. I've never been more ashamed than I am when I nod.

'Shantal . . .' Anjali, in all her innocence, can still afford to live in this rose-tinted version of how the world works, but now, that same innocence drives poison-tipped arrows between my ribs, making it harder for me to breathe with every word she says. 'If you keep wasting your time searching for a name for this feeling . . . let me tell you, you're never going to find it. Because look how much he loves you.' She gently taps the gold macaw bracelet that Darien had given me, his mother's bracelet, still on my wrist. I haven't removed it since we parted ways. Conflicting emotions cross her face as she lets out a small sigh. 'Look how much you love *him*.'

Chapter Fifty-Six

Darien

It's the last race of the season, and I'm not quite sure what I'm doing.

We're in Abu Dhabi for this one, as we are every year. It's a grand affair – the usual fanfare, the chaos, the flamboyant atmosphere. But it's like trying to get your headlights to illuminate a road through dense fog. I can't tell exactly what I'm seeing, where I'm going. Amid everything else, Shantal dominates my thoughts.

I tug my race suit on in silence in my personal room, fastening the Velcro with a heavy exhale. I extend my bad wrist, my right, out in front of me, and push the layers of fabric covering the scars back. There they are, one a neat incision that's now a pale line extending from my wrist to halfway up my forearm, a row of evenly placed puncture marks from the suture on either side. The other is a jagged gash on the opposite side of my arm, dragging through my tattoos like a surgeon went in blind. They'll be here for as long as I live now, but they no longer remind me of the accident as much as they do Shantal's graciousness after it.

I'm just starting to work my muscles when there's a knock at the door: Celina.

'C'mon in,' I call.

My trainer slips inside, her usually no-nonsense glare one of concern. Her rose hair is half up in two space buns this Sunday, the kind of cheery style that doesn't quite match the occasion.

I haul myself to standing from the exercise table. 'Tell me something good.'

She just shakes her head with what almost appears to be a guilty expression on her face. 'You'll have to go it alone today, Darien. Please, please. This is what you excel at. This is the last hurdle to the Championship, and I really, really need you to concentrate. Win this, and it's all in your hands at the end of the season. Please,' she repeats.

Cel's as desperate as I am.

We'll take a win right now, any win, after the recovery I had to make just so I could race. There's no question Heidelberg will take home the Constructors' at the end of this – Miguel and I are the top points earners on the grid. But that Drivers' Championship battle now sits at mere points between us. That makes Abu Dhabi winner takes all. I win, I secure my contract, the Ring, and a bright future for Redenção and its homegrown talent. For my home. This victory could be *everything* for me – it just doesn't feel that way. Celina was crucial to how rapidly I healed on the outside, but so was Shantal, and she found a way to start mending things deeper than the broken bones and bruises. How do I do this without her?

'I'll try' is ultimately the only reply I can give Celina. I have to give it to myself. *Your dad, Darien. Your dad. Make him proud. Do him justice.* I remind myself that this is how I find him, in the race. I think it'll do me good. But inside, the pressure only mounts.

308

Everything depends on this race outcome. And I'm missing half of my heart for it.

The start dawns upon us as the sun drops closer and closer to the horizon. After the formation lap, lined up on the grid, I start at a not-so-ideal P4, but I'll have to make the best of it. In front of me is the rear wing of Diana's Revello, and beside me, Peter's car of the same livery. I'm surrounded by friends, but in this moment, with seconds till the race start that could change the trajectory of my career for ever, all I see are opponents.

When you're part of a sport that requires that kind of aggression from you, and you find someone who's in your corner no matter what, who you can count on even when you're in the midst of the battle, you hold on to them. You hold on to them for dear life.

The first red light flashes on.

Five.

I ask Shantal if she thinks racing is risky, dumb. She tells me it's a part of me no one can take away.

Four.

Shantal offers a prayer for my health in Singapore, even when I don't think I'll get that health back.

Three.

She tells me about her sister, and all I can do is hold her.

Two.

We'll see each other again. Even if it's years later. Decades. Even if she has a family of her own.

One.

She kisses my cheek before the race at Silverstone. *Go fly.*

The lights go out.

Let's fly.

Chapter Fifty-Seven

Shantal

I brought Sonia's photo with me to Dubai at the last minute, grabbing the frame off my bedside table and taking it with me in a well-packed suitcase to ensure it didn't crack. Now, with a pit of guilt building in the bottom of my stomach, I am back where I started: in the guest room of Navin's house in the Emirates, with Sonia, hoping she can give me some kind of answer.

'You won't get to see any of this, will you?'

I catch the sob that begins to creep up my throat as I meet my sister's eyes. Perfect. She was perfect. And she was so, so tormented.

'My engagement. My wedding. You won't get to see me off when I leave Ma and Babu.' I push tears from my cheeks with a force that takes off some of my fresh makeup. 'What would you have wanted, huh? I feel like that's always been the question. Would you have wanted our parents happy, or me? Because the more I think about it, the more I realize – we can't have both.'

They're happy. But I'm you now.

I picture Darien lining up for the race in mere hours – Abu Dhabi, the race that will decide the outcome of his season. He's points from Miguel. This is his chance to prove himself, and he's doing everything in his power to make that chance worth it. I can't even begin to define who I am, what I stand for. Am I myself, or am I the weight that was placed on my shoulders when my parents found out why we lost Sonia?

When the doctors talked to my parents, Ma had fallen into Babu's arms with cries so horrible they made my stomach turn. She couldn't believe Sonia would hide such a thing from us for so long. None of us could, and I don't think any of us accepted the *true* reason she made that choice because of it. We were in shock. We didn't want to think about the sacrifice she'd made. We are still in shock, and instead of recognizing that something went awfully wrong, we made her a martyr.

Sonia did everything right, with meticulous skill. Dance, teaching, pageants. But there is a sharp sting that stabs at my heart when I think of the emptiness in her eyes that last night before she died, when she turned to me with those final words. 'Don't waste your time in making everyone else happy.' *You think I've done it all right. But this is evidence that I have not.*

I stand up, set my sister's photo in its frame back on the nightstand. I shake the wrinkles from my *lehenga*, my engagement dress, a pale lavender embroidered with gold designs and glimmering pearls and diamonds. I check my face in the mirror, make sure nothing is out of place, straighten the *dupatta* pinned to my bun. This is what it's going to be now. I can hear the commotion in the yard already, all the guests waiting eagerly as I sit here and pray for the minutes to pass by until I no longer have any choice but to leave my room.

I look terrified.

311

I grab my phone from off the bed and shoot Anjali a quick text. I don't think I can make it down there on my own. But just as I've hit *SEND*, she bursts through the door.

My yap-happy cousin is dead silent as she paces the room for a full three minutes before sitting down on the bed with dramatic emphasis and looking up at me, eyes heavy with disappointment.

'Seriously?' she finally says. 'You're still *here*?'

'What do you mean?' I reply slowly, with a hesitant gesture to the windows beyond which the ongoing party is visible. 'All these people are—'

'Shantal, to *hell* with all these people!' she sighs, voice rising. '*These people* dictated everything we did all our lives. They've been telling us what to do for ages, and never once has it made sense to me. Sometimes we're told to keep our chins up and be good wives. Other times we're told to lower our heads and have some emotion. Sometimes we have to put on makeup and curl our hair. And other times we're ridiculed for the extra effort. We get assigned a role in society, and when we raise our voices about it, we're told we have options.

'I'm sick and tired of being the perfect daughter. Of being the perfect *girl*. Our parents suck all the love out of us, take us for granted, and then ask us why we don't love harder. Everyone always tells us to be quiet, until they hurt us, and then they ask us why we weren't louder. Look at Sonia, Shanni. Perfect daughter, perfect sister, perfect dancer, perfect teacher. None of us realized that something else was going on behind all of that. So tell me, what kind of a world are we living in? Are we living in it, or is it just using us like everybody else is? And are you going to let it use you as well?'

Anjali's eyes fill with tears as she deals the final blow. 'When are you going to realize that it's time for you to stop being the listener, *didi*? To stop sitting there with nothing to say, listening and listening? Someone *sees* you, and you love him. If you don't – if you stay here and do this, I'm just scared you're going to keep serving everyone else until you just . . . disappear. And then there won't be anything left for him to see.'

My eyes slowly travel to behind Anjali, and they widen significantly as I realize it's not the two of us alone here.

'Ma,' I barely whisper.

Wrapped up in her purple and gold saree, my mom takes quivering breaths, her hands shaking as she takes in this entire scene, this tangle of lies she's just now getting the truth about.

'Vaani, what's—'

My father stops in his tracks directly behind Ma. Babu's glasses slide down his nose, and he pushes them up with urgency, his line of sight flitting from me to Anjali and back to me. 'Shanni, what's wrong?'

'Babu . . .'

Anjali clutches my hand in hers, and then my rebellious cousin does something that I fully believe comes from both herself and my Sonia. She tells the truth that undoes everything I've hidden from my parents since I got back.

'Aunty, she's in *love*. She's in love, and it'll cost her everything. She's willing to sacrifice all her dreams, the life she wants, to make you happy. She'll do whatever it takes, even if it means pleasing everyone before herself, just like Sonia did. And I know, I know this isn't my place, but that would be a mistake. She wasn't born to be Sonia; she was born to be Shantal.'

They are both silent for a long minute as they take this in, and then my father looks up at me with what I think may be disappointment. Is it disappointment? I can't tell, but it's the worst kind of stabbing pain.

'I just . . .' My words are slow, a long time coming. 'I know

313

you know Sonia was everything to us, but what happened to her . . . It wasn't fair. It wasn't. Now it feels like she's brought me the answer, and he's everything I never thought I'd have the heart to love . . . ever again. He's my way to something happier, something that's . . . truly and deeply mine. My kind of love. No obligations, no fine print, just . . .' My voice cracks as I remember what I'd told Darien that day, what my mum used to tell me. 'The other half of my heart.'

Ma takes a step forward, her fingers brushing the curls and flowers of my *mehndi* as she takes my hands in hers. A soft breath escapes her lips, and she meets my gaze with eyes brimming with tears.

'The drive to Abu Dhabi is an hour.'

At first, the words don't register in my brain. They don't even sound real, and then they do. They click together piece by piece, and I question how this is even happening – any of this.

'Vaani?' Babu says quietly.

'I will talk to the Kumars myself. I don't want,' my mother replies, more to herself than anyone else, 'to lose another daughter.'

Babu takes off his glasses, focuses on the ground, and then he wraps an arm around my mother, taking my hand in the other. He swallows hard. Says, 'That drive is more like forty-five minutes if you've *really* got somewhere to be.'

I don't think I've ever driven the way I do when I whip my parents' grey sedan out of Navin's parking lot and onto the road. I peek at my GPS for only a moment, making sure to get on the right highway, at which point I press my foot straight to the floor of the car. My chest feels as if it's about to burst from the thumping of my heart. Is it too late? Is this a mistake? Does he even want to see me?

'Shut up,' I mutter to myself. My eyes dart in search of police officers. None. I speed up even more. There's nothing to lose, anyway. Either I get there and he'll hear me out, or I get there and he won't. I'm too far to turn back now.

Heading off at the exit, I hit the traffic unexpectedly quickly; a flood of cars cramming the roads. Honking is the chosen mode of communication, with a couple of joyous middle fingers thrown up as necessary. No one is going anywhere right now. I check my phone. The race starts in less than an hour. The teams will be getting ready soon and, once that's started, that will be my chance gone. Darien will be on the track. It's a wonder if I'll be able to get in and find him any time after that.

I put my car into park and pat the dash longingly, checking in front of me one more time. No movement. Well.

I tug my heels off, and pull my Hokas from their tote bag in the back seat, yanking them on as I open the door. I grab my paddock pass and step out of the car. Once I'm satisfied that all the lavender-tulle material of my *lehenga* and *dupatta* have escaped the driver's seat, I slip my lanyard around my neck and slam the door shut.

With a deep breath, I peek down at my shoes. *Don't fail me now.*

And I run.

By the time I'm at the turnstiles for the paddock, I'm so out of breath that I nearly throw my badge at the machine to scan in. I rush through the paddock itself, ignoring strange looks from team members and a principal or two. The Heidelberg motorhome is close to the front, just beyond Revello and Jolt, and I grab the *lehenga* so I can run up the stairs, bursting through the doors. I'm a mess, I know it – my hair falling out of its jasmine-wreathed bun, my makeup melting off my face, dress crumpled, but I have one thing completely intact, and that is my audacity.

'Mr Demir!' I catch sight of the team principal right away and set a beeline.

His eyes go wide when he sees the state I'm in, looking over me with deep concern. 'Shantal! You're . . . God, are you all right?'

'Yes,' I manage. 'Darien?'

Afshin, bless his heart, sighs a resigned sigh, gesturing to the track, from which the roaring of cars already emanates. 'In the car. He's gone out there. It's all down to the wire here.'

No.

I collapse onto the nearest chair, my *lehenga* flying up around me, and I press a hand to my forehead. *Down to the wire.*

Please, please, please. I need you to know I'm here. I need you to know I'll never leave your side again.

'Shantal . . .' Afshin begins, brow wrinkling, but I hold out a hand.

'Hang on.' I look up at him, and I hope with all my heart that I can convey the desperation of the situation to him. 'I need to go out to the fences.'

'You think . . .'

'I know it.' I purse my lips and nod, every exhale a ragged, shaky puff of air. 'I know he will.'

Chapter Fifty-Eight

Darien

I'm up into P3, with Diana up ahead, and Miguel in P1.

We pit about a third of the way through the race, at lap twenty-six, and screw on a set of medium compounds. Diana, I get word, is going to go out on the same, which removes tyres from the list of things that I could use to get a leg up on her.

I manage the compound as long as I can, until I finally get my delta and my DRS.

'There's Peter about one-point-six behind. Be careful. On the attack,' says Afonso.

With a grunt, I dart forward, trying to position myself directly behind Diana, get the slipstream while I can. The force is astronomically more than I've felt all race, and maybe, just maybe, that's my dad helping me out, because it's like a tow from an enormous hand tugging me forward when I move out and get right ahead of Diana on the straight.

'That's P2, P2, Darien.'

I don't celebrate early this time. We're racing for survival. We want P1. There's a reason people like to say second hurts more than third. I can't end this knowing there was something more I could have done to get that Championship. The Ring is at stake. My home is counting on me.

'Can we . . . let's gamble, Afonso. Can we do scenario D?'

'Sorry, you said D? That's . . . it's a bit hot out here. Your delta is two-point-six.'

'Cover ground now, switch out right before the overtake.'

'Okay. Affirming, Darien, you . . . clear on D.'

Scenario D. The riskiest plan we have at Heidelberg, perhaps the riskiest of the race. I'll have to pace myself and manage my mediums in hopes that my teammate, Miguel, in front of me, will suffer enough wear over time to slow down, and to get me ahead. His tyres have been on for a couple laps more than mine, which means now it's all about strategy. If this is the right call, I'll pit for softs and come out with a significant speed advantage, even if he goes in before me. No team will be using soft tyres in this kind of heat. It's a big chance we're taking. I can almost see my mom in the pits, biting her nails down to the beds.

I hold it together for another thirty laps, during which Miguel enters the pits and puts on a set of hards – the hope must be that they'll last the rest of the race, but that's even better news for me as I roll in and get my soft tyres. He's going to be slower, especially when I initially get out: that's my chance. I need to stay methodical, though. I have just about twenty laps left in the race and can't afford to pit again after this.

On the exit, Afonso comes in with an update. 'You're going to come out maybe two seconds behind Miguel, Darien, two seconds. Still clear to fight. Let's pace and push once we have the delta.'

It's incredibly difficult, but I obey. Ten laps left, and I've paced myself enough while Miguel's lost speed. I inch into the one-second range. Time to bring it.

'Ten laps, make the move when you have the window.'

'Sure. Searching for gap.'

Miguel favours the outside, with a slight weave that allows him to close the door on overtakes without disobeying the racing line. I imagine Shantal watching from the pits the way she always has, pointing out troughs and peaks in our charts to Afonso, learning the different modes we employ in the sport just so she can push both of us to our limits. In this moment, it serves as both an advantage and a disadvantage, because Miguel, to his credit, has a slice of my technique under his belt after the pre-season training. He's had it all year, and it could very well end my Championship chances if I'm not careful now.

I close in on the straight, but the second I get to a turn, he refuses to give me entry. I'll have to go from the inside.

I curse under my breath. 'Well . . . if you insist.'

The next straight brings me so close that I could knock his right rear tyre with my left front one, but instead of doing so, I exit early into the turn, and bump around the kerb with a ferociousness that leaves my head pounding. Once I'm level, I see Miguel's Heidelberg in my rear-view.

'Yes! That's in P1,' reports Afonso. 'Manage, manage, you'll lose speed fast. Don't want to let him close.'

And even though tyre management has never been my strong suit, I pull some kind of miracle out of my bag of tricks. The last lap, I pull across the finish line well clear of Mig and anyone else, with a whoop I hope they can hear in the stands, over the popping of fireworks that decorate the sky above the track, pumping my fist hard as I pull close to my team hanging off the fences to get my Brazilian flag, screaming into the radio in hysterics with my wonderful engineer.

'DARIEN. DARIEN CARDOSO-MAGALHÃES—'

'HAVE WE DONE IT????' I nearly roar into the mic.

'YOU ARE A FORMULA 1 WORLD CHAMPION, DARIEN!'

'I'M A *WHAT?* I'M A *WHAT*, FONSY?'

'CHAMPION, MY FRIEND!'

As I near the fences, it's almost a mirage, the way I see her leaning over as she passes the banner over to me, blowing a kiss just before our hands brush, and she waves me off. God, I wish she were here. I wish Shantal were here.

And then I realize that I am wrong. She's not a mirage.

It's her.

I nearly shunt my car into the wall when it hits me, when I hear her voice behind me, so faint but so prominent over the growling of the engine, 'IT'S OKAY! I'LL WAIT AROUND!'

'Let's send this car off in style,' Afonso instructs me with a laugh. 'Give me some big loop-the-loops, please.'

'WHOO!'

I feel like I could probably burst from anticipation as I wrench my steering to the side and bring the car around for a doughnut, and then another, and then another. It's the end of the season, and with no other use for the Heidelberg car, the tyre burnout and doughnuts you earn as a champion are some of the most fulfilling moments of your life. Except there's only one moment I can think about right now, and it's definitely not the doughnuts.

I pull up to the P1 board triumphantly, with my third consecutive win under my belt. My heart is pounding triple-time, my entire body weightless, my limbs shaking with an overload of adrenaline. It's so bad it takes me an extra minute just to get up on top of my chassis, fists pumping as I raise the Brazilian flag, keep my neck on a swivel, in search of Shantal. *Where is she?*

320

'DARIEN!'

It's Miguel, who has climbed out of his car in P2. He tucks his helmet under his arm and gestures behind me with a broad smile on his face. 'LOOK!'

My entire body turns involuntarily, on edge from the already insane day I've been having, but the seed of hope deep in my chest bursts open when I make out the figure far in the distance, the crowds parting to let her through.

She's running down the track in a massive lavender traditional dress embroidered with flowers and leaves and peacocks, way faster than she should be with all the netting on the skirt. She grabs hold of it to give herself enough room to run, the soles of those white Hokas of hers slapping the asphalt. Her eyebrows are knitted out of exhaustion, and the lanyard of her paddock pass flaps about uncontrollably. I can see the tears shimmering on her cheeks as she storms towards us, a tempest of a woman.

Shantal Sanjeevani Mangal.

Before I can register anything, I've run towards my team. She smacks right into me, and I hug her tight, my eyes squeezed shut as she breathes heavily. She smells of expensive perfume and peaches, and she trembles against my chest, her hands digging into my back, her face buried in my shoulder. It's been months, but we still feel right in each other's arms, as if nothing has changed, and in a way, it hasn't. I've still pictured nothing but her face before every race, and her face in the crowd after each one. It's surreal that she's back, that I'm actually touching her right now, that she's not just a part of my imagination.

'Dar, I'm . . . I'm so, so sorry—'

'It's okay. It's okay, Shanni. Just stay with me.'

'I'm so sorry.'

'Don't be sorry. Stay, just stay.' I hold her tight, crushing the veil pinned to her head so hard that it slips down. I don't

321

ever want to let go of her again. 'What happened? You're . . .' Hesitantly, I pull away to regard her get-up. 'Tell me you didn't . . .'

She shakes her head vehemently. 'No, no, I just decided . . . I decided it was time to open my eyes, I suppose. With the help of a very, very insistent cousin."

'Well, don't stop now.' I let out a nervous laugh before taking her into my arms one more time, as if to confirm that she's truly here. 'I'm still fucking proud of you, Shanni.'

'I'm prouder. Of you.' She holds my face in her hands, presses her forehead to mine. 'World Champion.'

'I love you, Shantal,' I blurt, and I'm not totally sure where the courage comes from, but it's the moment – the cameras flashing behind us, the fireworks bursting above us. Everything is perfect, and she is perfect.

'You make my heart *whole*. I don't think the word has been invented yet,' she whispers, 'for the kind of love I feel for you, Darien.'

Maybe it hasn't. But I feel every drop of that love when I bring my lips to hers, and I kiss her, wrapping my arms around her, unable to let her go. Part of me feels that even if I hadn't gotten that Championship, I would still have won, because I have her here in front of me again, and that, in itself, is a miracle.

Chapter Fifty-Nine

Darien

When a Formula 1 team wins a race with either of their drivers, they are able to choose a member of their staff to come up and accept a second trophy awarded to the constructor. For this one, in Abu Dhabi, the finale of the season, the vote is unanimous.

Shantal climbs the podium, now free of the dress and wearing her team T-shirt and shorts, hoisting the trophy for Heidelberg Hybridge. Later, she'll attend the prize-giving held by the FIA to accept the Constructors' Championship, along with the rest of our team.

I feel weightless when the Brazilian anthem plays, for the first time in years, for a Brazilian champion, fans screaming every word of the hymn with me. It's almost surreal that this has finally happened, and in the year I suffered the injury I thought would end my career for good. All the tribulations of the season are left behind as I stand on the top step of the podium. And even though I was only on that top step for a couple of minutes, the feeling of being on top of the entire world doesn't dissipate.

I extend the flag wide behind me as the anthem comes to an end, complete with roaring and applause. I wave animatedly to the fans at the fence. And for a moment, I think I see Pai's face among them, beaming as he holds up the Brazilian flag as well, calling out my name with tears of happiness in his eyes.

When I bring the fabric back around myself, there are tears in my eyes, too.

It feels like my Pai is giving me a great big hug.

Demir is the first person to reunite with me after the ceremony. The guy's clearly had an evening, his hair plastered back from his forehead with sweat, his sunglasses gone missing, and confetti sticking to his button-down. 'Darien!'

'Hey, man,' I chuckle as he gives me a big hug full of stray confetti pieces. As ruthless as Demir can be, I have to give him credit. If he hadn't taken a chance on me those few years ago, we wouldn't be here. With a title, and a legacy in the making.

'I do have to say.' He gives my back a firm pat before pulling away and regarding me with pride. 'You took everything this season gave you and turned it into your *magnum opus*. I'm afraid, Darien, you will never be able to top the year you've had.'

That gets a laugh out of me. 'I'll find a way.'

'Then there's only one thing left for me to do.' Demir holds out a hand, looking me in the eye with a grin. 'I'm giving you the next three years with this team. You *and* Redenção, if you're ready for the fantastic change this will bring about.'

I've waited all year for this. And I'm finally a handshake away.

I took the brunt of a vehicular collision, recovered in a fraction of the expected time, suffered reinjury, had my heart mended, broken, and now mended again, and I'm a handshake away.

If Demir notices my eyes welling up again when I give his hand a firm shake, he doesn't say anything.

Shortly after, the entire crowd dissipates, everyone going their separate ways after the grand finale to the Formula 1 season. I'm not totally sure I can believe it's over, and I'm not totally sure where I go from here, to be honest. This Championship was my finish line for such a long time that I've never really thought beyond it. Yeah, I'll go home, back to California, bask in the title with my mom, who's in the States now. We'll have a family Christmas, family New Year's, and then it will be February again. Redenção will shift to the Ring, Heidelberg will start training our young talent, Brazil will get her time in the limelight. The season will come, and then it'll go, and then we'll do it all again, and again, and again, hopefully for a good, long time.

I wrap an arm around Shantal as she sits down beside me on the podium, the Brazilian flag coming with me so it engulfs us both from behind like a sort of blanket. She lets her head fall to my shoulder, and I press a kiss into her hair.

'I think I might stick around,' she whispers.

'Where?'

'In your world. This world.'

'You . . .' I almost can't believe it. 'Wait. You're gonna leave England to . . .'

'You've won it all, haven't you? You know Conquest is joined at the hip with Heidelberg now. I'm sure you know *damn* well I'll do whatever it takes to personally stay with the team for round two.' Shanni beams, and I think she beams for herself, a little gesture that melts my heart. 'I never thought this . . . *push*, straight out of my comfort zone, would give me my life's passion back. And besides, I can't leave you again,' she says, giving my shoulder a reassuring squeeze. 'It's about time I loved for the sake of loving, is all I know.'

'Even if that means suffering through another season of this crap?' I remark, more as a joke than anything else, but Shanni's smile in return is full of resolve.

'*Especially* if that means suffering through another season of this crap. With you.'

And in that moment I know that no matter what next season has in store for us, no matter how difficult it gets, it will be easy for the both of us. Easy in the way our bodies are made to hold each other, the way our hearts don't need to share feelings; in the way that, off the track, I won't have to worry about counting deltas and wasting time.

I'll already know that every second belongs to the one I love.

ONE MONTH LATER

Chapter Sixty

Shantal

The entirety of the Formula 1 universe, it seems, has gathered in Santa Maria del Mar on this chilly Saturday afternoon, cramming the pews shoulder to shoulder in dresses and suits. As cold as the weather may be outside, it doesn't stop the guests filing in from creating a special sort of humidity inside the church. I add a little extra *oomph* to the fancy hand fan I've borrowed from Diana, who'd been bustling around so quickly since morning that she's got to be on the verge of bursting a blood vessel. You couldn't tell, though. That's part of why I adore being on the inner workings of Formula 1 so much. The public sees one thing when they look at the drivers – like Diana, who will put up a strong front when she needs to – but I get to see the real Diana: the raw emotions, the feelings and experiences that I think genuinely make her such a force to be reckoned with.

Darien is still in awe at the church, glancing all around like he's never been in a church before. I have to elbow him out of his stupor when the entire room begins to rise, shooting reassuring smiles at the ever-so-nervous Miguel, standing at the front of the church in a suit, hair neatly combed, shadow of a beard in order, the terror apparent in his eyes. The things a powerful woman will do to you, I suppose.

The double doors at the end of the aisle open, and first comes the flower girl, who just so happens to be none other than Henrique Oliveira Miranda himself in a flower crown, throwing petals every which way from a comically small woven basket. Laughter ripples its way through the crowd, and when Darien lets out a particularly loud snort from beside me, clearly amused seeing the baby of Heidelberg Hybridge fully embrace his role, I can't even bring myself to scold him.

And then she steps into the aisle, Diana Zahrani, the driver who strikes fear into the hearts of those on the grid. She exudes grace and poise, in a stunning long-sleeved white dress, lace climbing down the bodice into a skirt so full she looks as if she's floating. The veil trails far behind her, edged with bespoke handmade pearl beading. Tears prick my eyes when I see the ones beginning to trickle down Miguel's cheeks. It is the realization that Diana, for all the blood and sweat she's put into sport her entire life, has found someone who truly understands that sacrifice – and loves her all the more for it.

Darien tucks a ridiculously large pack of tissues into my hand as I sniff, nodding knowingly in that dumb, infuriating way of his. I roll my eyes, but I dab at the corners of them, and the guests once again seat themselves while the officiant begins to address us all, declaring the intention of sanctifying this marriage between Miguel Ángel de la Fuente and Diana Heba Firouzeh Zahrani.

Just as he had that night in Imola at the dinner, Darien still feels what I feel strongly enough that he wraps an arm around me on instinct: nothing said between us, nothing required. I lean into him, and we watch the most stunning marriage unfold in the church in Barcelona. It is atypical, an Emirati girl and a Spanish boy, both race-car drivers for the top series in the world, but I can't ever think of a time when typical has been enough. I look to Darien, intently watching Diana and Miguel exchange vows with what I believe is a hint of very slightly watery eyes, and I think of the way I'd have felt being here just over a year ago. Indifferent, pained, maybe even resentful. Believing love to be some sort of trial by fire, something difficult, maybe impossible.

But now I know it isn't. A very wise man once told me that loving someone doesn't have to be any harder than we make it, and sitting beside Darien, it all makes sense.

I realize that I am extremely fortunate. Because it is so easy for me to love everything about Darien Cardoso-Magalhães.

Epilogue

Darien

Shantal's right. I'm pretty great. Maybe it's easy to love me, but it's easier to love her. Even easier to finally propose to her, two years later.

Shanni and I become the Magalhães-Mangals when I marry her twice. First, in a traditional ceremony at the Sri Mariamman Temple in Singapore. Second, in my backyard in Santa Teresa, where Miguel de la Fuente pronounces us husband and wife. The whole affair lasts five days. The backyard catering is immaculate. We order cheese pizza, no hidden vegetables.

Shanni works a kick-ass job at the very top of the pyramid, at Heidelberg, of course. We have a happy family with two kids, both as awesome as she is. Our oldest keeps asking when he can drive (he is only three). The two of us look at each other with that indulgent look parents have when their child does something far too mature for his age, and then we look back at him, and decide we will probably have to put him in karting in due course.

I finally have that WDC title, and it happens again in 2028. It's a long wait between titles, though it is completely and utterly worth it. All three of the loves of my life get to see it this time. I hold my children in my arms and kiss my wife up on the podium once everyone has gone from the audience.

A lot of stuff has changed. Perhaps we are not old and tired, but we have definitely grown up.

Something that has still not changed a bit is that I am eternally proud of Shantal. I think of her when we are inches away from each other. I think of her when I am racing halfway across the world from her. I think of her all my life. All *our* lives.

Shanni names our son Nico.

I name our daughter Sonia.

Author's Note

Grief is a feeling that we, as humans, are unfortunately made to struggle with. We become attached to our friends and family. We love, and then we lose, and it is one of the most incredibly painful experiences a person can endure. This novel is, truly, to anyone going through a period of grief. It is different for each and every person, but there is hope.

If you or someone you know is in a situation where grief deepens, prolongs or pervades day-to-day life, this may be a sign to seek help. If you live in the US, you can call 988 for the Suicide and Crisis Hotline, and if you are in the UK, you can call NHS 111. The Samaritans programme is also a judgement-free option for emotional support at 116 123.

Finally, we don't often know what someone is going through behind the face we see, even if we see it every day. We may well never know. But if you believe something is wrong, it is always worth seeking help, even if it is for a friend or family member. It is never wrong to do so, and it could save a life.

Acknowledgements

First, to my parents, who left their home country to bring up three NRI children in the Midwest. I love you. Thank you for raising me in a flurry of love and culture and education. To my mom, thank you for reading every line I write, even when you don't have the time. To my dad, for showing me what it means to keep on keeping on. To Aakash, always my first homemade audiobook listener. To Aashna, who will always tell me what I need to hear. To my Bas and Dadas times two.

To Amy for bringing this one to fruition, and for the fantastic title we get to squeal over. To the entire team across the pond at Avon for making Round Two even sweeter and giving me a space to represent the culture while yapping about motorsport.

To Batz, for teaching me how to feel through words. To Liebs, for giving me a place to put them.

To Bridget, partner-in-crime on the F1 scene. Ruby, my bookish big sister. Teigan, Peter Albrecht's first wife. Chloe, Aquaplane's auntie. Ams just because Ams is literally fantastic.

Caylynn, for being absolutely *hysterical*. Megan, for always checking up. Apoorva, for the endless amazing recs. Ava, Bal, N. M., Riya, my favorite Desi girlies in literature (you too, Ruby). A special thank you to Lochi for answering all my questions to make sure Shantal's Guyanese heritage shone through just right. Simone, Megan, Grace, Soraya, Salma, Viki, Becca, Danielle and so many more. If I've forgotten someone, my immense apologies, but I want to thank you all *millions* for giving this chaotic writer a space to bloom.

To Ilaria, Ria and Isabelle for 'hearing me out' no matter what it is I have to tell them. Specially to Ilaria and her high school principal for the inspiration behind the mega-bed from chapter thirty-four. To Jahanvi and Chandana for the late-night tears. To Jahanvi's *daal* recipe. To Sophie, Ana and Maria for the memories. I like my cake upside down and on the ground. To Emma for adoring Miguel perhaps as much as Diana does, probably more. To Lina for keeping it 100, even across state lines. To Alicia, Hiruni, Charlie and Anushka. To Walk It Out.

Unfortunately, a book like *Overdrive* comes out of some emotional Friday nights spent oversharing and bawling in the car and/or at Walmart, so I want to thank everyone above a little extra for helping me through the minefield of feelings that spawned the second half of this book. This includes the guy at Walmart who approved of our ten p.m. chocolate cake purchase.

To the ESL (English Second Language) community. I hear y'all.

To anyone who has grieved.

To anyone who has thought they were not enough. You fumbled nothing. They fumbled everything. Your Darien or Shantal, the person who will truly complete you without any complaint or conditions, is out there. They *will* find you when the time is right.

To everyone and anyone who has read or is reading this now, I don't think I can verbalize the way that means the *world* to me. Those posts and DMs and stories and comments: I hope you guys know I read each one and I adore each one of *you*. You are why I keep doing this. Thank you for sticking around.

Content Warning

This novel contains themes some might find upsetting, including explicit language and sexual content, mention of grief, depression and trauma, panic attacks, sibling and parent death, brief mention of death of an unborn child, racism and discrimination, and vehicular accidents both related and unrelated to motorsport.